ALL OF US IN OUR OWN LIVES

Also by Manjushree Thapa

FICTION
Seasons of Flight
Tilled Earth
The Tutor of History

NON-FICTION
A Boy from Siklis: The Life and Times of Chandra Gurung
The Lives We Have Lost: Essays and Opinions on Nepal
Forget Kathmandu: An Elegy for Democracy
Mustang Bhot in Fragments

ALL
OF US
IN OUR
OWN LIVES

MANJUSHREE THAPA

ALEPH

ALEPH

ALEPH BOOK COMPANY
An independent publishing firm
promoted by *Rupa Publications India*

First published in India in 2016
by Aleph Book Company
7/16 Ansari Road, Daryaganj
New Delhi 110 002

The author gratefully acknowledges the support of the
Canada Council for the Arts, the Writers' Trust of Canada
and the City of Toronto through Toronto Arts Council.

ISBN: 978-93-82277-11-8

1 3 5 7 9 10 8 6 4 2

For sale in the Indian subcontinent only.

Printed and bound in India by Replika Press Pvt. Ltd.

In memory of my Dai Bhaskar
And for my Sister Tejshree

I am part of a large family.
And that's enough for me.
—Great Lake Swimmers, *Ongiara*

~

(What kind of place is this
not unknown to me, my own village
where in the bright light of midday
a whole life has vanished
Do you know where I might find it?)
—Bimal Nibha, *Cycle*

~

But she said, sitting on the bus going up Shaftesbury Avenue, she
felt herself everywhere; not 'here, here, here'; and she tapped the
back of the bus; but everywhere. She waved her hand, going up
Shaftesbury Avenue. She was all that. So that to know her, or
any one, one must seek out the people who completed them;
even the places. Odd affinities she had with people she had
never spoken to, some woman in the street, some man behind
a counter—even trees, or barns.
—Virginia Woolf, *Mrs Dalloway*

~

Every one is really responsible to all men for all men and for
everything.
—Fyodor Dostoyevsky, *The Brothers Karamazov*

IF SHE COULD get those ten days back, she'd swim to the whalerock every day. She'd sunbathe on its surface, and then plunge back into the water. She wouldn't waste a single day if she could get those ten days back.

On her desk lay a hundred and seventy-one folders, stacked from her attaché case out to the crystal pyramid that she'd got as a deal toy from the Toralan file, which stopped everything from sliding into the dustbin. Once she located the documents on Burnett's uncollected receivables, the file would be straightforward. MacKenzie was buying out Burnett and Sons, but Gordon Burnett would retain an ongoing interest, including a seat on the board. Both parties had already signed a letter of intent and a confidentiality agreement. They'd reach a deal by the end of the week.

Ava picked up a folder, put it down, picked it up again. Why hadn't Cory Stewart assigned her a new file yet? She'd generated MacKenzie and Burnett from her own contacts, which was fine, but if she were going to be a partner she'd need large files, files like Toralan. She'd spent eight stressful months on that file as the only associate assigned to it from M&A. Over that time, unhappiness had settled like a fog in her life, but in the end the deal had succeeded, and the celebration at Harbour Club had been awash in champagne. Then her mentor Lester Prease left the firm, and Cory Stewart became the head of the corporate department, and the fog in Ava's life thickened.

Fuck it. She flipped the file aside and looked out the window. At which point, on seeing that you've taken a wrong turn, do you change direction? At which point does it become too late? From the forty-fifth floor of Canada Tower, Lake Ontario gleamed like some unattainable dream of happiness. Lester Prease left her stranded on Bay Street.

No, it was her fault. She should have gone straight into a non-profit after law school. Lester had convinced her to do otherwise. He'd recruited Ava as an articling student. After law school, he'd invited her to join Peckham and Poole as a junior associate in the corporate department, where he'd persuaded her to focus on his own specialty, mergers and acquisitions. 'Look, I used to be—I still am—a hippie,' he'd said in his compelling way, 'but nothing has laid bare the framework of human civilization more clearly than the files I've worked on in M&A.' For seven years, he'd mentored Ava through increasingly complex transactions, taking her to the brink of partnership. And now he'd left to provide

1

bench strength to First Nations in their negotiations with the Crown, doing exactly the kind of work that Ava had dreamed of in law school. At his farewell dinner, he'd said, 'I believe that in our lifetime the First Nations are going to redefine what it means to be Canadian. We're innovating an entirely new configuration for citizenship and statehood. I'm tremendously, tremendously hopeful. Miigwech and mahsi cho.'

'Hey!'

Ava turned around.

Lori Schiff was at the office door, dressed, as always, in a gorgeous DVF wrap. 'You up for a girls' night out?' she said. 'Oh, and did I tell you I saw Cory at my parents' club? He was with his girlfriend, the one he left his wife for!'

Ava smiled. 'I can't wait to hear the gory details.'

'Great! See you at Ki at six-thirty!' Lori twirled in her DVF and left.

Back to MacKenzie and Burnett, Ava told herself. Instead, she got up and went out to the kitchenette. The floor was exceptionally quiet today. She knew half the M&A team were in New York on the Goldfarber matter. Why hadn't Cory assigned her to that deal?

She turned on the kettle, fished out her cell phone and left a voicemail for Gavin, letting him know that she'd be out tonight. Then she remembered that he'd be out too. For a function at the bank? For dinner? For drinks? 'Av, I'll be at...' What exactly had he told her this morning?

Jesus. How had her life become so dreary, how had she become so dull? She who'd been born to the jagged world: she knew there were alternative lives for her. She and Luke used to talk about this all the time growing up. When their parents brought Ava from Kathmandu to Overland, Ontario, they set her off in one direction, but she could choose another direction for herself. She could even reverse course if she wanted.

The kettle reached a boil and popped off.

Heading back to her office with green tea, she saw Cory Stewart barrelling down the hall. She ducked into the washroom to avoid him. There she put down the tea. She checked the mirror, touched up her mascara, washed her hands, straightened her shirt. Then she stood around regretting those ten wasted days.

Talking to Gavin had left her even more dissatisfied. 'Remember, Gav, when we got out of law school—we were different. I wanted to do something, remember? I didn't want to end up at Peckham and

Poole. You didn't want to work at a bank. We're in a rut, Gav.'

'A pretty damn comfortable rut, Av.'

Georgian Bay had glittered around them as they spent every day—not arguing, because they never argued, but—deliberating. They hadn't got around to having sex even once. Ava couldn't actually remember the last time they'd had sex: was it after Gav's thirty-fifth at Oyster Boy? Or... She'd been overwhelmed by the Toralan file, and Gav had stopped initiating. Why had he stopped?

When she went to her office, Cory was there, pacing back and forth like a caged animal. He had a blunt manner that bordered on aggression. 'Ah-vah!' he said. He'd told her, early on, that he found the pronunciation of her name pretentious. 'What, were you camping out in the ladies, Ah-vah?'

With a flick of a finger he indicated that she should sit. Then he moved into her desk till his thighs pressed against the Toralan deal toy. He said, 'Here's the thing, Ah-vah. Your evaluation's coming up, and, as you know, I'll be writing it this year.'

A fog began to swirl around Ava.

Cory's voice floated in from far away. 'Now, we all know Lester was soft on his protégés, otherwise why would he have recommended you for partnership? But my view is? I'm not seeing a lot of motivation from your side. You want a future at Peckham and Poole? Then you and I, we need to level.'

Ava was already gone.

IN HIS NARROW room in Sharjah, they lay entwined in the sheets, wrapped in each other's warmth and contentment. Maleah was talking, Gyanu was caressing her hair. On their days off, he loved to lose himself in her words, to swim in the swirl of the sea in her stories and drift in the melody of her voice. When Maleah stopped talking he murmured, 'Tell more, meri maya.'

She smiled. 'What more you want me to tell, mahal?'

'Tell me: the men who catch fish.'

'You always want to listen about the Philippines.'

Maleah nestled in closer and told him about her father and brothers going out on their nightly excursions. Gyanu could see the lamps glinting off the water as the trawlers receded into the night. He could hear the roar of the sea in her voice, he could taste the saltwater in his mouth. The trawlers returned at sunrise as lorries rumbled into the village, setting the day in motion. The tuna catch was transported to a cannery, from where it was shipped to towns all over the South China Sea.

Some of the leftovers ended up in the village homes. 'Every day we eat fish, depends on the season,' Maleah said. 'There is rice and plantain, my mother cooks that first. My father and brothers come back, then she cooks'—and her English fell away—'Bilong-bilong, apahap, kabayo, lapu-lapu.'

She often cooked sea bass for Gyanu, infusing his room with the aroma of coconut, lemongrass, lime leaf: evocations of her fishing village. Usually they shared leftovers from Five Spices, though when there was time, Gyanu also cooked: he made meals flavoured with fenugreek and mustard, turmeric and fried chives, the hard rock and soil of his childhood in Nepal.

He found escape from his past in Maleah. He wanted to know everything about her. He knew she'd married young. At sixteen she'd run away with a boy from a town called Ramon. Ramon kept bad company, but he was tender to her. She was happy till his body showed up in the cannery garbage dump. Their son Crisanto now lived with his grandparents. 'My anak will never know his father,' Maleah had once said, and her sadness had unlocked Gyanu's.

Maleah was talking, now, of happiness: the meals her mother used to cook as she and her father and brothers sat around the kitchen, waiting to eat. 'There was nothing,' she said, and he felt the innocence

4

of childhood: a feeling of plenty. 'There was no big house, no fancy furniture, no nice clothes, no money. But there was love, so there was everything.' She turned to Gyanu. 'Like when you were a boy, mahal?'

He nodded. He still remembered the day Ma brought him to the village by the blue hills, to the house of the stranger who would become his Ba. Gyanu was fortunate. His stepfather was a kind man. After Sapana's birth, the scandal around Ma and Ba's marriage subsided, and their family was whole, till encephalitis took Ma. Now cancer was sapping Ba's life. The last time Gyanu called home, his sister had said their father was asking for him: 'Ba needs a son to light the funeral pyre, Dai. And he wants to see you one last time.'

Maleah noticed his silence and asked, 'You talked to your sister, mahal?'

'My father will not live long, meri maya.'

'You booked the ticket?'

'I booked it,' he said. He hadn't , however, asked Shantanu Kumar for leave. The manager of Five Spices was fond of Gyanu; he called him his Nepali Beta, his Nepali son; but Gyanu knew that no one was indispensable in the desert. He'd learned this over his years as a busboy at the Al Majaz in Abu Dhabi, a kitchen hand at the Safeer Café in Sharjah, and as a mess chef in the Ramla Restaurant in Burj Khalifa. Only when Shantanu Kumar hired him as a sous chef at Five Spices had Gyanu found stability. It worried him to have to risk it.

He didn't say more on the subject, and neither did Maleah. They were accustomed to living in uncertainty in this land where they could never settle. Maleah had come here on a two-year contract. One of her roommates had trained as a child minder to work as an au pair in Europe. Another was looking for new options. Maleah was enrolled in an English class and had convinced Gyanu to do the same. She sometimes talked about moving. She wanted to live with Crisanto somewhere, anywhere, where she could give him the kind of full, free childhood that she'd had.

For now, she gave Gyanu all her love. Their few hours together always raced by. It was already quiet next door: the Tamil construction crew had left for the day. The neon sign at the Al Faraby Hyper Express blinked on as the dusk deepened. Maleah would have to leave soon.

Gyanu propped himself up in bed and looked at her. Maleah Balana. He'd seen her one Sunday while accompanying his roommate Jairus to church: her head bowed, her face framed by lace. 'Our father who art in heaven, hallowed be thy name.' He'd heard her whispered incantation. 'Thy kingdom come, thy will be done on earth as it is in heaven.' How had he won her love, how was he going to keep her? Moving his hands over her shoulders, he felt the grace of her in his life. He removed the sheet and took in the sight of her paleness against his dark skin. They'd been lovers for a year and he couldn't envision a life without her.

'Mahal,' she whispered.

'Meri maya.' My love. He leaned in to kiss her and she arched her back, drawing her legs up to close him in to her.

OF ALL THE European cities Indira had been to while travelling for work—London and Brussels, Helsinki and Cologne, Copenhagen and, of course, Frankfurt, several times—Paris was definitely the prettiest. She'd been here before, eighteen-nineteen years ago, for her first ever international conference, a UNIFEM summit on women: she remembered it as a blur of national costumes and inspirational speeches. There'd been a tour of the city at the end. The delegates had been taken to the famous boulevard, the Champs-Élysées, and from a stone bridge Indira had taken photos of the Seine. Where were those photos now? Lost in time. Awed by all she'd seen, she'd vowed to return, and now here she was, back in Paris.

A fashionable lady in stilettos sashayed by. A boy on a blue scooter drove up the sidewalk and stopped at an automated teller. A tall man in a tailored suit cavorted down the sidewalk, smoking a cigarette. Indira shadowed him so as not to be spotted by the organizers of the Women's Empowerment Initiative.

There were, in her experience, two kinds of conferences in this world. The first was organized by veterans from the developing world, who understood that formal interactions were greatly enhanced by informal activities such as sightseeing or gift shopping. Indira had formed lasting bonds at such conferences. Years later, she still kept in touch with Abena Kwasima from Accra, Rudo Gamble from Cape Town, W. Werry from Jakarta, Mei Wang from Shanghai, Juana Hernández from Lima, and the formidable Kadri Pütsep from Tallinn. Together they formed a sisterhood of global change-makers.

The Women's Empowerment Initiative was, however, the other kind of conference, the kind organized by amateurs, usually American, who tried to squeeze too many outcomes out of too little time. This time, from the very first 'inspire breakfast' onward, Indira had had to pursue an asset-based approach using the principles of appreciative inquiry to discuss her work at WDS-Nepal. All day long, she'd been trapped in lectures and workshops, and in the evenings she'd had to attend 'solidarity dinners' with overly earnest cultural shows: a one-woman play set in Ciudad Juarez, an all-woman Roma folk band. Tonight there'd be a slideshow on female genital mutilation. And tomorrow morning she'd leave.

Why organize a conference in Paris at all? Why not meet, as WDS-International had one dire, under-funded year, at an airport hotel in

Frankfurt? Why not save money, and teleconference, for that matter, or video chat, Skype-shype, Viber-shiber?

The tall man turned into an alley. Just ahead lay a stately stone bridge. Indira hurried towards it. Having stolen out of a session on role-playing, she had two hours, or maybe three, to buy a present for Aakriti for having passed out of ninth class. She also had to pick up something for Muwa, though nothing would ever please that old witch. Aakaash was easy: she'd buy him a computer game at the airport duty-free; and two bottles of Johnnie Walker Black Label would suffice for Uday Sharma.

She reached the bridge, and her heart fluttered. Wasn't it—it was! It was the same bridge: it was the very same bridge she'd been to many years ago. She reached for the railing as she would for an old friend. The stone was smooth and hard and warm to the touch. Oh! She had once been young here.

She walked the length of the bridge, steeped in nostalgia.

On the far side of the bridge was a row of boutiques. A mannequin in a slinky dress stood in the window of the first boutique. A dress would be perfect for Aakriti, she thought—not this one, the neckline was low, but a dress from Paris would be perfect for her daughter.

The next window contained an array of jars filled with fruits, vegetables and nuts: dried, oiled, marinated, pickled, preserved. Yet another window was decorated with white lace panties. Another contained nothing but wine. Here, she lingered. The bottles—white, red, rosé— glinted like precious gems. She imagined Uday Sharma lifting a long-stemmed goblet and toasting, 'To you, Indira Sharma. To our marriage of twenty years.'

'To us.'

'No, to you.'

It wouldn't happen, not in this lifetime. Whenever she was in the developed world, Indira always regretted the way she, as a Nepali, had to blunder through life, without refinement, without joy, merely getting the needful done. Emotionally it saddened her, though rationally she understood why this was so. There was no comparing and contrasting her life with the lives of people from Paris. The developed world was the developed world, and Nepal was Nepal.

Next to the wine shop was a beauty parlour. She went in to buy a face cream for Muwa. A bell tinkled. The interior smelled like roses. A red-headed saleslady came to her, high heels clacking, and after babbling in French switched to English: 'May I help you, madame?'

'I need a face cream.' Indira pointed at a jar on a shelf.

'Ah, oui, there is much desiccation.' The saleslady whisked out a magnifying mirror and held it up to Indira's face, assaulting her with a vision of the furrows and grooves, dots and patches, stains and blotches on her middle-aged face. The lines under her eyes had deepened, and her complexion, once clear, was mottled. The saleslady said, 'I strongly recommend a treatment, for you it is urgent, madame.' She mentioned something called Eau Vitesse. 'That will make the skin tight, but my advice is to go for microdermabrasion. It aids the revitalization of youth.'

The saleslady herself had flawless complexion, even though she was, how old? Quite old. 'How much?' Indira ventured to ask.

'Just one hour, madame.'

'No, no.' She meant: 'How much is it costing?'

It came to over twelve thousand rupees.

Twelve thousand rupees for a beauty treatment! That was just immoral! Though, of course, her per diem could easily cover it, and it wasn't unreasonable when you converted the cost into euros. Plus a treatment, as the lady said, was urgent for her. A global change-maker ought to look smart. Also, a beauty treatment in Paris: when would she ever get such a chance? But then again—twelve thousand rupees!

Oof. Chances taken and opportunities missed, longings and qualms, desires and disappointments pulsated through Indira—yes, no, yes, no— till with profound regret she decided: 'I will take one face cream only.'

'Bof. Your choice, madame.' High heels clacking, the saleslady took a jar to the cash register.

The bill came to nine thousand rupees.

Nine thousand rupees for a jar of face cream! A high-quality cream, to be sure, a cream from a beauty parlour in Paris. She shouldn't waste it on Muwa. It would be a gift to herself.

As Indira left, the saleslady called out, 'Au revoir!'

'Bonjour,' Indira replied grimly. Outside, she felt just awful. What was she doing buying a nine-thousand-rupee face cream for herself? What did she think, that it would bring back her youth? That Uday Sharma would notice? And they'd recover their marital happiness? What?

Walking past the boutiques looking for a dress for Aakriti, she excoriated herself. Look at yourself, Indira Sharma. Tchee. Look at yourself. Just look at what you've become.

A WATERY LIGHT filtered through the banana plants, dappling the lawn with crazy dancing shadows. The lawn was turned away from Kakarvitta bazaar, overlooking a bridge. The land on this side of the bridge? This was Nepal. And the land on the other side was India.

'Can't we go?' Sapana asked, though she knew they couldn't. 'Just for a minute,' she said. 'Just so we can tell everyone at home that we've been abroad.'

Around her, the women tittered. They were waiting passively, indolently for their midday meal on this, the final day of their study tour. They were worn out from all the activities of the past five days. They'd visited a cooperative dairy, a pig farm, a carpet factory, a fish hatchery and a tea estate. They'd gone to a silk factory and seen silkworms feeding on mulberry leaves. They'd met women who made money selling baskets, brooms, cardamom, vegetables, nuts, dried fruits and just about everything else. Every day had been full of discovery, every evening had been full of fun.

If only Chandra had been on the tour, it would have been perfect, Sapana thought. She was hoarding all her observations to share with her friend when she returned home. There should have been more girls of her age on the tour, really. Sapana had, herself, been included by favour of her Thulo Ba only after old Laptanni Budhi pulled out, saying her family couldn't spare her. Ba couldn't spare Sapana either, but Chandra had insisted: 'Ey, girl, aren't I here to care for Ba? Haven't I been here for him all these years? Don't miss this chance. Go.'

As far as Sapana could tell, this study tour was the only thing her Thulo Ba's sham CBO had ever done for the women's committee. The committee was itself a sham: half its members couldn't read or write. No one in the village knew why the CBO had even bothered to set up the committee. But then the CBO—which, Sapana had learned on the tour, meant 'community based organization' in English—was just a means to fund Thulo Ba's politics. There was no point expecting much from it.

But this was no time to be negative: this was a moment to savour, she thought. The light, the lawn, the women. There, past the bridge: India. 'Can't we go?' Sapana asked again.

Rama Bhauju, who was sitting beside her, called out to their minder, the widower Jeevan Bhatta: 'Lau, Secretaryji, you're going to have to turn this into an international tour, re.'

The others tittered.

Jeevan Bhatta flashed a loopy grin. He looked a fool but was the secretary of the CBO, and Thulo Ba's most trusted political worker. 'If I were to take you across the border,' he leered, 'the police would nab me.'

'Why?' Rama Bhauju demanded. 'Is it against the law to go to India?'

'They'd think I was going to sell all of you to a brothel!'

'Haaa!' Rama Bhauju's face soured.

Jeevan Bhatta guffawed.

What a horrid joke. It immediately made Sapana think of Chandra's lost sister, Surya Di. After failing out of tenth class, Surya Di had decided not to marry. She was going to work instead. She'd always been a different kind of girl: plucky and bold. A family friend knew a manpower agent in Kathmandu. Over the phone, the agent said he'd find Surya Di a salaried job in India's capital, Delhi. 'I'll be the son you never had,' Surya Di had told her Muwa Buwa. 'I'll send money home so that Chandra and little Tara can study.'

The lodge owner began to serve dal-bhat-tarkaari, steaming hot in aluminum thalis, but Sapana didn't feel like eating any more.

What excitement there'd been on the day Surya Di left. Sapana and Chandra had escorted Surya Di all the way to the highway. 'You girls, don't be like me,' Surya Di had said sternly. 'Study hard. Pass out of school. Make something of yourselves. Take care of Muwa Buwa. Help raise little Tara.'

The agent was waiting at the highway with a van. He had a wiry moustache, and Sapana and Chandra kept looking at him and giggling. They found that moustache so funny. Two of Surya Di's friends were also going with her. After they arrived, the van drove away, and Sapana and Chandra raced home.

A few days later, when Chandra's Muwa Buwa phoned the agent, they found his line disconnected. Neither they nor the other families ever heard from their daughters again.

'Ey, girl!' Rama Bhauju nudged her. 'Your food's getting cold.'

'I'm not hungry, Bhauju.'

'It's a twenty hour bus ride! Think about how hungry you'll be in six hours, and eat!' Rama Bhauju burst into laughter. 'That's why I'm fat—I'm always eating because I think I'll be hungry in six hours!'

Sapana looked at her. Good-natured Rama Bhauju. Just last year, Rama Bhauju's schoolmaster husband left her for a young new wife.

Rama Bhauju was raising their four children all by herself, but looking at her you'd never know she had any troubles.

The others on the tour—Jethi Didi, Laxmi Aama, Kanchan Bhauju, Naina Di, Hasta Ma—all had their own troubles too, as of course, did she. Sapana had lost Ma only a few years ago, and now she was losing Ba. But then all of us experience sorrow, she thought: and yet here we are, across the country, on a study tour, in an animated discussion about—what?

Yogurt. 'The yogurt from here is famous,' Jethi Didi was saying, prompting Naini Di to say, 'Ssss! A bowl of fresh yogurt would be so refreshing at the end of this meal!'

'There's nothing in this world like fresh yogurt,' Rama Bhauju said.

'Ssss, now I really want some!'

'Sahuji!' Rama Bhauju called out to the lodge owner. 'Give us some yogurt, will you?'

The lodge owner shrugged. 'The batch I made this morning is finished.'

'Buy some from another hotel!'

'Do that!' The others chimed in: 'We came all the way across the country to try the yogurt.' 'Lau na, Sahuji!' 'We won't leave till we have some world famous yogurt!'

With another shrug, the lodge owner went to find them some yogurt.

A cheer went up at this small victory. Sapana had to smile. As much of a sham as this women's committee was, it was fun to be part of. The tour had given her a respite from the sadness of the impending loss of Ba. She was lucky to be here. She felt grateful—to the committee, to Thulo Ba, and even to Jeevan Bhatta, for if the old widower hadn't started the women's committee, this tour wouldn't have taken place at all. So what if he and Thulo Ba were profiting off the CBO? Whoever had given them the money for the tour had also enriched Sapana's life.

And anyway, maybe there's no such thing as 'my life' or 'your life', she thought. Maybe everyone's life is part of a whole. It felt so to her, because when she thought about it, she felt that the actions of one person shape the lives of others, and...don't all of us in our own lives shape the lives of others? They do. It's like a pattern, she thought. Not a pattern, but some kind of design, some kind of order. Chandra always said there's no God, and maybe she was right, but to Sapana it felt as though...

'Ey, girl! Eat! Or, you'll be hungry in six hours!'

Sapana smiled. She loved Rama Bhauju. She loved all the members of the women's committee; and actually, right now, she loved life. She drew the dal-bhat-tarkaari towards her and began to eat.

'GYANU?'

'Hm?'

'Let's live in Nepal, all of us. Mount Everest and all—it's beautiful, na?' Jairus said. 'You and Maleah can raise her son as a mountain boy. I'll bring my wife and daughters from Karachi. We can start a tour business; there are big dollars in that, hey.'

Gyanu knew his friend was only trying to soothe him.

Jairus patted him on the knee. 'Don't be upset, Gyanu. These things happen. Nothing comes from dwelling on them. You have to forget.'

'I know.'

'I mean it, friend.'

Earlier in the evening, Jairus had stopped by Five Spices to pick up kebabs, and had found Gyanu, and the rest of the staff, subdued. One of the servers, a young Nepali brother, had hung himself.

'Come with me, come, come, come.' Jairus had brought Gyanu along for the first part of a tour to Ras-al-Khaimah. They were in the dunes outside Dubai, in a tent at the back of the tour company's compound. Jairus's clients, IT entrepreneurs from Tamil Nadu, were in the main tent, where a belly dancer was gyrating to a Lebanese pop song. The clients looked bored. Serving them dinner, the tour company's staff looked bored. Even the dancer looked bored.

'Jairus?' Gyanu said. Between them they spoke a mix of Hindi and Urdu. 'He was a nice boy. Always smiling.'

Fucche: small boy. That was the server's nickname. Bright-eyed and quick to laugh, he was one of nine siblings—disposable, he used to say. 'A burden to our parents, that's all we are.' His gaiety must have masked a deeper desperation. He'd got into debt and borrowed. Then he'd got deeper in.

'He was happy on the outside,' Jairus said, 'but who knows how he was suffering inside? It does no good to dwell on it, friend. Look at the dancer, she's from Turkey, she has green eyes. See, how pretty she is.'

Fucche's body would have to be flown home. His room-mates had notified the embassy in Abu Dhabi. Gyanu had helped Shantanu Kumar call his parents in Kathmandu... And Gyanu had other reasons to worry. He'd asked Shantanu Kumar for leave, but wasn't sure the manager would grant it.

'Jairus,' he said, 'what if Shantanu says no?'

'Why would he say no to his Nepali Beta?'

'Look after Maleah when I'm away?'

'You don't have to ask, hey.'

Gyanu said, 'What will we do? Maleah and me.' He meant: how were they going to forge a life together?

Jairus understood him. In his calm, wise way, he said, 'You have to look at the world through a wide-angle lens, Gyanu. People like us, we've done all right, friend. How many of your brothers and sisters in Nepal come into this world just to suffer—and how many of my brothers and sisters in Pakistan? In this world we're powerless, na. Everything is in God's hands. You and I? We must have faith.'

In the main tent, one pop song ended, and another one screeched on. The belly dancer went on gyrating. After dinner, Jairus would drive on to Ras-al-Khaimah. Gyanu would catch the bus back to their shared rooms in Sharjah.

Jairus picked up a kebab and offered it to him. 'You want?'

Gyanu shook his nead no.

'It's good, hey, tender and juicy. You should know, you made it!' Jairus laughed.

'You eat it, you'll need strength for the long drive.'

Gyanu got up and left his friend to his meal. Beyond the tent, the sky was glittering with stars. He walked out, to the far edge of the tour company's compound, to a stall overlooking the dunes. A camel tethered there snorted as Gyanu approached. Its minder, a thin man in a dusty thobe, sat on a pallet smoking a cheroot. With a nod he invited Gyanu to sit.

The screech of the pop songs was muted here. The golden lights of Dubai glowed on the horizon. The dunes were velvety. The smoke from the minder's cheroot wafted, sweet and heavy, in the air. A shadow darted through the scrub. Gyanu took a deep breath. He loved the desert: its starkness felt honest to him. Outside of Nepal, the desert—the Gulf—was the only home he'd known. It was a difficult thing to love a land you could never call your own.

Jairus was right. He was fortunate. So many Nepali brothers and sisters suffered at home, and then came here and suffered even more. So many, like Fucche, perished. Everyone who worked in the desert recognized the haunted expressions of the distressed. In the past month alone, six workers from Gyanu's home district had been cheated by a manpower agency. A Nepali sister had been raped and became pregnant.

One of the other servers at Five Spices kept breaking down in the middle of work, but wouldn't say why. The desert could be ruthless, Gyanu knew: but it had given him everything he had. His livelihood. A future. True love.

The camel shuffled in the stall. The smoke from the cheroot kept wafting. Gyanu scanned the sky till he saw the familiar giant, Orion, and across from it, his birth sign, Gemini, its stars splayed in a pleasing symmetry. Early on, he'd pointed it out to Maleah from the shores of the Sharjah canal. She'd shown him another constellation, higher up, Auriga: a herd of goats. 'When I think how life brings us together, I think—like that, mahal. From so far, we come together.'

Gyanu looked, now, for the goats, but couldn't pick them out in the sky. From the corner of his eye he caught a movement: a satellite. He followed it. It was gliding so fast, it was hurtling, it looked as though it might crash into a star, though of course it didn't. He followed it across the sky till it vanished into the golden lights of Dubai.

'MUMMY, WILL I ever be pretty?' Aakriti scowled at her reflection in the gilt-frame mirror.

'You are pretty, Chhori, you're the prettiest girl in the world,' Indira said, wanting to add, you look exactly like I did at your age, but holding back, because given the way she looked now, how was that reassuring?

'But I'm not—it's not—I don't! I look like a skeleton in this.'

The dress was too big for the girl. The sashes drooped, the bows sagged, the buttons hung limp from the holes.

'It's my fault,' Indira said. 'I bought it in a size you can wear next year.' She cinched the dress at the waist. 'The tailor will take it in, and it'll be perfect, though even without a dress from Paris you're the prettiest girl in the world, Chhori.'

Her daughter only scolwed harder.

'Listen to me, Aakriti Sharma. Boys will have to line up to marry you one day!'

'It doesn't matter because I'm going to be a doctor in America and who cares about boys anyway!' Aakriti stomped out of Indira's room, the dress billowing behind her.

Oof. Indira followed her out. The girl slammed into her room and bolted the door from inside.

'Aakriti?' Indira knocked on the door. 'Listen to me, Chhori, you're very pretty, but you're right, it doesn't matter—'

From inside came a wail.

'Open the door, Chhori. Open the door. Open the door for just one minute.'

Another wail.

What to do, what to do.

Durga shuffled into the hall with a tray bearing kheer and milk. 'Snacks, Hajoor.' The servant girl looked frightful, like a beggar, a vagabond. She'd stopped grooming herself after the vegetable vendor she'd abruptly got engaged to just as abruptly abandoned her.

'Kheer!' Indira cried with feigned enthusiasm. 'Aakaash's favourite! Did you put cardamom in it?'

The girl nodded.

'And cashews?'

'Yes, Hajoor.'

'Go and serve Aakaash.'

17

The girl shuffled to Aakaash's door and knocked.

Indira jiggled the handle to Aakriti's door. 'Snacks, Chhori, snacks, Durga's made snacks,' she said. Her daughter despised kheer. 'Open the door, I say.'

There was no reply.

There was no reply, either, from Aakaash. Durga muttered, 'Babu never hears me knocking, he just stares at the computer, I knock and knock but he never hears.'

He was playing one of those games Indira had bought for him at the duty-free. Indira went to her son's door. 'Open, ey, Aakaash. Durga's made your favourite kheer.'

Silence.

'Open, I said!'

'He never hears me, Hajoor.'

'Aakaash, open the door, open the door, open the door!'

Oof, that boy, he was useless, Aakaash was a useless, useless boy.

Indira picked up a bowl of kheer and a glass of milk from the tray. 'Take the rest back to the kitchen. The children will eat when they're hungry. And Durga,' she added, 'wash your face. Comb your hair. Make an effort to look respectable.'

The girl shuffled away glumly.

What was the point, there was no point. They were all useless, her entire family was useless.

Kheer and milk in hand, Indira went down the hall to Muwa's room. Even from outside, the smell of incense was cloying. The old witch prayed constantly, though her fevered piety never lessened her witchiness. Indira hated her mother-in-law. Nevertheless, a Nepali daughter-in-law had to do what a Nepali daughter-in-law had to do. She called out, 'Snacks, Muwa,' held her breath and entered a miasma of myrrh.

A TROPICAL BREEZE tumbled in through the window, warm, fragrant, forgiving. The 112 was lined with billboards advertising cheap flights to Cuba, El Salvador, Jamaica. Past a palm grove, Ava turned off on the exit to the 195. She checked the speedometer: she was twenty above the limit as the rental car swooped down to a causeway on Biscayne Bay.

There was something about America, Luke had said after moving here, that freed you. Being one of three hundred million: that scale. In Canada, even in a world-class city like Toronto, everyone was from some small place. Your past held you in. 'Man, I'm never coming back,' Luke had said to her. 'I'm out of there, Big Sis, I'm gone.'

Following his directions, Ava drove past the pastel art deco buildings and crowded high streets of Miami Beach. Luke lived in North Beach. She recognized his apartment complex from his Instagram postings. She parked on the street and took out the single suitcase that contained everything she hadn't stored in her parents' garage. She wheeled it and carried her attaché case into a sprawl of stucco and tile: her little brother's low-budget paradise.

The key to Unit 4 was under the doormat. The apartment was furnished just as perfunctorily as Luke's old Kensington Market studio, with an unfinished table, an outrageous pink chandelier and a few dented metal chairs. One of his paintings, a yellow monochrome, was drying on the wall. Everything smelled of linseed oil.

Ava had the afternoon to herself. Outside the apartment was a lawn full of sunbeds. She changed into a bathing suit, grabbed a towel and went out. Lying on her back with her eyes closed, she listened to birds—thrushes? larks?—chirping exuberantly over the lawn. The heat of the sun melted in from her skin into the muscles, the sinews, the bones, easing away Cory Stewart and her last humiliating months at Peckham and Poole. The fog had lifted, was still lifting, from her life. She turned over and let the sun warm her back, easing away the pain of Gavin and his confession, their confusion, her sharp decision.

She was heading in, feeling light and limber, when Luke arrived.

'I see you found the sun.' He smiled.

'Little Brother!' She hugged him. 'What a place!'

'Don't you love it?' He grinned. He looked luminous. Back home he used to be wan, but his platinum hair and grey eyes had found a corresponding light here. 'Let's get you dressed,' he said. 'Hector Duarte

19

from the sculpture department has an opening tonight, the party's going to be epic.'

Before long, they were heading out in his battered red Mini. This was how it always went with Luke. Fuelled by impatience, he flitted from activity to activity, unble to sit still. 'You caught some of this on your way in?' He waved towards the art deco buildings. 'We'll come here tomorrow for a birthday bash. But first, tell me, what news of Mom and Dad?'

'Did Mom tell you about the Halloween parade?' Ava said.

'Her latest dust-up with Mayor Jenkins?' Luke pointed at a wrought-iron gate. 'That, by the way, was where Versace was shot. So listen. I've got to teach tomorrow, but a friend, Anthony, he's in the film department, he's offered to show you around.'

'You got me a babysitter?'

'He's a sweetheart. Plus he's local, he knows all these cool spots. I figured you might like a change of scenery.' He glanced over. 'You doing okay, Big Sis?'

Discussing the separation, Ava stuck to the facts. She and Gavin had signed an agreement. If they chose to file for divorce, they'd do so jointly. 'Of course, it's difficult,' she said. 'Six years, you know? Gavin will stay in the house till it's sold. The agent's saying we should be able to sell up.'

'So everything's hunky-dory.'

Ava ignored his ribbing. 'I'm really excited about this new job.'

'You'll be the director of women? At what—the forum to save the world?'

'The International Development Assistance Forum. It's called IDAF for short.'

'And since when have you wanted to get in touch with your roots, Big Sis?'

She could never get anything past her brother. Their parents had had him immediately after adopting her. The two of them had grown up like twins, closely, jealously attuned to one another. Ava said, 'Remember my friend Kim Armstone from Osgoode Hall? She's in Juba, in South Sudan, she does humanitarian work there. I got in touch with her on Facebook, and she put me in touch with a colleague, a guy from Quebec who works in Kathmandu. He gave me the lead for this job.'

'But we hated Nepal when we went there, remember?'

'We were kids, Luke.'

He arched an eyebrow. 'Whatevs.'

Their parents had raised them liberally, teaching them about Ava's 'birth country'. One Christmas, they went on a family trip to Nepal. Ava and Luke were fourteen at the time. From start to finish, the trip had proven a disaster. The orphanage—'Oh, this is where we first met you, honey'—turned out to be a crumbling wreck out of a Charles Dickens novel. A group of children playing ball stopped to stare at them, immediately grasping the story of a white family with one brown child. Ava had recoiled from their gaze. The family had walked through a warren of cold, empty rooms to reach a draughty office, where a dour official translated the few notes on file. 'Mother passed away in childbirth. Father is unknown. Name was given for official purposes.' He'd pronounced her name as it was spelled in the adoption papers, with an aspirated 'b'. 'Abha: it means early morning light,' he'd said. He had no information about Ava's biological parents. 'Caste is unknown.' He'd looked her up and down and pronounced, 'Skin is dark, but—only God can know.'

For the rest of the trip, Ava had refused to leave the hotel, and back in Overwood she'd thrown herself into her life—her real life, her Canadian life. Her rejection of Nepal had been total.

'You know how I feel about the whole roots thing,' Luke said.

They'd been having this conversation all their lives.

'I know,' Ava said. 'I don't have to connect with my past, but the timing feels right, Luke. It's a, I don't know, a kind of instinct.' They were passing a strip mall with Spanish shop signs: Gigante, Tapito, Maya Market. 'Remember Lester Prease?' Ava said. 'After he left Peckham and Poole, I felt trapped in a career I didn't want. And with Gavin, too, there was this—fog.'

'Well, here comes the sun.' Luke parked in a neighbourhood of converted warehouses.

The sculpture exhibit, Masculinities: Plural, consisted of a room of glandular plastic protrusions. 'It's conceptual, not retinal, it's not meant to please,' Luke said, walking Ava through it. At the front, the sculptor was making an incomprehensible speech about masculinities. When he was done, the crowd scattered around a cash bar.

Luke's friends were always bohemian, or perhaps feckless. Ava couldn't imagine living the way they did. That evening she met a painter who'd shown at Art Basel—'Just jumping through the art market's hoops.' She listened in on a debate between a journalist and a poet who refused, on principle, to publish: 'The world urgently needs more silence.'

'But you gotta pay the rent, man!' The poet turned vexedly to Ava. 'What do you think?'

'I, um, well.'

She was rescued by a heavily pierced woman: 'Hey, I'm Revolution Mary, you want another drink, babes?'

'Oh. No, thanks. I'm good.'

'Aw, come on. I'm a performance artist, it's my social practice to make everyone dirty martinis.'

The martini went straight to Ava's head. And so, late at night, when a man—tall, dark and handsome—came up to her with a flirtatious: 'So, Masculinities: Plural. Yes or no?' she flirted right back: 'Well, my husband and I just split up, so I guess that's a yes.'

'I'm extremely sorry to hear that,' the man said, sounding not at all sorry. 'Hi there. I'm Anthony Watson.'

'I'm Ava Berriden.'

'Luke's sister, right? I'm hoping to show you around tomorrow, if you're up for it, that is.'

~

The next morning, Anthony picked up Ava and drove to Coconut Grove, where his family had first settled. 'Bahamian immigrants—though we're all mixed in now,' he said. They walked under the big blue sky, past a mural. Then he took her to a taquería for lunch. 'You ever had mahi-mahi? And you've got to try the local microbrew, it's simply the best.'

The tacos were hot and the beer was cold. Later, they sat in a park with elderly Cuban men playing chess. 'I can see why Luke loves it here,' Ava said.

'Yeah, people think Miami's all art deco and beaches, but there's a lot of history here, a lot of African-American history. And now it's like the centre of South and Central America. Hey, Luke told me you're on your way to Nepal. I read a bit about it this morning—one of the poorest countries in the world, huh. So, you were born there?'

'Did you know they're drafting a new constitution?' Ava said, deflecting his question.

'Is that why you're going there? To draft a constitution?'

'That would be well above my pay grade.' Ava laughed, and asked about his films.

His last documentary was on the Maras of Guatemala. 'They're not fooling around, our cameraman almost took a bullet,' he said. 'I'm dying to start a new project already. Anything going on in Nepal?' He shook his head. 'Just my luck. I meet this gorgeous woman—and she moves away across the world.'

Ava shot him a look and he winked. She blushed involuntarily, surprised, embarrassed, not displeased. This, she remembered, was what it was like to flirt. This was what it used to be like, once, with Gavin.

~

That night, Luke took her to a South Beach club for Revolution Mary's birthday bash. The music was deafening and the strobe lights blinding. The air was heavy with perfume, marijuana, sweat and lust. There was no talking to anyone. Everyone drank dirty martinis and danced.

The following day was Ava's last one here ahead of her flight to Kathmandu. She and Luke spent the day on the beach. He was kitted in a Hawaiian shirt and Bermuda shorts. She picked up a new bikini on Lincoln Street. They lay on lounge chairs, sipping Campari tonics, gazing out at the moss green sea.

They were due for a talk. They always spent the first days of get-togethers studying each other, saving a heart-to-heart for the end.

Ava started it off: 'So, Mom wanted me to find out if you've met anyone.'

'You know Revolution Mary?' She and I are in an open relationship.'

'Oh.' A heavily-pierced performance artist. Her brother had always had bad luck, or poor judgement, in relationships. 'And how does an open relationship work?' Ava asked, keeping her tone neutral.

He shrugged. 'She sees other people, I see other people, but we have to pass it by each other. There are all these rules.'

'Don't you ever get jealous?'

Any hint of disapproval made Luke bristle. 'I hate to be indelicate; Ava, but you're not a great spokesperson for monogamy right now.'

'But is it the kind of relationship you'd prefer to have?' She persisted. 'Given a choice, is this what you'd want?'

'When have I ever done the right thing?' He said, 'I like things fucked up, you know? I could never be like Mom and Dad—so upright and proper, so unbearably correct.' He clinked the ice in his drink, then laughed. 'Fucking do-gooders. Remember all those causes Mom and Dad went on? Mom's mission to end world hunger, or—oh God! Remember Dad's Black Power phase?'

'He was just trying to fill me with pride.' Ava smiled. 'Remember Mom's solidarity potluck with the only gay man in Overwood?'

'Dad's environmental phase! All those trees he uprooted because they weren't native to Ontario!' Luke groaned. 'I hated it! I still hate it. Mom and Dad, setting out to right all the world's wrongs: you know how it makes me feel? Like I can't just—exist. Like it's not worthwhile to just be.'

'You know they mean well.'

'And now it's your turn to save the world,' he said.

'That's not what I'm doing.'

'I think it's worse,' he said. He'd obviously given this some thought. 'I think, Big Sis, that you're going to Nepal because this rich Canadian dentist couple rescued you from a life of Third World poverty, and you think you don't deserve it, you think you have to repay the debt.'

'That's not fair, Luke.'

He said, 'Gavin's been calling me.'

'What?' Ava sat up, stung. 'Why's he calling you? What's he been saying?'

'He sounds really sad. He says the separation was your idea, he wanted to work things out, but—'

'He cheated on me, Luke! With an equity sales director! Did he tell you about Leez Anne Williker? Ask him about her!'

'You want to throw away everything because of one indiscretion?'

'Our marriage wasn't an open relationship!'

'Touché.' He got up. 'Want another Campari tonic?'

'No!'

He said, 'Oh, don't be mad at me, Big Sis,' and sighed theatrically. 'Okay, maybe I'm being selfish, maybe I want you to remain the stable, boring kid so that I can be the one who's fucked up. Because if you get fucked up, I'll have to become stable and boring just to balance out the family dynamics.'

Ava said, 'I've finally found a career I can believe in, Luke. Nepal relies heavily on aid, and do you know how bad things are for women there? I've been doing some background reading, women can't even confer citizenship to their children—'

'Just promise me you'll be okay.'

'I'll be okay.'

'And if slumming doesn't work out, you can always come back.' He strolled off to get a drink.

Ava got up, rankled, and walked to the waterline. Her brother could be so cutting, so barbed. It was just how he was: angry. He judged their parents so harshly—for no real reason. It wasn't as though they'd transplanted him from one part of the world to another. He never had to wonder about his origins.

Two girls were playing with shells at the edge of the water. A couple was playing Frisbee nearby. A wave surged up to Ava's ankles. She followed it in, her feet sinking into the cold, wet sand.

She couldn't believe Gavin had been calling Luke. He'd also been calling Mom and Dad. Last week in Overwood, Mom had pleaded with her not to file for divorce. 'We're not saying you shouldn't go to Nepal, honey, of course you should, but we just... I hope you understand. We love Gavin too.'

The next wave surged up to her calves. Ava walked in deeper, till the waves lapped at her thighs. The water was cold, but she continued on, jumping the waves till the water was waist high. Then she plunged in.

Through the shock of the cold, she swam into the churning waves and came back up where the ocean was swelling on a gentle roll. She floated there awhile, observing the lightness of her body in saltwater.

Even Dad had said that it wasn't like her to be so rash. 'You've always been cautious,' he'd said in Overwood.

But that had been exactly the problem. She'd always been too cautious.

She swam out to the depths.

On her return, she encountered a current. It was mild, but she noticed, after fighting it awhile, that she was swimming in place. For a while more she tried to fight the current. Then she stopped, and let it sweep her out to the depths, where it released her with a wide, gentle spin.

~

That night, Luke took her for a farewell dinner to the bar where Revolution Mary worked, by a shipping channel. All of Luke's friends were there, including Anthony.

'Ms Berriden.'

'Mr Watson.'

'I was thinking, you should forget about Nepal and move to Miami instead.'

Anthony was impossible: smart, charming and attentive. It pleased

Ava that they sat together all evening. After dinner, they sat at the edge of the bar and watched cargo ships glide through the inky black channel. The air was lush. The stars were out. They talked easily about nothing much.

At one point Anthony said, 'So, are you upset about your split-up?'

What needs, what exigencies, make strangers feel as though they know each other? Ava said, 'I guess, I'm going through a lot.'

'Yeah. You know I'd never do anything to make you uncomfortable, but if you want to talk or anything, I live just a few blocks away.'

Ava thought of Gavin. Her caution. The fog. 'I'd like that,' she said.

And after a quick whisper to Luke—'Don't wait up, Little Brother!'— she strolled out with Anthony into the tropical night. Daring herself to explore all that was there. To follow unknown paths and unexplored trails, to wander, to stray, to get lost and be found. To walk out of the life she had into an alternative life.

THE VILLAGE WAS asleep, the house was silent. In her room, Sapana switched off the Petromax and slipped in between the mean, frozen sheets. Her teeth chattered involuntarily. She whimpered. Chandra had oiled her hair earlier in the day, and she smelled sumptuously of coconut. Sapana snuggled up to her for warmth.

Chandra grunted.

'Move over,' Sapana hissed. 'Let me into the warm spot.'

'How's Ba?'

'Move over, will you? I can't even talk, it's so cold.'

As soon as Chandra shifted, Sapana burrowed into her side of the bed, taking in the heat, the comfort, of her body. Chandra was bigger than Sapana, and stronger too, with sinewy arms and muscular legs, though her belly was nice and soft. If she positioned herself right, Sapana could warm her whole back against Chandra. Curling into position, she felt Chandra's toenails poking into her. She'd cut her nails for her tomorrow. She'd cut her own nails too. Ba needed constant attention. They'd both been so busy with him, they'd neglected themselves.

She warmed up, and eventually stopped shivering. She could tell from Chandra's breathing that her friend was wide awake. She said, 'Ba's aware of everything that's going on, Chandra. He can hear us. I told him, just now, that Gyanu Dai's coming, and—it wasn't a smile, but a peaceful expression came over his face.'

'When will Gyanu Dai get here?'

'You know what he's like, I've stopped asking, but I'm sure he'll come. Or—you don't think he'd stay in the desert, do you?'

'I'll go to my Muwa Buwa's house while he's here,' Chandra said.

'No! You have to stay, Chandra, remember, we're going to live together after...' She couldn't speak about Ba's passing.

Chandra shifted in bed. 'Just for a few days. How long will Gyanu Dai stay? I'll move back then.'

'Maybe he won't leave, though,' Sapana said, battling away her sadness. She'd been sad for so long with Ma, and now with Ba: she was sick of being sad. 'Maybe Gyanu Dai won't leave, Chandra. Maybe we'll all live here together,' she said, and the thought cheered her momentarily. Then the sadness returned. 'The other day I was thinking: after Ba goes, no one will ever call me Chhori.'

'What kind of talk is that.'

'I won't be anyone's daughter anymore.' Sapana hated crying, but couldn't help it.

'Tch, tch, tch.' Chandra put her arms around her, and held her tightly. 'I'll be here for you, won't I? I'll be here for you, and you'll be here for me. And yes, maybe Gyanu Dai will stay on, and we'll all live here as a family.'

'Maybe, hai?' Sapana wiped away her tears.

'Talk about something else. Tell me more about the study tour. You were telling me about the pig farm earlier. Tell me more about that.'

'I don't feel like it.'

'Then tell me again about the silkworms, tell me again what they looked like.'

'I don't want to talk about that. I don't want to talk about anything right now.'

'Then go to sleep.'

'Hold me till I fall asleep?'

'Come.' She drew Sapana closer in to her.

Sapana could hear Chandra's heartbeat, slow and steady, in her chest. It felt good to be held, to be touched. After Ma left, Sapana had longed to be able to touch her once more. The sudden absence had been bewildering. With Ba, now, she spent all day holding his hands, wiping his face, cleaning him, rearranging him on the bed, because soon he'd be gone and all she'd be left with was his absence. Listening to Chandra's heartbeat, she thought: hold me always, Chandra. Be here, right here, where I can feel you.

'Chandra?' she said.

Chandra grunted.

'I can't sleep, Chandra.'

'Close your eyes and think about something nice.'

'Like what, Chandra?'

'The study tour. Think about something on the study tour.'

'La, I'll try, hai. Keep holding me?'

'Of course.'

'La, I'll sleep now.'

'Try.'

'I'm sleeping now.'

'You're obviously not sleeping if you're talking.'

Sapana smiled in the dark. 'I'm sleeping, I'm actually asleep.'

'Idiot.'

'Honestly, believe me, I'm talking to you in my sleep, ah-ha-ha.'
'Go to sleep!'
'I'm asleep, ah-ha-ha-ha-ha, I'm really asleep!'

MALEAH, MALEAH. IF she could see his home, would she love him more, would she love him less? She of saltwater waves and drifting tides: what would she make of these backbreaking hills? From the water tap Gyanu looked out at the ancient, familiar village. He could see the stand of bottlebrush trees, the mud huts and concrete houses and the terraced fields, thick, in this season, with corn. The mist was fine this morning. The mad river was visible in the distance, as were the low blue hills where he and his friends used to pick wild berries as boys. The land looked deceptively abundant. From his first glimpse out of the airplane window through the long drive from Kathmandu, he'd been struck by its greenness, its fecundity. How accustomed he'd grown to the desert.

The cold tap water quickened his pulse, ridding him of the stiffness of the thirteen days of austerities, and awakening him to the world.

He'd got to the village in time for Ba's last breath. Then he'd shorn his hair, worn white clothes and lit the funeral pyre, as he had for Ma. For thirteen days he'd received the company of mourners from all over the village. At mealtimes he'd eaten unsalted food, and at night he'd slept fitfully under thin, unstitched sheets. With the completion of the Shraadha ceremony yesterday, his filial duties were done.

As he washed, his sister called out from the porch: 'Aren't you finished, Dai?'

Sapana was standing exactly the way Ma used to, with her hands on her hips. Since Gyanu's last visit to the village, her sharp eyes and dark lips have become more defined. She was fine-boned like Ma, with the same agreeable manners that disguised a more willful depth. She called out, 'Hurry up, Dai, I've made all your favourite dishes.'

'Coming, Bahini.'

When he went in, she sat him down at the old laminate table, which had been there since the day he came into this house. It had been a novelty then: Gyanu had never seen laminate. Now the surface was scratched and chipped.

His sister put his plate on the table. 'It's good to see you back in your own clothes, Dai. All these ragged old rituals—I hated seeing you in white. Will you have hot water with your food?'

'Cold is fine.'

'It's been so long since I cooked for you.'

She'd made a simple meal of dal-bhat-tarkaari: rice, black dal with dried chives, and cauliflower with potatoes. After she served herself, they sat and ate together for the first time since his return.

They didn't talk about anything pressing—How long will you stay, Dai? What will you do now, Bahini?—but lingered, instead, over diversions. Gyanu asked after his boyhood friends: 'How's Ram? Did Bisnu come back? Is Kisne around nowadays?'

Sapana asked about his life in the desert.

He told her that most of the staff at Five Spices were Nepali. 'We live together in the same building. We speak Nepali, we eat dal-bhat. If it weren't for the heat, we'd think we were in Kathmandu.'

'How hot does it get there, Dai?'

'In the summer time? It's unimaginable.'

A vision of Maleah came to Gyanu: Maleah lit up by the neon sign of the Al Faraby Hyper Express on their last night together. Earlier that day, Gyanu had bought a coin from Suleiman Bhai, a Nepali jeweller in Deira. Four grams: enough for a ring. When he gave it to Maleah, she had looked at him with questions in her eyes.

He waited for the vision to pass, then said, 'How are you doing, Bahini? It's been hard for you, all these years, taking care of Ba.'

She didn't want to dwell on her sadness. She talked, instead, about a study tour she'd gone on a few months ago. 'They took us out east,' she said, smiling at the memory. 'Out there, it's not like here, it's completely different, Dai. They don't farm for food the way we do. They think of the market and plant cash crops like fruit trees and cardamom and broom.' Gyanu noticed that she said market and cash crops in English. Thulo Ba's CBO had organized the tour. 'In the beginning, everyone kept calling it seebeeyo, seebeeyo,' Sapana said, 'I didn't understand.' She laughed: 'They were saying CBO in English, for community based organization.' Then she grew earnest. 'The CBO has a women's committee, Dai. I wouldn't have been asked on the tour, but old Laptanni Budhi, she's the committee's chairperson, she dropped out. It was me and nine other women—we had such fun!'

How memorable this tour had been for her, Gyanu observed. How small, how sheltered his sister's life had been.

Sapana got up to serve seconds. 'Have more, Dai.'

'I've already eaten too much.'

'You didn't like the food. It's not as good as the food you make,' she said.

'It's the best meal in the world, Bahini.'

He got up to help clear away the dishes, but Sapana snatched away his plate. 'Leave it, Dai, I'll do it.'

'Ey, Bahini,' he laughed, 'in the desert I wash my own dishes, and the dishes of others—'

'But you're at home now,' she said, suddenly grave. 'You know, Dai, with Ma and Ba gone, it's just you and me now. We're all that's left of our family.'

She turned away, her eyes glistening with tears, and began to clatter about to fend off emotions. Whenever Gyanu tried to help, she protested. 'Put that down, Dai! Do you want tea? I'll make tea. Don't do anything, just sit there and drink your tea.'

At the end, she was back to her usual self. 'Dai, what are you going to do today?' she asked. 'Are you going to visit Thulo Ba? He'll be expecting you.' She hesitated, then said, 'It's been so long since I've left the house, I'll go out too, all right, Dai?'

'You don't have to ask for my permission.'

'Rama Bhauju, she's the secretary of the women's committee, she wants to talk to me. I think she's going to ask me to join the committee, Dai. Do you think I should?'

'Do you want to?'

'I really do! Tchee, look, there's an oil stain on my kurta, I'll have to change first.'

She left in a flurry of excitement.

~

Alone in the house, Gyanu walked from room to room, reacquainting himself with it. Ba had broken away from the ancestral home that Thulo Ba and he had inherited to set up a new life with Ma here. The house was small but proud. It had fallen into neglect over the years. The kitchen table and chairs needed repairing. Everything needed repainting: where earlier the doors and windows used to be a deep sea green, they were now a muddy brown. When he came back for Ma's funeral, Gyanu had had the house wired, but neither Ba nor Sapana had been able to connect it to the power line. They still used Petromaxes for light.

He checked the larder and saw that it was stocked with last year's potatoes and corn, lentils and rice. There were tomatoes, onions, garlic bulbs and ginger roots and the usual spices—cumin and coriander, sesame, fenugreek, turmeric, dried chillies. But there were none of the finer spices: clove or nutmeg or saffron, certainly no nuts or dates or raisins or lemon grass, lime leaves, galangal. Back in the kitchen, he saw that the pots and pans were rusty. All the knives were dull. There were no shelves; everything was stacked—tidily, but without any system—on the countertop.

He'd realized, over the thirteen days, that he was now Sapana's guardian. He needed to set her up: but how? 'Thirty days, Beta,' Shantanu Kumar had said when granting him leave. 'Not one day more.' There were only two weeks left.

The morning mist had burned away by the time he set out for Thulo Ba's house. Down the way, by the bottlebrush trees, blind Gharti buwa was sitting on a straw mat, sunning himself. Gyanu greeted him: 'You're looking well, Buwa.'

'It's already been thirteen days, Babu?' Gharti buwa turned up.

'The days pass by.'

'Your Ba was a very wise man.'

They talked for a while about family: Sapana on Gyanu's side, and Gharti Muwa, Chandra and little Tara on Gharti buwa's side. Then Gyanu walked on, passing Gharti buwa's hut. Their family had always been poor, but a pall had fallen over the family after their eldest daughter, Surya, disappeared. This entire stretch of the village felt blighted. Next to Gharti buwa's hut was an empty house, abandoned by the family after their only son died in a bus accident. Beside the empty house, a brick house had been divided in two after the sons launched a court case for their inheritance. By the time they won the case, both parents had died and the sons had emigrated. Both halves lay rotting by the path.

But the rest of the village wasn't desolate. Further down, were concrete houses that had been built from the earnings of family members in the cities, or abroad. From there, the path dipped past the terraced fields to the large feudal estates. Gyanu passed the bungalow of the Amatya clan whose son was a doctor in Kathmandu. Nearby were the spread-out mustard fields of the Sah clan. Then came Thulo Ba's vast plot, marked off by stone walls.

Ba's plot abutted Thulo Ba's. It was large enough to have sustained the family once. After Ba's cancer diagnosis, Thulo Ba's family had taken to farming it in return for half the yields. That arrangement would have to continue, though it had occurred to Gyanu, over the thirteen days, that he ought to transfer the land deed to Sapana.

Thulo Ba had had the old ancestral house painted pink, as though to flaunt its owner's prosperity. Gyanu found his uncle in the courtyard, surrounded by his usual coterie of party cadres, favour-seekers, hangers-on and lackeys: the eternal unemployed of the land. Dressed in a traditional labeda sural, Thulo Ba looked every bit the patriarch. Governments had fallen, regimes had changed, a Maoist insurgency had started and ended, the monarchy had been abolished. Allying with every new power in Kathmandu, Thulo Ba had remained ascendant throughout. Though he held no official position at the moment, everyone called him the Chairman.

Gyanu bowed to him.

The old man proffered his blessings. 'You've changed out of white, already, Gyanu Babu?'

'Just this morning, Thulo Ba.'

'Well, no one expects you to observe a whole year's mourning,' his uncle said.

Old hurts—the wounds of family life—winced through Gyanu. He said, 'He was the only father I knew, Thulo Ba.'

'And you've been a true son to him. Sit, Babu.' The old man turned to his lackeys. 'Make room, ey, boys, make room for Gyanu Babu. Move. Move at once.'

'I was hoping to talk to you alone,' Gyanu said.

His uncle nodded, and with a flick of hand dismissed everyone.

When the last of his coterie straggled away, Gyanu said, 'I need advice, Thulo Ba, about Sapana.'

The old man's eyes glazed over in boredom. He'd anticipated this talk. 'Yes, I tried to bring up the subject of Sapana Nani's future with my brother,' he said, 'but...ey, I don't have to tell you, he was a dreamer. He always told me: that girl's got fire, she'll look after herself. But you and I know it's not easy, Gyanu Babu. Did Sapana Nani tell you, I sent her on a study tour? The CBO had no budget, mind you. I sent her at my own expense.'

'She benefited. We're grateful.'

'It's our dharma to look after our own,' he said. Then his tone hardened. 'We'll continue to look after your Ba's land—unless you'd rather take responsibility yourself. Though how could you, if you're going back to the desert?'

'I'll have to go back.'

'And how can Sapana Nani manage it all by herself?' his uncle said. 'Also, Gyanu Babu, she shouldn't live in that house any more. A single girl. She can move in with us, we've got room. We'll cover her expenses from your family's share of the yields.'

Thrown by this, Gyanu tried to steer the conversation back. 'I was thinking that we should put the land in her name, Thulo Ba.'

The old man fixed him with a hard gaze. 'Sapana Nani would just have to sign a few documents. Ey, don't worry about small things like that, there are bigger concerns. Sapana Nani takes after your mother,' he said, 'and as a man you understand that that kind of beauty attracts bad men. The wickedness of the world only increases. Even here, in the village, we hear: this family was tricked, that girl was sold, that girl died of AIDS in a brothel in Mumbai. As her guardian, you must talk to her. What your sister needs is a groom.'

Gyanu hesitated. He wanted more for his sister than an early marriage—though what other life could Sapana possibly live in this village? Even if she were to move to Kathmandu, she was only a high school graduate: and he wouldn't be there to look after her. She'd missed the deadline for enrolling in the Plus Two in Butwal Bazaar. Should he take her with him to the desert? Still unsure, he said, 'There's so much to think about.'

'It's true. Your entire family structure has changed, and it's too early to think about worldly matters. There's the prayer on the forty-fifth day. You'll stay for that, won't you?'

'I should.' Gyanu was immediately stabbed by remorse. He had to leave.

'We'll talk about everything in time, Babu.'

'I look to you for guidance, Thulo Ba.' Gyanu bowed again and left.

For form's sake, he then sought out his aunt. She was in the yard behind the house, picking stones out of a basketful of rice. 'You won't stay awhile, Gyanu Babu?'

'Another day, Thuli ma.'

'You and Sapana Nani come for a meal.'

'We will, Thuli ma.'

Gyanu left, feeling trapped. He should have expected obstructions, he should have expected delays. It took wherewithal, and patience, to undo the knots of obligation, debt, need—and power—in the village. Thulo Ba hadn't come to be known as the Chairman for nothing. He wanted to control everything, even his dead brother's assets.

On his way back, he stopped on a ridge to survey Ba's plot. When he was a boy he'd helped Ba till the plot, plant crops, repair the irrigation canal and harvest the yields. On hot days he and Ba used to rest beneath an aged willow tree. The tree had been chopped down, but its stump still remained. How much would the plot fetch if they were to sell it?

Any such decision would be Sapana's to make, he knew. This was her inheritance. Gyanu had more than exceeded his claims after Ba sent him to Kathmandu to enrol in a hospitality course, and to find his way in the world.

Sapana was still out when he got home. The house felt deserted. It made him restless. He checked his mobile phone. Maleah would be at the gift shop right now. There were no phone signals in the village. He'd have to go to Butwal Bazaar to call her. He'd do so tomorrow.

Today, he'd prepare the evening meal: he'd make something special for Sapana. He went to the backyard and found a head of cauliflower, some mustard greens, two carrots. There were chives in the yard, there was basil. Further out, tender young shoots were sprouting in the bamboo grove. By the grove was a lime tree. He plucked a few of its soft, tender leaves.

By the time Sapana returned he'd finished cooking the meal.

'Ey, Dai, what are you doing?' she cried, seeing him at the stove.

'Tonight, Bahini, I'll feed you a five-star meal.'

He served rice with toasted sesame, crispy mustard greens, stir-fried cauliflower, and fragrant lime tea. Sapana delighted over everything. 'What's in this, Dai? I've never tasted anything so...how much do your customers pay for a meal like this?'

'For a dinner for two? About ten thousand rupees in our currency.'

'Tch, when will we Nepalis ever be able to afford a meal like that, hai? Ey, Dai,' she said. 'Rama Bhauju asked me to join the women's committee, not just as a member—as the treasurer!' She said, 'I didn't realize the committee members have been paying a hundred rupees' due every month. They've been giving out interest-free loans with that money. I thought the committee was a sham—and it is, Thulo Ba and Jeevan Bhatta are profiting from it, but today, listening to Rama Bhauju, I was thinking about what Ba always said: there's nothing you can't do. Even in this village, if you try, there's nothing you can't do, Dai.'

She sounded so much like their father: lofty. 'Bahini,' he said, 'do you want to move with Thulo Ba?'

She looked at him, startled.

'I went to see him,' he explained. 'He suggested it.'

'Do I have to?' she said. 'I don't want to, I really don't want to. Dai, Chandra and I made a pact,' she said. 'When the doctor said Ba would go, we decided to live in this house together. I've been meaning to ask, Dai: Chandra's miserable in her Muwa Buwa's house. Would it be all right for her to move back?'

'Of course.'

Sapana beamed. 'I'll tell her you said so!'

Gyanu tried, again, to talk about her future: 'Are you going to enrol in the Plus Two next year, Bahini?'

'I guess I should.' She hesitated. 'Chandra and I talk about it sometimes. She can't afford the fees.'

'That shouldn't stop you.'

'I know.' She became evasive, and began to talk, again, about the women's committee. 'I can't believe I'm going to be the treasurer, Dai. These old women, they need help even to do simple addition and subtraction. They should bring other girls in, girls like Chandra and Ritu and Namrata.'

Gyanu listened to her, wondering whether this—her life in the village—would be enough for her. Perhaps, for now it would be. And as for the future, well, it was chance that propelled people forward, wasn't it? Maleah had started off in a fishing village in the Philippines, and was now in Dubai. Who knew where she would end up? Who knew where he would, himself, end up? He, who didn't even know where he'd been born: for Ma's life before Ba had never been mentioned in their family. Only at the very end, on her deathbed, had Ma acknowledged it. 'You had to give up your past so I could live,' she'd said to Gyanu. 'I couldn't even give you your own identity.'

Could a man who didn't know where he started ever know where he'd end up? Everyone, everyone followed chance, Gyanu thought. This would be true for Sapana, too: who knew where she'd end up? He'd enrol her in the Plus Two. This would be a start. He'd transfer the land deed to her name. And then, and then: he could leave.

IDAF'S OFFICE FELT like a fortress: ringed by a high stone wall—a rampart—topped with metal spikes. At the front gate, a flank of former Gurkha soldiers whisked visitors through a metal detector, and scanned bags and examined incoming vehicles for bombs. The office had received threats during the Maoist insurgency. The conflict had ended, and the threat had passed, but the security measures remained. Ava learned from a risk assessment report that the office building had also been retrofitted to minimize the risks posed by earthquakes. Kathmandu fell in a seismically active zone. All the building walls were reinforced and the windows fitted with shatterproof glass. The office was hermetically sealed, as though to keep Nepal out. Entering the conference hall for a senior staff meeting, Ava noted that but for the country map on the wall, there was no indication as to which part of the world she were in.

She found this unexpectedly soothing. The hotel she was staying in was part of an international chain, and it bore only a few decorative traces of Nepal, though her room did look out onto a crooked brick house. At night, Ava would stare out the window, both attracted and repulsed by the flimsy structure, its moss-covered tile roof, its dirty windows. The people of the house huddled together on the floor in a cramped room, their faces lit by the flickering blue light of a television screen. Being in Nepal was harder than she'd anticipated. The drive from the airport to the hotel alone had revived painful memories, and she'd recoiled like a wounded child at the shabby streets, pell-mell crowds, ugly concrete-block houses. There was garbage festering openly on the street leading to her hotel. Fortunately, her daily commute to the office was short. She'd have to immerse herself in Nepal eventually, but for now she was grateful for the barriers that existed. She wasn't ready to breach them just yet.

'It's donor shopping, plain and simple!' Andrew Scheiffer from Employment Generation strode into the conference hall with a woman Ava couldn't recall from the staff chart in her orientation package. 'These NGOs beg us for funding.' Andrew's voice boomed. 'But if we demand accountability, they go to another donor. I'll bring this up at the next donor harmonization meeting. In fact...' He whipped out a cell phone. 'Hello, Greg? It's Andrew Scheiffer from IDAF. Andrew Scheiffer. Andrew Scheiffer. I said it's...' He turned around and strode back out of the hall. 'Can you hear me?'

Without as much as acknowledging Ava, the woman sat at the far side of the hall.

This was in keeping with the institutional culture at IDAF. No one at the office smiled or said hello to each other; or none of the international staff did. The secretaries—all Nepali women—talked constantly among themselves, gathering in groups in the halls, in the offices, in the women's washrooms. Their names were Geeta, Sharmila, Indu, Prativa, Meera—Ava couldn't yet match the names to the faces. They always greeted Ava with a punchy, 'Namaste, Ava madam!' pronouncing her name in the Nepali way: Abha. Early on, one of them had said, 'You are so pretty, madam, a black beauty, like our own girls from the Tarai, in the south,' and another had chimed in, 'I was thinking that also!' Ava had since avoided the secretaries. Not that they seemed to mind, or indeed to notice. There was an unspoken, if rigorous, hierarchy at IDAF separating the support staff from the programme staff. Only two of the programme staff were Nepali. They were paid considerably less than the internationals—in keeping with local rates, apparently—and they were placed below the internationals in the chart. They were tasked, essentially, with assisting the internationals.

One of the Nepali programme staff, Vishwa Bista, came into the hall and sat beside Ava. 'Is this chair free?' He'd brought a paper that Ava had drafted in her first days of work, a paper on Gender Responsive Budgeting. She'd had to learn about the subject overnight. She'd be presenting the paper at a stakeholders' meeting with senior government officials later in the week.

She watched Vishwa pull out a Mont Blanc and mark up a passage, and asked, 'How is it?'

'Mmm. One or two small things, nothing major.' Vishwa had studied in the US, at Ohio State University, and he had an American accent. 'I'll come by your office later to discuss it.'

'Thanks.'

'Sure.' He made a note on the margins.

Vishwa was responsible for guiding Ava during her six months' probation period. He was a helpful man: he did more for her than called for by duty. He picked her up at the hotel in the morning, and dropped her off at the end of the day. He ate lunch with her at the canteen, and every afternoon he brought her a cup of the sweet, milky Nepali tea that he brewed in his office. He had debriefed Ava on safety, helped her buy an earthquake kit and had even found her a real estate agent so that she could move to a place of her own.

Jared Lukkinson from Peace Building entered the conference hall with Shova Simkhada, the other Nepali programme staff. Shova worked with Andrew Scheiffer on…something. Ava hadn't quite grasped what when she'd gone to Shova's office to introduce herself.

Everyone knew Herman Banke from Social Inclusion wouldn't be coming to the briefing. He'd dispatched a circular this morning—I OBJECT IN THE STRONGEST POSSIBLE TERMS!!!—protesting IDAF headquarters' directive to downgrade his programme to a short-term project on resilience. He had appealed to headquarters to reconsider the directive. Meanwhile he was refusing to work, spending his workdays sending furious circulars: SOCIAL INCLUSION IS THE MOST PRESSING ISSUE BEFORE NEPAL!!!

The deputy country director Claire Ross-Jones arrived with a slam of the door. 'Good morning, everyone.' She was direct and authoritative. 'We're waiting for William, he had a meeting at the Home Ministry, he's been held up, the student unions have blocked the roads.' She scanned the room. 'Jared, I wanted to make sure you've spoken to Dana Spinkof at Save the Children?'

Jared shot her a surprised look. 'We're cooperating on a joint strategy on non-compliance.'

'Will it touch on governance?'

'Naturally.'

'Super. Now, has everyone set up their sectoral briefings with our new director of Women's Empowerment Programme, Ava Berriden?' Claire turned to Ava. 'By the way, I ran into the Secretary of Health yesterday, and it occurred to me—how did Nepal do on MDG Six?'

MDG Six. Ava had brushed up on the millennium development goals, but couldn't remember what the sixth one pertained to.

Vishwa helped her out. 'I'm still briefing Ava on the MDGs, so let me answer,' he said. 'Nepal was a little behind on MDG Six, Claire. At first we saw significant progress on HIV-AIDS, but there was a reversal. The indicators on malaria, tuberculosis and other preventable diseases were also mixed. The key problem, Claire, has been resource gaps.'

Claire nodded. 'And will the paper on Gender Responsive Budgeting address these resource gaps going forward?'

This time, Ava was able to reply. 'It will. It'll also highlight Post-2015 Priority Themes.'

'And don't forget, you'll need to double your budget for the Five

Year Outlook.'

The country representative William Tomlinson came in at last, trailed closely by Andrew Scheiffer, booming: 'It's donor shopping!'

'Yes, yes.' William Tomlinson was rumpled and unfocused in the eye, like someone who'd just woken up from a nap. 'My apologies, everyone.' He sat heavily at the head of the table. 'These goddamn student unions, always screwing around. I don't know what they think they're doing. All right, let's begin.'

Claire took charge of the proceedings. 'We're here,' she said, 'to hear from Daphne Muirwood.' She nodded at the woman at the far end of the hall. 'Daphne has been deputed from headquarters to help us integrate the Paris Declaration on Aid Effectiveness into the Five Year Outlook. Daphne, please.'

'Thank you.' Daphne Muirwood gave the room a thin smile. 'I'm in Nepal on a limited mandate for six months. My brief is to innovate an internal implementation strategy in low-performance country offices in the Asia-Pacific Region as we draft the Five Year Outlook.'

Ava paid close attention, trying to follow her.

'The implementation strategy is envisioned as being two-pronged,' Daphne said. 'The implementation strategy addresses the latest updates on the Paris Principles. There'll be a modular component as well, which I'll apprise you of later. But first let me begin with an overview of the updates of Accra and Busan.'

~

Ava soon learned that her predecessor, Catherine Christy, had left after receiving a poor review for under-budgeting. Claire Ross-Jones was keen that Ava not repeat the mistake. She was granting Ava four months to draft the women's empowerment component of the Five Year Outlook, telling her more than once: 'I can't stress this enough: I need the budget doubled, Ava.'

Proposals for next year were also pouring in daily. It was part of Ava's brief, as the director of the Women's Empowerment Programme, to assess each one for funding. She began to spend all her office hours, as well as evenings and weekends, studying reports, policy papers, assessments, briefs, circulars and memos. Stacks of documents lay half-read in her office and in her hotel room.

And yet she had to scramble to keep up. A few days after the weekly briefing, at a briefing of the Employment Generation Programme—

'Paradigm Shift on Schemes for Employment Generation'—she couldn't even understand what Shova Simkhada was saying, in part because Shova's voice was so soft as to be audible. 'The application of cash transfers from transitional societies in sub-Saharan Africa to transitional societies in South Asia remains practically untested,' Shova said before a cough from Jared Lukkinson drowned out her words. For a while her lips moved soundlessly. Then Ava heard, 'Preliminary baseline study carried out by our partner shows that microfinance still has a higher point estimate,' before Shova's voice faded again, till: 'Nevertheless this paradigm shift must be acknowledged. Therefore, it is our recommendation that the Five Year Outlook allocate resources for cash transfers to our clients...'

'Stakeholders,' Andrew Scheiffer cut in.

'Stakeholders. Sorry. Yes.' Shova closed her eyes. 'Sorry, Andrew. I mean allocate transfers to our stakeholders, not clients. Stakeholders, stakeholders,' she said. 'Stakeholders. In conclusion, what I am saying is that in the Five Year Outlook we must allocate additional resources for cash transfers to our stakeholders.'

Was she recommending that IDAF hand out cash? Was this a common practice in the aid?

Ava never got a chance to ask, though she did stop by Shova's office several times in the following days. Shova was either in meetings, or on the phone, or out of the office. In fact, everyone at IDAF was extraordinarily busy, or if not busy, then preoccupied—so much so that Ava couldn't help but wonder if there was something wrong here.

She felt so especially on the day of her briefing with William Tomlinson. As she headed to his office, she rounded a corner and came upon Herman Banke and Jared Lukkinson arguing in the hallway. Or Herman had cornered Jared, and was shouting at him: 'Without social inclusion, what peacebuilding can there be, Jared? Inclusion is key to peacebuilding in this country! There are more than a hundred identity groups here, we cannot support their systematic exclusion by the PEON, the PEON, the Permanent Establishment of Nepal!'

Jared's hands were up as if in surrender. Unable to get around the two men, Ava stood by as Herman shouted: 'The government of Nepal tells us to write 'poor and marginalized,' instead of 'socially excluded,' and you comply! I demand that you put the term 'excluded' back in your report, Jared!'

'Naturally—'

'If you don't reinstate the term 'excluded' I'll fight all your work,

Jared! I'll undermine everything you do! I'll destroy you! There'll be no more peacebuilding for you!'

Jared stepped aside and walked away, hands still up.

Herman turned away, towards Ava, his face blotched with fury.

'Sorry, I'll just—' Ava passed by.

What had she stepped into?

The country representative's office complex occupied the sunny top floor of the fort. His secretary was seated outside the door. Was she Geeta? No, Geeta was Claire's secretary, who had a soft face. This woman had angular features. This was—Sharmila? Indu? Prativa? Meera?

'Good morning, Abha madam!' The secretary smiled. 'Please go in, William Sir is waiting for you only.'

'Thank you.' Ava stepped in.

William Tomlinson was on the phone, fulminating. 'The fucking minister, how many times do I have to tell him, how do I get it through his thick skull—oh, hello.' He sat up when he noticed her. 'Ava Berry. Were we supposed to meet today?'

'Berriden. We're scheduled for a briefing. I can wait outside.'

'Ah, I see.' He took a long gulp from a glass of—tea? It glinted like aged Scotch. 'Just a sec,' he said into the phone, and turned back to her. 'Look, I'm sorry, Ava, but the Minister of Youth and Sports has thrown us for a loop, he's demanding that we allocate extra funds for a stadium if we want his support on youth leadership programmes. Can we reschedule for next week? Oh, wait, I'll be in London next week, and then I've got family time in Luang Prabang—have you ever been?'

'To Luang Prabang?'

'It's out of this world. We'll have to postpone the briefing till after I come back.'

'Oh. All right.'

'Thanks for understanding, Ava. And on your way out, will you tell Sharmila I've run out of ice?'

IDAF *was* a major aid organization. It had a fine reputation internationally. Back in her office, Ava scoured the web to reconfirm this, to reassure herself. In Nepal, IDAF funded not just the government, but also some of the country's largest international and national non-government organizations. The problem was with her: she hadn't yet adapted to this new line of work. It surprised her, in retrospect, that her application to IDAF had been accepted at all. What did she know, after all, about women's empowerment? Her annual programme budget was upwards of two million pounds. What qualified her to oversee it?

Kim Armstone had emailed from Juba asking how things were going.

Ava sent a peppy reply: *I'm learning a lot!*

Did you meet Tomás Barba? Kim had written. *I told him you were adopted from Nepal. I hope that's all right?*

It wasn't quite. Ava didn't want anyone here to know about that. It felt too private. She hadn't put up family photos in her office, and when Vishwa Bista asked about her background, she lied: 'We have mixed ancestry—it's complicated.'

Now Kim's friend Tomás Barba knew. Ava and he had exchanged emails and cell-phone numbers, but she didn't want to meet him. At night, she ordered room service and looked out the window at the brick house. Kathmandu was going through twelve-hour power cuts, and on some nights the house was completely dark. She watched the invisible family, imagining their lives. She felt far away from Nepal. Several weeks into IDAF, she couldn't really tell what impact her work had on the lives of Nepalis. Outside of work, she didn't even know any Nepalis.

~

For now, Vishwa Bista was her sole source of companionship. He helped her prepare for the stakeholders' meeting, and, on the day, picked her up early, in one of the more ostentatious office SUVs, the kind that only programme staff were authorized to requisition. Vishwa had taught Ava how to requisition them for her own use, but she'd never had reason to do so. The meeting was at a resort outside Kathmandu. Ava had dressed in a formal suit. She was armed with her attaché case. She wanted to look authoritative.

The driver—one of many at IDAF, they seemed interchangeable, no one ever introduced them—steered away from the usual turn to the office, through a row of tumbledown buildings.

Vishwa was in a garrulous mood. 'We'll be taking a—what do they call it?' He smiled. 'When I was at Ohio State, a group of us—foreign students—drove from Columbus to Detroit once along a—that's it—a scenic route.'

The tumbledown buildings gave way to a stretch of concrete block houses. Much of Kathmandu was ugly, there was no sugarcoating it. The modern city was drab at best, and at worst squalid. There was something personal about Ava's disappointment in this. As they drove on, she found herself picking out fragments of beauty—a flowering cherry tree, carved woodwork on an old house, a shrine strewn with marigolds—in the fug of mist, dust and exhaust.

After weaving through traffic, the driver turned onto a four-lane highway. Vishwa pointed out points of interest as they drove on. 'You see there? That's the government department for herbs and herbal products. And that's the TB hospital, Ava, you know, tuberculosis. When we were growing up, this area felt so far away, in the countryside. Now...Kathmandu has really grown.'

'Has it?'

'You can't imagine. Now if we were to turn right here, we'd get to Bhaktapur. Have you been there yet? I can take you sometime. It's one of the three ancient kingdoms of Kathmandu Valley.'

He began to tell her about the valley's history. Parts of it were familiar to her. Her parents had made her and Luke read guidebooks before their Christmas trip, and she'd sought out books on history, politics and sociology after accepting this job. But she was happy to learn more.

And Vishwa was happy to talk. 'And so the lake was drained, you see, by the sword of the Bodhisattva...' He became eloquent, even flowery, describing Kathmandu's mythical origins.

The air cleared after they left the city. The sky shifted from grey to white to blue. They drove past terraced fields and small, scattered villages. The road meandered up into the hills. This was the Nepal of the guidebooks Ava had read at age fourteen: beautiful, exotic, alien.

On a high ridge, the driver turned off the main road, into a resort. Getting out of the car, Ava had to stop to take in the sweep of undulating green hills and steep black mountains, and beyond, the Himalayas: sharp, spiky, white, shimmering like a hallucination.

Vishwa said, 'Nice, huh?'

'I've never seen anything like it.'

Nothing in Kathmandu had prepared her for this. This, she thought, was what she'd barricaded herself against that Christmas. It was what she still was, consciously and subconsciously, barricading herself against: the risk of developing an affinity for this land.

Nepal was beautiful.

The stakeholders' meeting took place in a musty hall with no view of the Himalayas. There were about a hundred people in the hall. Ava and Vishwa sat at the front of the hall, but just as the meeting started, Vishwa excused himself and went to talk to a man in a traditional trouser-and-tunic costume and colourful cap. The official at the orphanage had worn the same costume, Ava remembered. It was the national costume. There was a name for it: she used to know it.

The presentations, when they began, were in Nepali. Was she supposed to have known about this? Ava glanced around, noting that she was the only foreigner present. Surely she wasn't expected to understand, or speak, Nepali? The language gushed and bubbled and lilted and popped. She wondered if it was difficult to learn. At one point, she looked at Vishwa to see if he could possibly translate for her, but he was absorbed in conversation with the costumed man. So she sat, discomfited, increasingly bored, as one after another speaker—all men—came to the podium. Even the PowerPoints—the charts, graphs, captions—were in Nepali.

When her turn came, she was rattled. She hated public speaking, and right now she couldn't even tell whether the audience understood English: though surely they did? She stood at the podium, trying to project confidence: 'Good morning. Namaste. Thank you for having me here.' The audience was mostly unresponsive, but a woman in the back was smiling at her and nodding, as though encouraging a child at a school performance. Ava went ahead and made her presentation. Everyone clapped at the end, but there was no telling whether anything she'd said—about Gender Responsive Budgeting, about the MDGs, about the Post-2015 Priority Themes—had made an impression.

The meeting concluded with a buffet lunch in another windowless hall. In the queue, Vishwa introduced her to the costumed man. 'Ava, please meet the labour secretary. Sir,' he said to the man, 'our new director of WEP, Ava Berriden, is from Canada.'

'Oho!' the labour secretary exclaimed. 'My daughter is also living in Canada, in Ottawa. She is having a job as software designer in a company. Very good salary.'

'Oh,' Ava said. 'That's wonderful.'

'My son-in-law is also having an office job. They are living in Blackburn Hamlet. You know Blackburn Hamlet?'

'No.'

'They bought one house there, in Blackburn Hamlet. They are saying to me to visit. Where I should apply for a ten-year super-visa, miss. In Delhi, or in Kathmandu itself?'

'Oh. I don't know,' Ava said. An awkward silence followed. She tried to break it. 'You'd probably be the right person to ask. I've been following the news a little, but can't tell—when will the constitution be promulgated?'

'Constitution, ha ha.' The labour secretary turned away, towards the buffet table.

As they picked over the greasy Indian-Chinese lunch, the woman who'd smiled and nodded during Ava's presenation came and introduced herself. She was the deputy co-director of an international NGO called World Development Systems-Nepal. She didn't mention her name. 'I am working on a proposal to submit to IDAF,' she said. 'WDS-Nepal is a longtime partner, as you know. Catherine Christy, she was my good friend. You are free on Friday, Ava? You come to my house for a Nepali dal-bhat: you and Vishwaji.'

Dinner at the house of a Nepali woman. Ava felt she ought to extend herself. 'If Vishwa's free,' she said, unsurely. 'I'd love to.'

'Sure, sure,' Vishwa said. 'Ava, you should know that Indira Sharmaji here is one of the seniormost Nepali women in the aid sector.'

'That is true.' The woman—Indira—beamed. 'I am seniormost!' Then she said something in Nepali to Vishwa.

He replied to her in English, 'But we can discuss this at your house, Indiraji.'

'Most definitely. Most definitely. It is confirmed, then. Friday at seven!' She shook hands with Ava. 'Looking forward to it very much!'

'Me too,' Ava said, still unsure.

By the time they left the resort, a haze had settled over the sky, and the Himalayas were no longer visible. Ava stared, nevertheless, at the undulating hills and steep mountains. There were houses scattered about in small clusters—villages. One or two houses stood alone, separated from the rest. They looked fragile, and unprotected, against the vastness. It was impossible not to think: I could have been born in of those houses.

On the drive back, Vishwa praised Ava's presentation. 'We got a great response from the stakeholders, now we'll have to build on that, Ava. Ah, look.' He pointed at a row of sheets drying beside the road. 'See that? That's handmade paper made from hemp, it's part of the handicrafts industry of Nepal.'

He talked about handicrafts as they drove out of the hills, into the grey fug of Kathmandu. He talked about papermaking, basket-weaving, wood carving, stonemasonry, metal work, jewellery design. He told her about the special repousse technique used to cast bronze statues of Hindu and Buddhist deities. Then he began to explain the deities.

By the time they returned to IDAF—the fort—Ava was exhausted.

In the washroom, she splashed water on her face. It revived her a little. But then, drying off, she suddenly felt very lonely. She wished she could talk to someone, someone from her world. Not Gavin. And not Anthony either, though Anthony had emailed: she owed him a reply. She wished she could talk to someone who knew her, who also knew Nepal.

Luke. She missed Luke.

On the washroom wall, by the dryer, was a cancer self-testing aid: a woman's breast, made of rubber. It stuck out of the wall like a gristly trophy. She gave it a poke and felt a lump on the sticky underside. Had she made a mistake coming to Nepal?

She took a cell phone photo of the breast and attached it to an email to her brother: *Help, there's a Nepali woman trapped in the wall, I don't know how to empower her. Talk soon? I need to vent! xoxoA*

OLD LAPTANNI BUDHI'S house stood at the foot of the hills on the far shore of the mad river. Sapana ducked in through a side door, shivering underneath her thick brown shawl. The mist was so dense this morning it seeped into the veins, chilled the blood. The members of the women's committee were huddled by the hearth. Kanchan Bhauju patted a cushion next to her, and Sapana sat cross-legged on it. Jethi Didi and Naina Di shifted to make room when Hasta Ma and Laxmi Aama came in. One of Laptanni Budhi's countless daughters-in-law served everyone hot, steaming tea.

Laptanni Budhi looked around. 'Where's the Secretary gone? Ey, where's Rama? She was here just a moment ago.'

'I'm here, I'm here!' Rama Bhauju hurried in and sat in the centre of the room. 'Something's wrong, I need to pee all the time, I should go to the medical shop in the bazaar.' She took a cup of tea from the daughter-in-law and said, 'Lau, let's start the meeting.' Then she became officious. 'The agenda of today's meeting is: accounts. Now that Sapana Bahini is the treasurer,' she said, 'she'll have to do the accounts for us.'

'Lord Shulinbaba sent us a treasurer just in time!' Laptanni Budhi said. 'My nephew Jit told me we have to do the additions and subtractions in writing.'

'In writing?' Rama Bhauju gasped. 'He wants it all in writing?'

'That's what he told me,' Laptanni Budhi said. 'He told me the CBO's asking for money from foreigners. We have to tell them how much money we collected, how many loans we gave, what profits and losses everyone made.'

'And we have to do all that in writing!'

This stumped everyone. For a while, the room fell silent.

Then Laptanni Budhi said, 'If the foreigners give them money, my nephew will take us on another study tour next year.'

This reanimated the room. 'Another tour would be fun!' 'We had such a time!' 'They talk funny out there, remember how hard it was to understand the woman at the pig farm?'

'Quiet, everyone!' Rama Bhauju turned to Sapana. 'Lau, Bahini, that means you'll have to do the accounts for us—in writing.'

Sapana wanted to laugh out loud, but held back. These old women were shameless about making her do all their work. She didn't mind, actually; and in fact, it felt good to be needed. She'd brought an old copybook from school. She opened it, and said, 'You'll have to give me all the information about the committee.'

But it turned out that no one knew much. Laptanni Budhi claimed that there were seventeen members in the committee, but then she listed twenty-two names. Sapana hadn't realized that Chandra's Muwa was also in the committee. No one could remember who'd joined when, or for how long they'd paid the monthly due. There was no record of the loans the committee had given, or of the repayments it had received. And worse, when Sapana asked how much money the committee had, Laptanni Budhi held up a battered tin box and a stack of loose hundred rupee notes. 'I lost the key to the padlock, we haven't been able to open it for more than six months, Nani.'

'You store your money in a box?' Sapana was aghast. 'You should put it in the bank, it'll earn an interest there.'

'We discussed that once,' Rama Bhauju said. She turned to the rest. 'Didn't we discuss that once?'

'We did, that was that time we met at my house,' Hasta ma said.

'The time you made that anarasa roti! Ssss! That was so good.'

'We had it with tomato achaar.'

'Ssss! That was the best.'

Laptanni Budhi hushed them. 'Sapana Nani's right. We should put the money in the bank. So do it for us, Nani. You know how to do it. Do it.'

But as soon as Sapana said that the bank required the presence of the chairperson, secretary and treasurer, she and Rama Bhauju began to fuss: 'Who has the time to go to the bazaar?'

'I don't have the time.'

'We don't have the time. Do the accounts first. Then we'll see.'

They were so lazy. Sapana agreed, of course, to do the committee's accounts. 'I'll have to meet all the members, so it'll take a few days, but I'll do the accounts for you—in writing.'

'Jaya Shulinbaba!' Laptanni Budhi handed over the tin box and loose notes.

Everyone immediately got up, relieved. 'Our work's done, isn't it?'

'I have to go, I have so much to do.'

'Me too, I can't sit around, my mother-in-law will kill me.'

The room quickly emptied out.

Laptanni Budhi asked Sapana to stay on. 'My daughters-in-law are cooking fresh corn.'

But Sapana wanted to go to Chandra. 'I can't be the only one with nothing to do!' she shot back impishly. 'I also have to go.'

~

The mist was still dense outside. It would probably remain so all day. Every winter, there was a cold spell when the sun never came out, then it would rain, and the seasons would turn.

Sapana crossed over the mad river and went up the hill, to Chandra's house.

Chandra's Buwa was sitting, as he did every day, by the bottlebrush trees. He heard her and turned his face up. 'Is that you, Nani?'

'I don't think the sun will come out today, Buwa. Shall I bring you a blanket?'

'I'm fine as I am, Nani. Go in. The other girls are also there.'

Chandra's Muwa was in the courtyard, bottling a batch of fresh radish pickles. Sapana could remember a time when Muwa wasn't so pinched, before Surya Di disappeared. She said, 'Muwa, I didn't realize you were in the women's committee.'

Chandra's Muwa smiled wanly. 'I joined last year to see if I could sell pickles.' She looked exhausted, as always. 'You know.' Her brows furrowed. 'If you girls didn't visit, Chandra wouldn't do anything at all. Was she like this at your house, Nani? All she does is lie in bed, reading.'

'She reads too much.'

'She hardly even speaks to us. She acts as though we've harmed her, Nani.'

Sapana felt bad for her. She said, 'It's not that, Muwa. It's, well, you know what Chandra's like.'

Obstinate: that's what she's like, Sapana thought, going into the house. She knew Chandra blamed her parents for what happened to Surya Di. It was unreasonable, but Chandra felt that if they weren't poor, Surya Di wouldn't have had to go to India, and nothing bad would have happened. Even little Tara protested, 'That's not fair, Di!' But Chandra just couldn't forgive her Muwa Buwa.

The house was dark, with a sour air. Surya Di's old room was used for storing pickles. A fermented stench wafted out of it. After passing the door, Sapana saw someone in the shadows.

All three sisters—Surya Di, Chandra, little Tara—had smooth hair that cascaded down in black sheets. All three had flashing eyes and a mannish build. Among them Surya Di was the tallest. Her eyes were dull as she gazed at Sapana.

Sapana couldn't move or think or breathe for the longest time.

Finally, she stammered: 'What—what happened to you, Di?'

I died, of course.

The world convulsed. Sapana reeled, lost her balance, reached for the wall for support. There was no one there, the hall was completely empty, it was just a shadow in the shape of a person.

Heart pounding, she burst into Chandra's room, and found, to her great relief, that everything was normal there. Little Tara was in a corner, mending a torn shirt. Ritu and Namrata were sitting on the floor, talking, and Chandra was lying in bed above them, leafing through a book. Sapana flopped down beside her friend, trying to calm her heartbeat.

Chandra turned to her and eyed the tin box. 'What's that?'

Sapana forced herself to smile. 'I robbed the women's committee!'

'Ey, Sapana,' Ritu said, grinning. 'Is it true that Jeevan Bhatta begged you to join the committee?'

Ritu was a gossip: you had to be careful what you said around her. 'I joined it for you,' Sapana joked. 'I did it to arrange your marriage to him.'

'Who'd marry that old widower?' Ritu made a face. 'Besides, he's already got his eyes on you. Tch, Sapana, it would make him so happy if you were to marry him!'

'I'd never marry that old man!'

'Well, I'll never marry anyone,' Chandra said.

'Me, neither,' little Tara chimed in from the corner. 'I'll never marry!'

Ritu pouted. 'Me, I want to get married, otherwise how will I ever leave my parents' home? But I need a husband who's young and handsome, and rich too. Ey, Sapana, isn't your brother looking for a wife?'

'You want me to talk to him for you?'

'Not for me. For her.' She pointed at Namrata.

Poor Namrata, she was so proper, and so easy to tease. 'I'll kill you, Ritu!' she hissed.

Ritu cackled. 'Gyanu Dai must earn a lot, working in a five star hotel. Is that true, Sapana?'

Chandra scoffed. 'Can't you talk about anything but boys, Ritu?'

'Namrata and I aren't like you two,' Ritu shot back. 'We're not smart, we didn't pass out of school, and we're no beauties either, so we can't be picky, we'll have to marry the first boy who'll have us, right, Namrata?'

'Be quiet!'

As they bickered, Sapana turned to Chandra. 'Ey, girl. What are you reading now?'

'Why should I tell you? You won't read it anyway.'

'I don't understand all those big words you use.' Sapana laughed. 'Progress and materialism and—what? Historical necessity.'

'So, then?' Chandra wouldn't show her the book. 'You don't need to see what I'm reading.'

Ritu looked over at them. 'Is it a dirty book? Remember that book you were reading once, about the girl who loved two boys at the same time? Is it like that?'

'Yes, it's exactly like that,' Chandra said. She held up the book and read from it. 'He entered her like a hot knife in butter.'

'Tchee!' Namrata cried, scandalized.

'Gasping, she submitted,' Chandra went on. 'She gave up her most cherished womanhood.' She rolled over to face Sapana, and lowered her voice seductively. 'He looked into her eyes and said, "I love you, darling. Do you love me too?" "Yes, I love you," she said. He cupped her breasts with his hands, and thrusting harder, said, "Do you truly love me, darling?" In ecstasy, she moaned, "I truly love you, darling, I love you, I love you, I love you!"' At this, Chandra drew in and kissed Sapana on the mouth. Her lips were soft, and she tasted of milk.

'Tchee!' Namrata cried again.

Ritu cackled wickedly.

Little Tara squealed.

'You're crazy!' Sapana tried to extricate herself from Chandra's arms.

'Ah-ha-ha!' Chandra sputtered. 'I love you, darling, I truly love you.' She kissed her again, and collapsed on the bed, laughing.

'Let me see that book.' Sapana lunged for it, and wrested it from her friend's hands. Then she saw that it wasn't a dirty book at all—it was someone's life story. 'Idiot!' She tossed it back.

'Ah-ha-ha!' Chandra laughed. 'You wanted to read a filthy book, didn't you? You wanted to read about hot knives and butter, ah-ha-ha!'

'Be quiet!'

'You want a hot knife in your butter, ah-ha-ha!'

'Be quiet, will you?' Sapana said, though in truth, she loved to see Chandra laughing.

It took forever for Chandra to stop. When she did so at last, she wiped away her tears and explained that the book was the life story of a Maoist woman. 'She ran away from home at fourteen and joined the revolution. She learned how to use guns, she raised money for arms, she even went to battle.' She hooked her arms through Sapana's. 'Come, let's run away, you and I. Let's run away and become revolutionaries.'

'Lau, we'll do that, but first, move back with me,' Sapana said.

Chandra looked at her.

'I asked Gyanu Dai, and he said you should move back, Chandra.'

The others were looking at them. They knew how much Chandra hated being in this house. Even little Tara knew that. 'If you go,' she said, 'I'll have this whole room to myself again, Di.'

Ritu joked, 'You can move back, ey, Chandra, but Gyanu Dai's booked for Namrata.'

'I'll kill you, Ritu! I'll really kill you!' Namrata hissed.

Chandra kept looking at Sapana. 'Really?' she said.

'The house is empty without you.'

NOWADAYS IT WAS impossible to buy a simple kurta, one that wasn't marred by beads, embroideries, sequins or mirror-work. Indira covered the gaudiness with a plain black pashmina shawl. She checked the mirror. She felt, and looked, fatigued: her monthlies had started, though she'd kept this from Uday Sharma, because how could she possibly supervise a dinner party if she were barred from the kitchen? She leaned forward and examined her face. Every morning she daubed on the beauty cream from Paris, but the furrows and grooves, dots and patches, stains and blotches remained.

'Durga!' she cried, stepping out to the evening's duties. The servant girl had aired out the house, but a trace of myrrh clung to the air. In the sitting room Indira plumped up the sofa and ran a finger along the shelves to see if Durga had wiped off the dust. She had. The girl had stuffed too many dahlias into the cut-glass vase. Indira loosened the bouquet and placed the vase at the centre of the oval marble-top coffee table from Luxury Home Decor.

'Durga!' She went to check on the children. Aakaash was playing computer games, as always, and Aakriti was hunched over a book. The door to Muwa's room was closed. May it remain so all evening, she thought. The old witch was growing crankier by the day, convinced as she was that Durga was whoring: 'How else can she afford to buy red lali for her lips?'

'I gave her one of my old lipsticks, Muwa.'

'That girl has very bad character.'

'Durga!' Indira cried.

The girl loped into the sitting room, her clothes torn and her hair a rat's nest. 'Hajoor.'

'Is the food ready?'

'The chicken's still cooking.'

'And the snacks? Are they done? Let's go and inspect, shall we?' She led the girl to the kitchen, where, sure enough, the crystal bowl was heaped with walnuts. 'How many times must I tell you, Durga: don't fill the bowl to the top!' she cried. 'People don't eat nuts by the handful; they take one or two at a time. Put half the nuts back—and seal the bag so they don't become soggy!'

The girl slouched miserably over her task.

Now Indira felt bad. 'Look, Durga, this party isn't for fun, it's for my office work,' she said. 'Now, don't forget: first, bring the nuts, then the dried meat, then the pakodas, then the momos. Only then serve the meal. But first: change into something nice. The guests will think I don't pay you anything. The red kurta I gave you last month? Wear that.'

'It tore.'

'You've torn it already?' She had to stop herself from shouting again at the girl. 'Then find something else, Durga. When I go to the office, I don't wear rags, do I? This house is your office. Of course you live here, it's your home too, but it's important for us working women to look our best.'

Oof, what was the point.

Indira went back to the sitting room, and found her husband at the bar, pouring whisky into a tumbler. It made her blood pressure shoot up. 'What kind of a host are you?' she cried. 'You're not even waiting for the guests!'

He gave her a drunkard's smile. 'Indira Sharma, you worry too much.'

'And you, Uday Sharma, worry too little!'

'Relax,' he said. 'I got your man a Black Label—not a Chinese knock-off: the genuine thing.' He took a gulp. 'Ho, that's smooth, all right.' He lowered himself slowly onto the soft black leather recliner. 'And there's brandy for afterwards. VSOP. Everything will be all right.'

Indira looked at him sprawled there, so cocky, so confident. 'How do you know that?' she wondered out loud. 'You don't actually know that, do you? You don't know, Uday Sharma. You have no idea what it's like to be a Nepali woman.'

'I'm telling you.'

'You really think?'

'A hundred per cent.'

Why was this so reassuring?

The doorbell rang. Indira shot to the door as her husband gulped down his whisky.

There he was, IDAF's senior programme officer, Vishwa Bista, with his smug face, floppy hair, pricey name-brand clothes and America-educated sheen of privilege. Behind him was the dark, twiggy woman who had replaced the American Catherine Christy as IDAF's new director of WEP. She was wearing a minidress and looked exactly twenty years old.

'I hope you like wine.' She held out a bottle. 'It's an Argentinian cabernet sauvignon, the best one at my hotel.'

Indira stepped aside so that her husband could handle the alcohol.

Indira introduced them: 'Ava, this is my... He is under-secretary at the Ministry of Works and Physical Planning.' To her husband, she said, 'Ava Berriden has replaced Catherine Christy.'

Uday Sharma leered at her. 'You are from Argentina, Miss?'

'Canada, actually.'

He deployed the same line on her colleagues. 'You please call me Mr Indira. We men should take second place, isn't that so? Today, I am on bartender duty. Can I serve you beer-wine-fruit-juice-soft-drinks?' For Vishwa Bista's benefit, he said, 'We also have Black Label.'

'I'll have that.' Vishwa Bista said.

'And for you, miss?'

'I'd love a glass of wine, please.'

The Canadian turned to Indira with a smile. 'You won't have wine?'

'No, I never—at home.' What would foreigners know of the restrictions on a Nepali daughter-in-law? 'I will have apple juice,' she said. Then she went to the kitchen to fetch it.

The chicken was bubbling furiously on the stove. Durga was nowhere to be seen. Indira turned down the flame, poured herself a glass of juice and returned to the sitting room, where her husband was decrying the latest scandal—the home minister had released an underworld don from jail.

'In all my years as a public servant I've never seen something like this!'

He was already slurring.

'You're right, it's shameless,' Vishwa Bista said, and the men were soon trading laments.

'In all my years!'

'It's utterly shameless.'

The Canadian listened, polite but uncomprehending. Indira wondered why she was so dark. Was she of African descent? Were there people of African descent in Canada? During a lull in the men's conversation, Indira asked her, 'You are from Ottawa, Ava?'

'No, I'm from a small town—you wouldn't have heard of it, it's called Overwood. But I've lived in Toronto since my college years.'

'I see.' Indira searched for something else to say about Canada, but nothing came to mind. She knew nothing about that country—just as the Canadian, likely, knew nothing about this one. This was invariably the case with IDAF's international staff. They wielded immense power over their local counterparts such as Indira, whose careers, and lives, depended on them. Yet, they knew nothing. And by the time their counterparts educated them, they were ready to leave, climbing the next rung of the career ladder after their stint in Nepal.

Nevertheless, networking with donors was a crucial component of her job, so in the next lull in the men's conversation, Indira turned back to the Canadian. 'You have ever had our Nepali dal-bhat, Ava?'

'When I move into my new place, my Didi will make it for me.'

Her Didi. She'd just arrived, and already had servants.

'You are living where?' Indira asked.

'Do you know where Catherine Christy used to live?'

'The house with the fountain.'

'It's too big for me, I don't have a family like she did, but, well, it's earthquake-proof, and when the agent showed me the garden, I couldn't resist.'

No family. How old was this Canadian? 'You must remember,' Indira said, repeating the old platitude: 'Kathmandu is not the real Nepal. Isn't that so, Vishwaji?'

'Absolutely, Indiraji. To see the real Nepal you have to go to the villages,' Vishwa Bista said.

'Yes, I'm hoping to fit in a field trip,' the Canadian said. 'Maybe next month, though there's a divisional meeting, and then there's a workshop on...is it best practices?' She smiled apologetically. 'I have to confess, my background is in corporate law, and it's taking me a while to get up to speed on IDAF's work.' She asked Indira, 'I was reading WDS-Nepal's report from last year, and I noticed that you work in areas which are high risk for trafficking.'

'Oh, trafficking is a big problem in Nepal.'

'I'd love to see that work. Maybe we could go together to one of your project sites?'

'To the field?' Indira shuddered at the memory of her last field trip. Even going to the toilet was indelicate when you were the only woman. And the evenings were especially intolerable. The men would go to a bar, fostering the boozy camaraderie that gave them a huge professional advantage, while she, to maintain her respectability as a woman, ate alone in her hotel room, as though she were untouchable. 'I will check my schedule,' Indira said, though she had no intention of doing so.

Durga—changed, washed, combed, if sullen-faced—shuffled in with the walnuts.

'Snacks!' Indira steered her towards the Canadian. 'Have.' The Canadian took one walnut. Indira then steered the girl towards Vishwa Bista. 'Vishwaji, have.'

'After you, Indiraji.'

'Have, have.' His tumbler was empty. She glared at her husband till he finally noticed, and got up for refills.

~

The snacks phase of the evening passed smoothly, in this manner. After the nuts, Durga brought the dried meat, then the pakodas, and then the momos, as instructed. Whenever the men stopped lamenting—'I've really never seen anything so shameful'—Indira exchanged pleasantries with the Canadian.

'You like the momos, Ava? You have eaten goat before?'

'Was that goat meat? I've had it—there was a Greek restaurant that I and my, um, that I used to go to near our—my—house.'

'Have some more momos, then.'

'It's delicious, but I'm stuffed.'

'Just one more momo.'

'Really, no. Thank you, Indira. That was a lovely meal.'

'No, no, no!' Indira laughed. 'This is snacks only! Dal-bhat is still coming.'

'Oh, my goodness.'

Through these surface pleasantries, Indira remained deeply attuned to Vishwa Bista. She was waiting for a signal from him, a sign, the merest hint.

It came over dinner. They were at the dining table. The power had gone off, but the inverter had switched on automatically, and the Belgian chandelier cast a sophisticated glow over the room. Durga had served them and had gone off to serve Muwa and the children in their rooms. The conversation had drifted to work. Vishwa Bista was going on, as he was wont to, about IDAF-this and IDAF-that, when Indira noticed a certain tightening of his voice.

'The main challenge for an organization like WDS-Nepal,' he was saying, still lucid on his fifth Black Label, 'is that you fail to prioritize the customization of the results logframe, Indiraji.' To the Canadian, he explained, 'You see, Ava, many of our partners don't realize that with us donors, the management response corresponds directly to the integration of a proper alignment agenda.' He flicked his floppy hair and struck a pensive pose. 'Especially with our ongoing commitment to donor harmonization, Indiraji, it isn't enough to incorporate the MDGs or the PRSP or even the CSP and CAP. It's also critical to match our policy priorities, wouldn't you agree? Otherwise'—and here his voice tightened—'how can we monitor and evaluate the reported outputs?'

Indira sat forward, clenched and prepared. She was ready. Here was the scenario that she'd been anticipating, in a way, for all her life. 'Vishwaji,' she said, 'in the process of donor harmonization.' Her voice unexpectedly quavered. 'Capacity enhancement for WDS-Nepal is the utmost priority.' Her pulse quickened. Her breath shortened. 'For example.' She coughed. 'Excuse me. For example, last year.' A liquid heat swirled inside her. 'All of WDS-Nepal's sectoral strategies were implemented successfully, though of course some operational approaches had to be modified due to local conditions.' Trying to sound as normal as possible, she explained to the Canadian, 'You see, in this transitional period there are many conflict-exacerbating factors at the ground level, Ava. WDS-Nepal has adopted the Do No Harm principles, and accordingly, we have to continually adjust our operational approaches.'

The Canadian looked lost.

'Nevertheless.' Indira soldiered on. 'WDS-Nepal has successfully met all the target outcomes and outputs. But Vishwaji, it may be the case that we must further emphasize monitoring of our partners, who lack capacity.'

'Sure, sure,' Vishwa Bista said. He took a long sip of Black Label. He wasn't going to make this easy for her. 'And yet, Indiraji, all we have to go by is WDS-Nepal's results logframe.' He shook his head like a disappointed parent. 'We donors see this all the time. All the time.' He turned to the Canadian. 'Our partners may be doing good—excellent—work, Ava, but there's no transparency in their reporting, which makes us worry about the delivery of tangible results to beneficiaries, especially when the size of the grant is large. That's why we, as donors, support organizations such as National Network Nepal, who emphasize the customization of the results logframe.'

Pleading with him now, Indira said, 'It is just a small problem of capacity enhancement, Vishwaji. At the grassroots level, all the target outcomes and outputs have been met. As you understand, our partners are unable to follow the format. We need to help them with customization. Reporting is not our partners' strong point. Vishwaji, they need additional help with capacity enhancement.'

'You may be correct,' he conceded.

She looked at him beseechingly.

'It may be that you're correct,' he said. 'It may indeed be a matter of greater capacity enhancement.'

'I really, really think so, Vishwaji.'

'You're right,' he said. 'The problem isn't with WDS-Nepal, Indiraji, it's with your partners—the CBOs at the village level. They urgently need capacity enhancement.'

'Yes, and National Network Nepal is an excellent organization for this,' she said.

'I'm glad you agree, Indiraji.'

'I agree very much with you, Vishwaji, I completely agree, thank you so much.'

'You're welcome.'

How she loathed him.

But with this they'd reached an understanding. Indira would increase the budget for capacity enhancement in her proposal to IDAF, and, on the condition that the funds could be routed through National Network Nepal—Vishwa Bista's cousin-sister-in-law's NGO—he'd ensure that IDAF would approve it. Thus, Indira would secure WDS-Nepal's largest grant ever.

Throughout their exchange, Uday Sharma had stared at his tumbler like those monkeys who saw, heard and spoke no evil. A stunned silence followed. The Canadian eased it away with a question: 'Have you been in this line of work for a long time, Indira?'

The question brought back memories from when Indira started off, full of dreams, at Help. She remembered all the development agendas she'd worked on: poverty alleviation, income generation, women and development, women in development, awareness raising, mainstreaming, rights-based development, sustainability, advocacy, empowerment. All the cynicism she'd eschewed. What's a DINGO? A development NGO. What's a WINGO? A women's NGO. What's a FINGO? A five-star NGO. All the reports, proposals, budgets, papers, summaries, evaluations that had passed through her desk. All the training, self-improvement, and professional development she'd suffered through. Battling her womanly shyness, she'd spoken up at meetings, workshops, seminars, conferences. For decades, she'd worked tirelessly, truly tirelessly, but only when the development agenda had come around to social inclusion had she been promoted to WDS-Nepal's deputy co-director, alongside a man, of course, her number one rival Chandi Shrestha.

She replied, 'Yes, Ava, I have been in this line of work for a long time.'

'So you'd be familiar with the entire range of non-government organizations, from the village-based CBOs all the way up to NGOs at the district and national levels.'

'Local, district, regional, national, international: everything I know.'

'I've been familiarizing myself with them.' The Canadian frowned. 'And I guess I'm accustomed to more structure, or to more of a legal infrastructure around organizations. Do you know what I mean? Some of these NGOs and CBOs seem, I don't know—flimsy.'

Indira looked at the Canadian and wondered whether she'd be an ally to her, as Catherine Christy had been. *You mustn't stop at deputy co-director*, Catherine Christy had always said to her: *you must become the first Nepali woman director of WDS-Nepal*. Which was true. The present director, an Australian hippie with the horror name of Rick Peede, was retiring soon, and WDS-International had announced that it would prioritize in-house applications for his replacement. The director's job came with a dollar salary that was more than quadruple what Indira earned. Which was why she'd had to bribe Vishwa Bista, because only if IDAF approved her proposal would she edge out her rival Chandi Shrestha for the job.

'Ava,' she said, 'I am happy to share my experiences. You call me with any and all questions.'

'Same here,' Vishwa Bista said. 'If there's anything, Ava, just call me—at night, during the day, Saturday, Sunday, holidays, it doesn't matter.'

'Thank you, you're both so kind.'

Durga shuffled in to serve seconds. Indira steered her to the Canadian.

'Oh, I'll explode if I have one more bite! Actually, I do have a question for all three of you,' she said. 'How hopeful are you about the prospect of getting a new constitution?'

Only then did Uday Sharma deign to rejoin the conversation. He slurred, 'Nothing will happen, miss! Constitution will never come!'

Vishwa Bista said, 'One of our consultants wrote a report, I'll give it to you, Ava.'

'Nothing will happen!' Uday Sharma roared.

Vishwa Bista said, 'I'll give you the report on Monday.' His tumbler was empty again.

The men had one more Black Label with the ice cream dessert, and then back in the sitting room, Uday Sharma insisted: 'One peg of VSOP, Vishwaji!'

'A small peg, sure.'

'Also for you, miss!'

'No, thank you. I should get going,' the Canadian said. 'Maybe the driver could drop me off and come back for you, Vishwa?'

'No, miss, you have one peg VSOP!' Drunkenly, Uday Sharma sloshed out three snifters of brandy.

The Canadian hardly touched hers.

The men returned to lamenting.

'Shameful.'

'This country is run by underworld dons.'

'In all my years!'

When they downed their drinks, the Canadian got up in obvious relief. 'That was lovely,' she gushed. 'Thank you so much, Indira and, um, Mr Indira. I had a wonderful time.'

Uday Sharma leered. 'You like our Nepali dal-bhat, miss?'

Elbowing him aside, Indira said, 'Come back for a proper dinner, Ava. You didn't have enough dal-bhat this time.' To Vishwa Bista she said, in Nepali, 'The proposal...'

He said, 'Submit it directly to me.'

When the guests were gone, Indira was overcome with revulsion—for Vishwa Bista, and for herself, too.

Remember? How innocent she'd been in her youth, how pure? On her first field trip for Help, in impoverished Jumla District, she'd cried, seeing flies on the mouth of a malnourished child. She'd vowed to dedicate her life to helping the poor—but today she'd offered a bribe.

She was corrupt. She was excrement. She was filth.

Her husband was pouring more brandy into his snifter. 'It went well, Indira Sharma, now relax, have a peg, I won't tell Muwa.'

'I won't have any brandy and you shouldn't have any more either!' she snapped, though she knew there was no stopping him now. He'd have his fill and stumble gracelessly into bed, reeking of booze from every pore.

For her, sleep wouldn't come easily tonight. She went to check in on the children. Aakaash was still playing computer games and Aakriti was still studying. 'Go to bed,' she said, knowing that they wouldn't. She stopped at the door to Muwa's room, took in the scent of myrrh. All was silent inside.

As a final chore, she went to the kitchen to make sure that Durga had cleaned up. She found the girl hunched over the sink, heaving and sobbing.

'Ey, what's this?' Indira rushed to her side. She tried to draw the girl up, but the girl kept heaving and sobbing. She put an arm around her. 'Tch, tch, tch. Don't cry,' she said.

Poor Durga. Poor, poor Durga. It was her fault, Indira thought: overwhelmed by work-travel-family she'd neglected the girl; and Durga had no one in the world. She'd come into this house wild-eyed at age twelve, the eldest of six unwanted daughters. Her father had taken her from house to house in Kathmandu, begging for work. The days of keeping a child servant were over, but who could reason with Muwa? The old witch had insisted on taking the girl in, saying, 'Village girls are hard-working.'

'Raise her, look after her, she's yours now,' the girl's father had said to Indira. To Durga, he'd said, 'Do as your masters bid, they're your gods now.' He never came back for her.

Indira had enrolled the girl in school, but she'd dropped out after class three, settling into the life of a servant girl. She was sanguine by temperament, and seemed content with her lot—till her disastrous engagement with the vegetable vendor. Now he'd abandoned her, and her life was ruined. She was just seventeen.

'What's wrong, tell me what's wrong,' Indira said, though she knew what was wrong.

The girl was disconsolate. She kept heaving and sobbing over the sink, as though the world were about to end.

'Tch. Durga, don't cry,' Indira said. 'I know it's been hard for you, but it'll be all right, I'll always take care of you, girl, you're like my own daughter. Durga? Tell me. Tell me, girl. Tell me what's wrong.'

THE ROAD TO the house was steeper than she remembered from the time she came with the real estate agent. The cab driver honked twice at the gate. A dog began to bark next door, its baying filling the air. The gate opened. A skinny guard waved them in.

The landlady, at the front door, was dressed in a blood red sari, as she'd been for the showing. She was tiny—four and a half feet at most—with jet-black hair pulled back in a tight, oily bun. The contract listed her name as Mrs Thapa. Ava stepped out with a box of office documents and her attaché case, stuffed with a gargantuan proposal from WDS-Nepal. Mrs Thapa screeched, causing the skinny guard to scuttle over to help. The driver unloaded Ava's suitcase from the trunk, along with the earthquake kit that Vishwa had helped her buy.

After the cab left, the landlady held up a bunch of keys. 'It is saancho.' She indicated, through mime, that Ava unlock the front door.

The main hall stretched through the house, to the back door, where a woman of indeterminate age stood, smiling shyly. 'Oh, hello,' Ava said, taken aback.

'Namaste, madam.'

'It is Luna.' The landlady launched into a babble of English and Nepali. 'Luna cooking, cleaning, ghar safa garne, pakaune, Luna making dal-bhat, tapain ke khane, food, you give money, Luna cooking cleaning shopping making dal-bhat.'

'Okay.'

The skinny guard toiled behind them, carrying in everything.

Mrs Thapa prodded Ava. 'You coming!' She pointed to a stack of electronics near the back door. 'Battery back-up inverter UPS Wi-Fi, you no touch, light going, battery power automatic, you no touch!' She produced a chit of paper from her blouse. 'Wi-Fi password.'

'Okay, thank you.'

'Coming.' She marched Ava out the back door, into the garden. The fountain at the centre of the garden had been on when Ava had come to see the house. 'No water,' Mrs Thapa declared, waving her hands at the sky for emphasis. 'Monsoon, then rain, then water, now no water, no water, no water.' She pointed to an old man pruning a hedge with rusty scissors. 'It is Jaleswor garden, he kaan sundaina, no ear, dherai kura gardaina, no talk. Here it is three servants: Harihar guard, Luna maid, Jaleswor garden. Salary you give to me, I give to servants, twenty thousand rupees, you give tomorrow.'

'Oh.' The contract mentioned the staff, but Ava had assumed that their salaries were included in the rent. Twenty thousand rupees: two hundred dollars—for a staff of three? 'Okay,' she said, discomfited.

'I go, you stay,' the landlady said. 'If problem, you coming to my house.' She pointed at a modern brick house across the garden. Then she marched across the garden, climbed a set of stairs carved into the compound wall, and disappeared, only to reappear on the balcony of the house next door. From there she waved at Ava.

Ava waved back.

The garden was an oasis, a tropical idyll: it was extravagantly beautiful in the midst of modern, ugly Kathmandu. The agent had identified the flowering trees for her—jacaranda, acacia, crepe myrtle—though she couldn't remember, anymore, which were which. She walked through them, feeling their barks, running her hands through their leaves. Green shoots were sprouting on some branches. There were fruit trees here too: pomelo and guava and kumquat and plum. Cane garden chairs sat at the edge, by a hedge—a jasmine hedge—on the verge of budding. She stopped beside it and looked out at Kathmandu: the dinge, the sprawl, the concrete maze hemmed in by hills. The agent had said that the Himalayas would be visible on clear days. All she saw was the usual grey fug.

When she turned back, Mrs Thapa was still on her balcony, staring at her.

Ava went into the house through the back door. She could hear Luna in the kitchen. Luna maid, she thought. Luna maid, Harihar guard, Jaleswor garden. The guard had deposited the earthquake kit in the main hall. Her suitcase was in the largest of the bedrooms upstairs. There were two more bedrooms upstairs, both, like this, with en suite bathrooms. The house was absurd. On the ground floor were a study, a living room, a dining room, a kitchen and a guest bathroom. She'd once lived in an orphanage in Kathmandu, she thought: and now she lived here in a mansion.

She unpacked and went down to set up the study. She'd have to wade through WDS-Nepal's proposal ahead of a meeting with Claire Ross-Jones next week. For now she set it aside and opened her laptop. The Wi-Fi password worked, but the connection was slow. She'd fallen behind on emails.

She fired off a note to Luke first: *Moved into the new place! I'm living in style, with household staff, three of them! My landlady introduced them as Luna maid, Harihar guard and Jaleswor garden. Yikes! Talk soon? xoxoA*

Then she turned to the emails she'd been avoiding. Gavin had sent two last week. She opened the first. Its tone was mercifully neutral. *The real estate agent had received offers on their house, but felt they'd do better if they held out for an auction. The market's booming, he'd written. The agent's confident.*

But his second email was a mess. *How's Nepal treating you, Av? Is your job everything you hoped for? Have you found what you were looking for? Are you happy there?* His words seared. *I miss us, I miss being Av and Gav. I keep thinking about it and don't really understand why I did what I did. You seem hell bent on leaving me, and if you want a divorce, the decision is yours, but I want to tell you I love you, Av.* At the end, he'd added: *I thought we'd be Av and Gav forever.*

She didn't have it in her to reply to him.

Anthony had also emailed. His message sat directly above Gavin's in the inbox.

The connection we had that night was magical, he'd written, and this made Ava cringe, though it was true. That night in Miami she'd crossed an important threshold. Anthony had given her company through that crossing. *I'm seriously thinking of visiting you in Nepal,* he'd written. *Let's have a FaceTime date sometime? Lots of love, Ax.*

Ax, she thought. Ax.

She couldn't reply to him either.

Her mother had written a long, chatty email. She turned her attention to it. *Dearest darling Ava.* Mom's voice instantly heartened. She was her usual self, going on about her latest cause: the lowered water levels of the Great Lakes. *Mayor Jenkins, of course, will hear nothing of it, it's his friends in the military-industrial complex across the border who are causing the water level to drop, after all. I saw him at the Christmas fundraiser. He was sitting next to Tom Boretta from Detroit!!! Do you remember Tom Boretta, honey? His son Jamie's out of rehab and back home now, working for his father's company...* She went on to gossip about all of Overwood.

Ava enjoyed the predictable arc of Mom's communications. All of her emails read like this. Only at the end did she veer to the personal: *Are you settled into your new job, honey? We're so proud of you for being there—but of course we worry. We want you to be happy with your decision.* She wrote: *Gavin came by for dinner last weekend. He seems to be coping, though sometimes it's hard. After he left, your Dad and I were talking. You've never asked us about it, but in case you want to know where the orphanage is, here's the address.*

Ava stared at it in dismay. She didn't want to go to the orphanage yet—or maybe ever. Not all adoptees needed to know their origins. She didn't; she needn't; there was no imperative.

She closed the email, left the laptop, paced in the study. Mom knew perfectly well how Ava felt. Ava had talked to both Mom and Dad about it endlessly, growing up. Or—did they think that's why she'd come to Nepal? Was that, in fact, why she came? Did she want to go back to the orphanage?

She was thirsty. There was a water filter in the kitchen. She went there.

Luna, Harihar and Jaleswor, who were eating on the floor, scrambled to their feet when she entered. They were eating with their hands, which were smeared with dal-bhat.

'I'm sorry, I—please don't let me interrupt your meal,' Ava said. 'I'll just get some water.'

'Water, madam!' Luna lunged to the sink, washed her hands, lunged to the cupboard, took out a glass, and lunged again to a water filter to fill it. She placed the glass on a tray before presenting it, decorously, to Ava.

'Oh. Thank you. There was no need. I could have—' Ava took the glass and backed out of the kitchen. 'Please—please finish your meal,' she said from the door, wondering what kind of employment arrangement she'd got into here.

She went back to the study and sat down with WDS-Nepal's proposal, flipping through it, unable to concentrate. Her thoughts kept skittering over the emails.

I thought we'd be Av and Gav forever.
The connection we had that night.
Here's the address.

Why did the household staff sit on the floor to eat, and not at the dining table? Renting this house—this mansion—was a mistake now. She should break the contract and go back to the hotel. Or she should cut all her losses and quit IDAF and go back home.

Her phone pinged. What time was it in Miami—would Luke be up at this hour?

It was Kim Armstone's friend, Tomás Barba: *Ciao Ava! Meeting friends 4 Newari-Russian dinner 2night. U free?*

A Newari-Russian dinner, whatever that was, with company, would beat spending the evening alone in this house. *Hi there!* She messaged back: *I'd love to join you and your friends for dinner.*

Gr8! He sent directions. *Come anytime, m aready here, at d bar.*

'AND, OTHER THINGS?' Gyanu asked just to keep Maleah online, to see her, if only in blurs and pixels, on the blue electric screen. He was in Butwal Bazaar, at an Internet café that had been set up at the back of a grain store. She was in a cyber café at City Centre. Gyanu had been to that cyber café with her, waiting by as she Skyped with Crisanto. Now she was there Skyping with him. On the screen she looked impossibly beautiful, impossibly remote. He said, 'Tell me—other things, meri maya.'

'What other things, mahal?' She folded the sheet of paper on which she'd printed Crisanto's last email. She'd read it out to Gyanu, as she did all her son's emails. This one had ended with a request for new building set. At age six, Crisanto loved to build castles with plastic blocks.

'Tell me how everyone is?' Gyanu said. 'How is Jairus?'

She told him that Jairus had come to the gift shop. 'He talked and talked: for two hours he talked, mahal! Only about you.' Quietly, she added, 'He is keeping your room.' Gyanu heard the unasked question in her voice. She told him about her roomates: 'Jojo is going soon. The agent has found her a job in Germany, in Hamburg, mahal. Susanna's contract will end in four months,' she said. 'Same like me.'

He knew she wanted him to ask if she, too, would go to the agent, but he feared that she'd say yes, so instead he said, 'You will have to look for another room-mate after Jojo.'

But then she came right out and asked, 'When you are coming, mahal?'

'Soon, meri maya, soon.' Gyanu closed his eyes. 'I will come soon to you.'

The days kept slipping by: the transfer of the land deed remained incomplete. Gyanu had discovered that there were generations of paperwork to update first: Thulo Ba and Ba had never transferred it from their father's name to theirs. After spending a futile week at the land revenue office in the bazaar, he'd had to appeal to Thulo Ba for help. 'Ey, you haven't got it done yet, Babu?' his uncle had said, acting surprised; then he'd dispatched Jeevan Bhatta to help him. 'He knows his way around government offices, Babu, let him handle it.' Jeevan Bhatta did, indeed, know how to move the files. All he required from Gyanu was money. 'Bribing officials is the only way to get work done,' he'd explained sheepishly. Gyanu had already given him twenty-five thousand rupees. For all he knew, the widower was pocketing it himself. What

Gyanu did know for certain was that at this pace, the transfer wouldn't come through by the end of his month off.

As though reading his thoughts, Maleah asked, 'You phoned Shantanu Kumar?'

Gyanu said nothing.

On the screen, Maleah turned away.

He couldn't bear to see her turn away from him. He should go to her at once, he thought. Sapana could follow up on the land transfer: she and Chandra could do it together. No. Thulo Ba would easily stymie them: he'd delay, he'd lie, he'd cheat. Gyanu wished Ba were still here. He wished he were back in the desert. He wished he'd never come here. He fidgeted in the booth. Perhaps there was no ideal circumstance in which to talk about the future, he thought. He said, 'What do you want to do, meri maya?'

'I want to live with my anak.'

She'd been waiting for a chance to tell him this.

He nodded. 'You will talk to the agent?'

'Yes, mahal.'

The thought was out there between them now, uttered and acknowledged: Maleah was going to leave the desert with or without him. A sadness began to spread through Gyanu. He tried to contain it. 'If you want to go, then go, meri maya,' he said. 'Germany, anywhere. Where you go, I will come.'

Maleah's face crumpled.

He said, 'I will come where you go.'

She wiped away her tears, and reached into her shirt collar to pull out the gold coin. She was wearing it as a locket on a silver chain. It felt as though an age had passed since Gyanu had gone to Suleiman Bhai's shop in Deira. He watched Maleah put the coin to her lips. Four grams. A wedding ring. A dream.

~

After they hung up, he walked past sacks of lentils, pulses and beans to the front of the store to pay for the computer time and a new thousand rupee recharge card. 'Where can I find women's clothes—which are the best new shops, Sahuji?' he asked.

'For your wife, mother, daughter?'

'Sister.'

'Children's clothes are there.' The shopkeeper pointed across the way. 'But if you're looking for ladies' fashions, there's a new shop one street over. All the pretty girls go there nowadays.'

Outside, Gyanu scratched the PIN number on the recharge card and topped up his mobile phone. He had to call Shantanu Kumar today. He'd do so later.

The grain shop was in the old part of the bazaar, which was as sleepy as it always used to be. A busy modern city had risen up around it. Every time Gyanu came back, he noticed new buildings, new streets, whole new neighbourhoods. The bazaar sprawled across both banks of the Tinau River, where there used to be open fields.

Following the shopkeeper's directions, he turned into the next street. As boys, he and his friends used to come to this part of the bazaar, Traffic Chowk, to seek out the urban entertainments. There used to be a DVD shop that screened Bollywood movies. It had long since closed. Gyanu and his friends had learned to drink at a cabin restaurant here. They'd once talked to a prostitute in that restaurant, tantalized but too terrified to follow her into a back room.

The clothes shop, New Nepal Fashions, was on the ground floor of a shopping complex that was still under construction. Rods and pipes stuck out of the sides of the building. The front window was lined with six headless mannequins in vermilion wedding saris.

Inside, the clothes were stacked tidily behind glass shelves to protect them from dust. A young salesman took out each kurta individually and held it up, modelling it against himself. Gyanu selected a simple one with blue stripes that would suit Sapana.

Leaving the shop, he came upon a row of empty plots: fifteen in total, each demarcated by a low concrete-block wall. He wondered how much the plots were going for. The price of land kept rising, and even after years in the desert he couldn't afford to buy in Kathmandu, but maybe here in the bazaar... Perhaps he and Maleah and Crisanto would end up here one day. Maleah sometimes asked him about the prospects in Nepal. His own misgivings kept him away.

He stepped over the concrete-block wall and went into one of the plots, where it was quiet. Then he placed a mobile call to Shantanu Kumar.

'Hello.'

He could almost see Shantanu Kumar. He'd be in his office: he practically lived there. He'd be tapping on the desk with his ring-covered fingers, looking out at the glass towers across the road. In Hindi, Gyanu said, 'Sir, it's Gyanu.'

'Hanh, Beta, I've been expecting your call. When do you come in? Speak.'

Gyanu confessed, 'I'm still in Nepal, sir.'

Shantanu Kumar coughed. Gyanu could hear tapping on the desk. Then Shantanu Kumar laughed, gruffly but not unkindly. 'You're a simple hill boy? You have no duties, no responsibilities? You'll have enough to live on, there, in the village?'

'I need a few more weeks, sir.'

'But I told you, Beta, when you left: thirty days.'

'I—sir. I have to, my sister—' He struggled to find the right words in Hindi. 'I have to make my sister secure,' he said, thinking, again: maybe he didn't have to, maybe Sapana and Chandra could take care of everything themselves.

'And how do you intend to make your sister secure?'

'There's some official work, sir, concerning my father's land.'

Shantanu Kumar drew a sharp breath. 'For a worthless piece of land in the hills you give up everything, Beta? What an innocent you are.' He laughed. 'You travel to faraway lands, you work day and night, you prove yourself, you advance—and then? You throw away everything for a fallow plot of land in the hills.' He grew stern. 'Where I come from in Bihar? There's nothing. My parents spent their whole lives working their landlord's farm. My mother died from poverty: we didn't have enough money to buy her medicine. Now look at me, Beta. Learn from me. Learn to be smart.'

'I'm learning, sir.'

'You're learning too late.'

'Just two more weeks, sir,' Gyanu begged. 'If you have to replace me I can take another position—assistant chef, even kitchen assistant. I'll clean dishes, sir, I'll wash the floors—'

'Thirty days.' Shantanu Kumar's tone was final. 'You know it's not easy what I do, managing a top restaurant like this. Think about it from my side: nothing can ever slow down, nothing can ever stop, everything must always keep moving apace, tak–tak–tak.' He sighed. 'You know I like you, you remind me of myself when I was your age, Beta, but I have my own constraints.' Before hanging up, he offered some advice: 'Free yourself from your entanglements there. The village is the past, it holds you back. The future is in the cities, cities like Dubai. For people like us, opportunities don't come by easily, Beta. You have to take them when you can.'

~

'Jairus?'

'Gyanu!'

'What am I going to do, Jairus?'

'What happened, hey? Why are you calling?'

Gyanu's throat hurt. He couldn't speak. If he opened his mouth he would cry.

Shantanu Kumar was right. The village was the past. If he didn't leave, it would trap him.

Jairus could feel his distress over the phone. 'Gyanu, don't worry, hey,' he said. 'Tell me what the problem is. Whatever it is, you know I'll do what I can from my side. I'll talk to Maleah, I'll talk to Shantanu Kumar, I'll talk to all the Nepali brothers and sisters here. Hey, Gyanu,' he said, 'you know who I ran into yesterday? Suleiman Bhai Sah'b. He was asking—did he make the ring, when's the wedding, what kind of feast will there be?' He said, 'Gyanu, you have so many friends, hey. Remember that. If you're in difficulty, everyone will help. So whatever happened, don't worry, Gyanu. Hello, friend? Are you all right? Are you hearing me at all?'

SHE WOKE UP parched, her head throbbing and her body stiff. She'd had too much to drink again. Tomás was trouble, he really was. Every time they met, he led her on a tear—and why did she follow so willingly? Last night, they'd started out at a low-budget den near his apartment. Then they'd caught a cab to a Tibetan neighbourhood, Bouddha, to meet Tomás's friends: 'Drukpas, nomads, yak herders—I met them last year on the Tibetan plateau.' The nomads turned out to be jean-clad hipsters who spoke not a word of English. At a diner overlooking a candle-lit Buddhist stupa, they'd had noodles and a fermented millet beer—tuba? Tumba? Something like that. Then Tomás took them to a nightclub: 'The Rox, it's where Kathmandu's rich kids come to let off steam.' They'd done tequila shots and danced to the relentless beat of Journey—'Don't stop believing, hold on to that fee-ee-ee-ling'.

She couldn't remember the cab ride back, but recalled, hazily, that Tomás had accompanied her home. Yes. He'd uncorked a bottle of wine, railing about international aid's complicity in perpetuating inequality in Nepal: this was his favourite subject when drunk. 'This isn't a poor country, what it needs is a redistribution of wealth. Aid is preventing Nepal from having a proper revolution.' Ava had suggested, several times, that they call it a night, but he'd gone on and on—'Only humanitarian work is justified in this country'—till she'd excused herself to go to bed, leaving him...where?

Warily, she glanced across the bed, and there he was, buried under sheets, pillows, clothes.

Jesus.

She slipped out of bed and went downstairs. The house was all hers today. Upon her insistence, Luna had stopped coming in on the weekends, though the landlady had come over to argue with her about it: 'Sunday no holiday Nepal!' Ava had refused to give in to Mrs Thapa. Jaleswar came in thrice a week. Harihar lived on the grounds, in a house by the gate—servants' quarters—but he kept to himself. Ava saw him only when he opened the gate for her.

She went to the kitchen and made coffee, enough for Tomás too, when he woke up. Tomás intrigued her. He was half-Montreal, half-Venice, effortlessly cosmopolitan. He'd left home early, and had worked in Sri Lanka, Indonesia, Afghanistan and Haiti before coming to Nepal. He was full of stories. And he wasn't bad to look at, with a lazy eye that gave him a dreamy look—though it was too bad about the gold tooth. He'd had an incisor capped after a trip to Tibet, and it glinted, sickly and yellow, when he smiled.

She took the coffee and two mugs out to the garden. Mrs Thapa's balconey was vacant. The landlady was no longer as hawkishly watchful as she'd been at the start, but every now and then she still came out to stare.

Only after pouring the coffee did Ava notice the view. It had rained during a recent cold spell, and the air had cleared. The city looked scrubbed and clean, and its concrete maze seemed delicate, and even fragile, cradled by a ring of green hills. Above the hills were the dark, jagged mountains she'd seen at the resort at the stakeholders' meeting. And above those mountains shimmered squat snow peaks.

She couldn't believe how close the Himalayas were. What a country this was, she thought. What a strange, difficult, complicated country. By now she'd caught up on background reading, and the indicators in relation to women were distressing. Women lagged behind men in health, education, income, mobility, opportunity, political representation. Many of the national laws violated international law. The statute of limitations on rape was three months, and the new constitution, if it were ever drafted at all, was likely to deny women equal citizenship rights. Nepali culture remained defiantly patriarchal. To add to this, Nepal's citizenry was divided into more than a hundred identity groups. Women's indicators varied widely by economic class, but also by their caste, indigenous and regional identities.

'Good morning, my dear.' Tomás came out, rumpled and dishevelled. He sat down beside her and poured himself a coffee. 'Ah, look. Ganesh Himal. It looks close, doesn't it, but it's up near the Tibet border.'

'Oh, tell me you've climbed it.' Ava smiled.

'I had to give up climbing after I broke my leg in the Wakhan corridor.'

She gave him a look.

'Some friends were going, I tagged along, but then I had to be rescued. It was embarrassing.' He shrugged.

How could she not like him? 'Hey, Tomás?' she said.

'Yes, my dear?'

'About last night.'

'You should have kicked me out.' He raised his hands, proclaiming his innocence. 'I hope I didn't, um, you know.'

'No.'

'Our spouses will be relieved to hear that.'

He was married?

He explained, 'Violeta and I are waiting for an annulment. In any case, I've taken a vow of celibacy—things were getting out of hand, I had to stop.'

Ava couldn't help but feel a twinge of disappointment.

Tomás said, 'Hey, did you mean it when you said you'd be up for a trek in the Spring?'

'Have we discussed this?'

'Last night, remember, at the Rox? It'll have to be an easy trek, because of my knee. Maybe Langtang.' With a yawn he stretched, his shirt riding up to expose a shapely belly. 'So what's for breakfast, my dear?'

'There's leftover dal-bhat in the fridge.'

'Let's go to the organic market,' he said, standing up. 'I'll introduce you to Richard and Luisa. He's Australian, she's Argentinian, they have a goat farm, they make cheese with a method from the Ardennes.'

A day that began with Tomás would surely end on another tear. 'Another time?' Ava said.

'Of course.' He leaned in to kiss her on the cheek. 'See you later, my dear.'

Ava watched him amble away, feeling a little sorry for herself. Tomás was her only friend in Nepal. They hadn't talked about her adoption, but the fact that he knew about it made her feel close to him, somehow, though in truth she hardly knew him. An annulment: was he an observing Catholic?

Harihar darted out of the servants' quarters to open the gate for Tomás. Tomás stopped to talk to the skinny guard. He'd taken language lessons, and could speak what he called 'bazaar Nepali'. He wasn't tall, but he towered over the guard. Tomás patted the guard on the shoulder.

After closing the gate, Harihar turned to Ava. His expression was— what was that? He was slack-jawed. Ava stared back at him, startled. Was he really judging her for having a man over—in her own house?

Out of the corner of her eye, she caught a flash of red. Mrs Thapa had come out to her balcony. An odd emotion—shame—crept through Ava. It quickly converted into anger. Was she expected to conform to Nepal's social mores? Why would she? And she deserved privacy: she was paying enough for this house. The rent had seemed reasonable when she'd signed the contract, but Tomás had blanched when he'd found out how high it was: 'I'm going to have to intervene,' he'd said. He'd since loaned Ava *Lords of Poverty, White Man's Burden, The Bottom Billion, Dead Aid* and two books by William Easterly—sharp critiques of aid, which Tomás derided as 'the aid industry.' Tomás himself lived in a small apartment in an unassuming part of town, though he earned just as much as Ava. It wasn't as though he couldn't afford a house like this. It was a difference of lifestyle: what he saved on rent he splurged on satisfying his wanderlust.

The clarity of the morning air was fading. Ganesh Himal was disappearing into the usual grey fug. Mrs Thapa was still staring. Ava got up and went in.

She had to comb through WDS-Nepal's proposal this weekend, ahead of a meeting with its largest partner, National Network Nepal. The proposal was so big, and so ambitious, that it intimidated Ava. She'd asked Claire Ross-Jones for permission to conduct an assessment before approving the grant. Claire had asked her to write a one-pager arguing her case. Ava needed to send the one-pager to Claire on Monday.

But when she sat down to work, she realized she was still irritated— about the guard, about the landlady, about the mansion she lived in.

~

She was halfway down the hill by the time Harihar scrambled to the gate. Picking her way past a pile of garbage by the neighbour's house, she walked to the main road, where a cab sidled up to her. 'Taxi, taxi, taxi!'

The driver looked ten years old.

'No,' she said.

'Taxi, sister!' The driver grew baleful. 'Sister, sister, and taxi.'

'Okay, okay.' Ava got in. 'Can you take me to...Bal Mandir?' She hesitated over the name. Then, as she'd seen Tomás do, she tried to bargain: 'How much?'

'And four hundred rupees, sister!'

Unlike Tomás, she couldn't haggle over what amounted, in the end, to four dollars. 'Okay.'

'Okay!' The driver cried as they started off. 'And you which country from, sister!'

'Canada.'

'And sister, Canada is too far!'

He launched a spirited, if garbled, conversation. She answered his questions politely—'Yes, it's far.' 'Yes, it's nice.' 'I like Nepal too, it's also nice.'—till he stalled for lack of a vocabulary.

Then the driver turned on the radio and sang along to a Nepali pop song, careening through the pocked, bumpy streets, swerving to avoid pedestrians and motorbikes. A sharp stench arose as they crossed a bridge. Ava looked in alarm at the befouled Bagmati River, which trickled below like an open sore, rank and infected. How could people put up with this?

They shot past a stretch of government buildings: the National Archives, the Supreme Court, Parliament House. The centre of town had wide streets and large, glass-front storefronts. She saw a crowd forming around a man, a performer of some kind. At the intersection, a woman traffic police waved them on, her face hidden behind a dust mask. Two middle-aged women at a bus stop were poring over a newspaper. A motorcyclist whizzed past the cab, loaded down with a family of four. This, Ava thought, was what she'd barricaded herself against that Christmas with Mom and Dad and Luke. All this. She hadn't wanted any of this to bear a relation to her.

Back in a less central part of town, the driver announced, 'Bal Mandir!' Ava tensed up reflexively as he drove through an open metal gate. She was thirsty from last night's excesses. She should have brought a bottle of water. The driver halted in front of a rambling old palace. 'And waiting here, sister?'

'No,' Ava said, then changed her mind. 'Actually, yes. Could you wait?'

'Petrol too big price today, and nine hundred rupees!'

'Okay. Just wait for me here, it won't be long.'

The orphanage wasn't quite the crumbling wreck she'd remembered it as. It was palatial, if run-down, and it was ornate, decorated with columns, arches, and balustrades. There were two entrances, each flanked by Greek-style fluted columns with Corinthian capitals. The paint on the façade was chipping, as it was on the doors and windows, but there was a faded grandeur to the building.

There was no one in the front lawn. Ava remembered the children who'd been there that Christmas: how they'd stared at her. That old wound prickled inside.

'Existential Earth?' a woman said.

She spun around, and saw a young woman with brochures of some kind. 'Oh, I thought—isn't this Bal Mandir?' Ava asked her.

The woman pointed at one of the entrances. 'That is orphanage side. This—she pointed at the other entrance—is Academy of Art side.'

She handed Ava a brochure. 'Please you are welcome to see, exhibition is on theme: Existential Earth.'

'Oh. Thank you.'

With a smile, the woman went inside the Academy of Art.

Ava turned back to the orphanage. The building was still. There was no movement in any of the windows. *This is where we first met you, honey.* Where were the children?

~

Not wanting to stand there too much longer, but not yet ready to leave, Ava went into the Academy of Art. Through the entrance was a large, empty foyer with a stone floor. She remembered the stone floor from that Christmas, and how cold the rooms had been. Dust motes swirled in a beam of sunlight from a side window. There was a sign pointing upstairs. The wooden staircase creaked as she climbed.

The art show was two floors up. It opened dramatically, with a life-size effigy suspended in thick black rope. There was a television screen beside the effigy. It displayed a woman, also suspended, swaying back and forth in the air. Sometimes the woman raised her hands as if trying to fly, and at other times she flailed, unable to find her footing.

Ava took a picture of the installation and emailed it to Luke: *Look, little brother, there's conceptual art in Nepal!*

The rest of the show consisted of what Luke would dismiss as retinal art: landscapes, figurative paintings, abstractions. Ava noted the prevalence of Hindu imagery: there were several gods from the pantheon, which she didn't recognize, certainly not in these interpretive renditions. There were too many paintings to take in in the show. They blurred together after a while.

She saw a balcony on the far side of the hall and stepped out onto it. It looked over an inner courtyard of the building, with an enclosed yard directly below.

The yard may have been part of the orphanage. There was a boy there, he looked about seven or eight. He had on a school uniform, but no shoes. Ava watched as he raised his arms and hurled himself into a cartwheel, letting out a triumphant whoop as he landed on his feet. He raised his arms again and was about to do another cartwheel when someone called out. He ran in.

Mother passed in childbirth. Father is unknown. Name was given for official purposes.

Abha.

She didn't know why she'd come here, but she was glad she had.

When she turned back in, the woman who'd given her the brochure was standing directly behind her. 'Oh! I didn't notice you,' Ava said. 'Sorry.'

'Please, you are welcome.' The woman seemed sweet. She was young, in her early twenties or perhaps late teens. 'That is by me,' she said, pointing at a pedestal with a small carving.

'You're one of the artists?'

'I am youth artist of Nepal.'

Ava went to look at her carving. It was about ten inches high, and made of clay. It was of a woman, maybe, though it wasn't clear. The style was—naïve? It had a kind of raw energy.

'It is, it is...' The artist struggled with her English. 'It is mother.'

'Your mother?' Ava asked. Or did she mean a universal mother figure?

'My mother is living in Kirtipur,' the artist said. 'It is not portrait of her, but my imagination.'

'Oh.' Ava wasn't sure what she meant. 'It's an interesting piece,' she said.

The artist smiled shyly.

Checking the brochure for a title—there was none—Ava caught the price, and on a whim, decided: 'You know what? I'd like to buy it.' It would be a memento of her visit—her return—to the orphanage.

The sculptor's eyes widened in delight. 'Oh, I appreciate very much your support! It is a big support, thank you for buying, oh, I am happy!'

She got into a tizzy over the payment, writing up a receipt, counting Ava's money, making change. She cradled Ava's business card in her palms as though it were a precious gift. 'I will deliver myself,' she said. 'I will deliver to your house after exhibition.' With a glee that both gratified and embarrassed Ava, she placed a red dot beside the piece. 'Oh, I am very happy today!'

Only once back in the foyer did Ava realize that she'd left behind the brochure. She hadn't asked, and the sculptor hadn't told her, her name.

Was it a Nepali thing not to introduce yourself by name?

Outside, she took a final look at the orphanage. She was done here: she'd never come back.

When she got into the cab, the driver said, 'Too long waiting, Sister! And one thousand rupees, okay!'

Ten dollars. 'Okay,' Ava said.

She badly needed a drink of water. As they started off, she checked her email. Luke hadn't replied to her: it was the middle of the night in Miami. She didn't really want to go back home. She needed a distraction—any distraction. She called Tomás: 'Hey, how was the organic market?'

'I picked up some two soft cheeses, a semi-soft with truffles, and a hard blue. What are you doing for lunch, my dear?'

'A cheese platter wouldn't go amiss.'

'Come over. I found a cab sauv from Margaret River in my corner shop. I'll open it so it can breathe.'

'LAU, GYANU BABU, let me know if I can be of any further service,' Jeevan Bhatta said. They crossed the bridge over the mad river. 'Send word anytime through your Thulo Ba. Anything the Chairman orders, I'll do.'

'We couldn't have done this without you,' Gyanu said.

Sapana, who was trailing behind by a few steps, also thanked the widower. 'We'll always remember your help.'

The widower gave her his usual loopy grin. 'My loyalty to your family goes back for generations.'

They parted on the shore. Gyanu and Sapana watched him go towards Thulo Ba's house. No doubt he was going there to report on his success. By the end, Gyanu had given him seventy-five thousand rupees to see to the stamping, sealing, signing and fingerprinting of a thousand documents. The land transfer was done.

After he disappeared around a bend, Sapana suggested they go to see the plot. Gyanu led the way, skirting around the feudal estates to reach the ridge. The corn was already standing tall: it would have to be harvested soon. Thulo Ba's fields were also ripening.

Sapana was in a wistful mood. 'Dai,' she said, looking out at the plot, 'I agreed to sign the deed only because you insisted, but it's not my land, it's ours. It's yours as much as mine, you know.'

He said, 'You'll have take to charge of it, Bahini. For now let the old agreement with Thulo Ba stand, but in the future—'

'I won't do anything without consulting you first, Dai.'

Gyanu was just relieved that the transfer was done. Sapana would be all right: for the first time, he finally felt so. To ease his last niggling doubts, he asked, 'Bahini, do you think you'd want to live elsewhere—in the bazaar, say?'

'Why would I want to do that?' She looked at him quizzically. 'Or—do you want to live in the bazaar? Is that what you're saying, Dai?'

'No, I was just wondering. I saw some plots for sale, that's why.'

'Don't buy land for my sake, but if you want—'

'It was just a stray thought,' he said.

Sapana kept looking at him, trying to read him. Then she gave up and grew wistful again. 'They're really gone, hai, Dai? Ma and Ba. I never thought there'd be no one above us one day,' she said. 'I mean, there's no one older than us now: there's no one between us and our own end.'

'It's the way of the world, Bahini.'

'I hate it, Dai. I know we all have to go one day, but I really hate it, I hate it so much.' She forced herself to smile. 'Shall we go? Chandra's cooking, she burns everything.'

'I'll come in a little while.'

'I'll make sure Chandra doesn't burn the food!'

~

After she left, he sat on the ground, leaning against the stump of the old willow tree. He'd received a message from Maleah at the land revenue office. He took out his mobile phone and reread it.

I m going 2 visit agent 2day mahal.

He'd shot back a quick response: *ok meri maya.*

He was at a loss as to how to proceed from here. He'd overshot his thirty days' leave by several weeks. Shantanu Kumar had given away his job. He needed to find another job now, and had telephoned the manpower agency in Kathmandu through which he'd first gone to the desert. It had closed after workers were stranded in the war in Libya. The manager had opened a new agency, though. Gyanu had tracked it down. 'Right now I have a line on Saudi and Kuwait,' the agent had said to him over the phone, 'and there's money to be made in Iraq, but you'd have to go through India.' He had no links into the UAE.

Now that he was free to leave, Gyanu had no way back to the desert. And by the time he returned there, Maleah might have left... He could barely stand to complete that thought.

From where he was sitting, he could see the low blue hills. The jungle there had thickened with springtime. Below the ridge, the mad river was seething, the meltwater from upstream having doubled the river's size. It was called the mad river because it often flooded without warning in the springtime. Two boys were standing in the shallows, casting nets. From the bridge, a man called out to them: 'Have you caught anything good, boys, or is it all sidre fish?'

One of the boys replied, 'We caught asala all morning!'

The man went to examine their catch, and selected a long, lean trout for himself. After he paid the boys, he came up the hill. Gyanu recognized his old friend and called out, 'Kisne!'

Kisne looked up. 'Oho, Gyanu, I heard you came for your Ba, I didn't realize you were still here.'

Kisne came over and sat with him, laying the trout on a clean patch of grass. He said, 'I felt sad when I heard about your Ba, but I guess the old man's at peace now. Are you going to stay on, Gyanu?'

'Only for a while.'

Kisne had been a peculiar, though not unlikeable, boy: and he'd grown into a peculiar, not unlikeable man. 'I was sure you'd be gone by the time I got back,' he said, picking a blade of grass and chewing on it. 'There was a wedding across the border, our aunt's son got married, I had nothing else to do so I went.' He let out a sudden, braying laugh. 'It was crowded and dirty—and the heat! It reminded me of the time I used to work in Bombay. I guarded a shop. Did I ever tell you I went to Bombay?' He shook his head. 'Everyone called us Bahadur, Bahadur: that's how it is in India, isn't it, Gyanu? The shop sold refrigerators and stoves, all kinds of electronics. There was a separate machine to heat bread, a separate machine to cut vegetables, a separate machine to mix spices. I worked there for more than four years.' He laughed again. 'What haven't we done, hai, Gyanu? In our lives? What haven't we done in our lives?'

Gyanu smiled. He asked after their friend Ram. 'I heard he was in Kathmandu.'

'He's still there, working at an office, an insurance company. Did you hear what happened to Bisnu?'

Their other friend had fled the bazaar after a pyramid scheme that he operated collapsed, robbing hundreds of investors. 'He ran away to Kathmandu—he lives in a seven-storey house, re, made all of glass. That's what people say,' Kisne said. 'Bisnu's not like you and me, Gyanu, he always knew how to make money.' He went on. 'Me, I've worked as a guard in Bombay, as a waiter in Allahabad, as a cleaner in Goa. Ey, Gyanu, did I ever tell you about the time I went to Japan?'

'Tell me.'

'These boys I knew in Goa, they used to go there to pick apples for a few months, and then came back to work on the cruise ships—I decided to go with them to Japan. I'd heard so much about Tokyo, Tokyo, but my luck? We ended up in a village on an island in the north!' He brayed again in laughter. 'Nobody spoke our language except for us: all the apple-pickers were from home. The pay was good, but it was freezing! I worked for one season and never went back. What about you, Gyanu? How have you fared in the desert? I heard you were working in a five-star hotel?'

'I've been lucky.'

All of Us in Our Own Lives

'Is it true that your uncle is bringing a hydro plant upstream?'

'Is he?'

'That's what I heard. It's going to earn ten lakh rupees a day, re, that's what everyone's saying. You're fortunate, Gyanu, you have him, he'll help you with anything you need. People like me, we have no one. Ey!' he suddenly cried. 'Can you connect me with a manpower? What else is there to do but leave this land? Give me a telephone number, Gyanu, I'll try it, I'll try anything once, though these manpowers—which are honest, which are cheats? One never knows.' He narrowed his eyes. 'You know Jiten from the bazaar? He went through a manpower, it took him to Doha, but there was no job, he had to come back, and he lost all his money.' He said, 'I have a cousin in Malaysia, maybe it would be better to go there, what do you think?'

'I've only been to the desert.'

'And you've never been cheated?'

'Lots of people suffer, you're right to be careful.'

They heard a ripple of laughter nearby, and turned to see two of Sapana's friends, Ritu and Namrata, crossing the bridge. The girls were absorbed in their own conversation and didn't notice them.

Kisne watched them go. 'You're not going to get married, Gyanu?' he said. 'And what about your sister—how old is she now?'

Gyanu changed the subject. 'Come by the house sometime. I'll give you the number of a manpower.'

Kisne was still looking at the girls. 'Womenfolk,' he said, 'they have their own difficulties and we menfolk, we have our own, don't we?' He tossed aside the chewed-up blade of grass and got up. 'I'll come and visit you, hai. Who knows? Maybe you and I will end up together in the desert.'

He picked up the trout and left.

Gyanu remained on the ridge, rereading Maleah's message and his reply.

I m going 2 visit Jojo agent 2day mahal.

Ok meri maya.

He thought about what Kisne had said: *What else is there to do in this land.* He was right. As was Shantanu Kumar: *The village is the past.* Gyanu would call Maleah tomorrow, they'd make a plan, a life plan. If they couldn't be together in the desert, they'd find a way to be together elsewhere.

He looked again at the blue hills, and recalled a day from boyhood.

He and Kisne and Ram and Bisnu had skipped school and gone to the hills to pick ainselu berries. They were scrambling through the brush. Ram was talking about a tiger that had killed a goat in the village. Gyanu was correcting him, 'A leopard, not a tiger,' but Ram was insisting, 'No, my cousin saw it, he said it was a tiger,' when Kisne shouted: 'I think it's been here, there's a dead goat here!'

Everyone ran over to Kisne and saw the remains of a carcass, pale and half-rotted in the underbrush.

'That's not a goat,' Bisnu said. 'What is it?'

Ram poked at it with a twig. 'It's a dog.'

'No, it's a baby!'

They crowded in to see.

'It's a dog.'

'It's a baby! Someone threw away a baby!' Kisne screamed.

A terror gripped them; they all panicked at once.

'Leave it! Don't touch it!' 'Its ghost will curse us forever!' 'Let's go, let's go, let's go!'

'IT WON'T TAKE long.' Sapana said, leading the others through the bazaar. 'Rudra sir will help us. You'll see.'

'Good, because I have so many chores at home,' Rama Bhauju said.

'Me too,' Laptanni Budhi said, though this was clearly untrue. She was waited upon by a retinue of daughters-in-law at home, and never had to do anything. 'I also have chores,' she said.

Poor old Laptanni Budhi. The women's committee was too taxing for her. She'd been so relieved when Sapana took care of the accounts, she'd passed the report straight to Jeevan Bhatta. Now she was back to complaining about him, 'My nephew, since boyhood all he's done is bother his elders. He told me this morning that the CBO is going to hold a big meeting, re. One of us will have to make a big speech.' She pinched Rama Bhauju's arm. 'As the secretary, you'll have to do it.'

'You're the chairperson, you make the speech,' Rama Bhauju said.

'My nephew forced me to be the chairperson—I swear I'm going to resign!'

'Why doesn't Sapana Bahini make the speech?' Rama Bhauju said.

'Me?' Sapana was intrigued. 'But I'm only the treasurer, Bhauju.'

'Do it, do it,' Laptanni Budhi said. 'Praise the committee. There'll be foreigners at the meeting. If they're impressed, they'll give the CBO money for another study tour.'

'As the secretary, I second the proposal that Sapana Bahini make the speech,' Rama Bhauju said. 'There, it's decided.'

Sapana laughed. She'd never made a speech before, but having met all twenty-two members, she now knew everything about the women's committee. The committee had done surprisingly well, though Rama Bhauju hadn't repaid her loan yet, and at least two other members would probably default: they'd frittered away their money on household expenses. But Naina di had earned twenty thousand rupees selling goats. Jethi Didi had planted an entire orange orchard. Even the poorest members had recovered their investment: Chandra's Muwa had just repaid her loan, and from here on, all the earnings from the sales of her pickles would be hers to keep.

They reached the bank. Sapana led them in through the front door, past the security guard. It was the start of the month, and the line was long. She asked the others to wait by the side and went to Rudra sir's cubicle.

Rudra sir was busy with a client. He was wearing a green shirt today: he always wore green shirts on Wednesdays. Whenever Sapana came to the bank, he came out of his cubicle to help her. When Ba fell ill, Rudra sir taught her how to manage the family's account. He always expedited Gyanu Dai's transfers from the desert, and he talked to Sapana about money management, stressing the importance of saving. Sapana could tell from his attentiveness towards her that he liked her: even the blind could see that, it was obvious. After he finished helping her, he always said, 'Let's have tea,' and sometimes she said yes.

When he finished with the client, he left his cubicle and came to Sapana.

'What can I do for you, Sapana Bahini?'

Rudra sir wasn't handsome, but his eyes were a curious golden-brown that shifted hues in the light.

Sapana said, 'We want to open an account, sir. I'm the treasurer of a committee. I've brought the chairperson and secretary.'

'Is the committee registered? Have you brought the registration papers?'

'Yes, and our citizenship cards.'

'Then I'll just have you fill in some forms.' He escorted the three of them to a side office, and methodically helped them write down all the information. 'Complete the top part of this page. And I'll need you to sign on that line. How many signatories do you want on the account? Will you need cheques? Can you come back to pick up the chequebook, Sapana Bahini?'

'I can.'

It took a while: and Laptanni Budhi and Rama Bhauju grumbled throughout. But when they were done, they were pleased. 'Our little committee has a bank account!'

Rudra sir escorted them out, to the front door. 'If you need anything else, come to me,' he said to all of them, though he was looking at Sapana. 'Are you sure there's nothing else I can do for you today?'

Sapana said, 'That's all for today, Rudra sir.'

'If there's anything.'

'I'll come to you.'

~

Laptanni Budhi was deeply impressed. After leaving the bank, she said, 'If we'd known it was so easy, we'd have done this years ago, hai, Rama?'

'Haaa!' Rama Bhauju laughed. 'It was easy only because—did you see how that boy was looking at Sapana Bahini?'

Sapana smiled knowingly. 'A plain boy like that is lucky to talk to any girl at all!'

'He seems like a good boy, Bahini.'

'He's the father of two grown sons!'

'Tchee, then why was he flirting?'

Before returning to the village, Rama Bhauju had to go to a medical shop; but first Laptanni Budhi wanted to buy some rice. They turned into a grain store. They were entering the store when Sapana heard someone calling her name. Rudra sir had come out of the bank, waving a sheet of paper. Laptanni Budhi and Rama Bhauju went in. Sapana waited outside.

When Rudra sir reached the grain store, he stopped to catch his breath. A delicate flush spread on his cheeks. 'I thought we'd completed all the formalities, but—' He looked at Sapana with his golden-brown eyes. 'I needn't bother the others, but if you have a moment, Bahini... do you have a moment? There's a little bit of information I still need.'

Sapana saw the way he was looking at her; and she saw the power she held over him. She enjoyed it. She said, 'I suppose I could catch a bus later. Let me go and tell the others?'

Inside, Laptanni Budhi was haggling with the shopkeeper. 'Why would I pay so much, Sahuji, when I can go to another store and pay half that amount?'

'Go, then, go to another store!'

'I'll pay you half the amount.'

'No, go! Go to another store!'

Unable to get her attention, Sapana told Rama Bhauju they'd have to return to the village by themselves. 'I also want you to call a new meeting, Bhauju. I think the committee should open cooperatives, like the ones we saw on the study tour.'

'Yes, yes, cooperatives—why not?' Rama Bhauju said, paying no attention to her at all. 'And don't forget about the speech!' she cried out, before turning back to resume haggling with the shopkeeper: 'We'd rather die of hunger than pay that much for your stale, broken rice!'

Rudra sir, standing outside, had overheard Rama Bhauju. When Sapana rejoined him, he asked, 'What speech is that, Bahini?'

Sapana told him about her Thulo Ba's CBO, and the meeting they were going to have. 'There are going to be foreigners there.'

'A brilliant girl like you, I'm sure you'll give a great speech.'

Sapana saw that he was appealing to her vanity. 'Do you really think so?' she said coyly.

'I have no doubt.' He opened his mouth to say something, and Sapana already knew what it was. He said, 'Do you have some time to spare for me today, Bahini? If so, let's have tea first, we can fill out the forms afterwards...but only if you have time.'

'I have time.'

'Then let's have tea.'

WOMEN WERE FOOLS, they were imbecile-moron-dolts, naive and gullible, ever willing to give up their most intimate selves to the first man who said, 'Oh, I love you.' They were simpletons, dunce-chumps, halfwits, saps: nothing but idiot-fools.

Durga had gone and got herself pregnant by the vegetable vendor. 'Hajoor, I should take poison and die,' she'd wailed that night, after the dinner party. 'No one will have me now. Muwa will kick me out when she finds out: aaaai, aaaai! Then, what will I do? Where will I go?' She'd got so worked up she could hardly breathe. 'I should die, Hajoor.' She'd keened like a wounded beast. 'I should just take poison and die!'

Indira shuddered to remember it. She was in the waiting room of a private clinic, waiting for the girl to come out. It had fallen on her, naturally, to help the idiot-fool. 'Tch, tch, tch! What are you saying?' she'd said that night, her mind galloping in all directions all at once, like a herd of wild elephants: how was she going to solve this, what if Muwa found out, what was she going to do with Durga? 'No one's going to kick you out, you're part of the family,' she'd said. 'Don't cry, girl. There's no use crying now. The time for crying has passed.'

'Aaaai!'

Fool.

The girl had gone into the doctor's office more than two hours ago. There was no one else in the waiting room, thank the gods. For extra precaution, Indira had chosen a clinic in a poor part of the city, where no one was likely to recognize her. She hadn't told a single person about this, not even Uday Sharma, because if she did, he'd blab about it to Muwa, and Muwa would undoubtedly kick the girl out.

When the door to the doctor's office swung open, the girl shuffled out, dull-eyed. They must have given her sedatives.

The doctor came out behind her. 'It was quite far along, I had to go in twice,' she said brusquely, snapping off the rubber gloves. 'You're her guardian? Who are you to her?' She appraised Indira with a withering glance. 'You must be her master.'

'I'm like a mother to her.'

'Then educate her about birth control!'

Indira paid a thousand rupees for the procedure, then led Durga out of the clinic. The poor girl was unsteady on her feet. Indira had to hold her by the elbow so she wouldn't trip or fall. 'This way, girl.

How are you feeling? Don't worry. The medicine will wear off, you'll be back to normal soon.'

The intersection by the clinic was choked with traffic. They crossed it slowly, and turned into a quiet side street, which was all shadows and discretion. There, behind a gate, was a concrete-block building with the sign: Heaven Hotel.

The hotel's front desk was unmanned, but Indira had already paid in advance for a three-day stay. 'Here we are.' She led the girl to the room at the end of the hall. The room was sunless, but it had a TV with a satellite connection. Indira helped the girl into bed and took out an extra blanket from the cupboard. 'There.' She tucked her in carefully. 'Don't do anything for a few days, Durga. Just lie here and watch TV,' she said. 'Now, listen: no one knows about this at home. I told everyone you've gone to the village to meet your family, understand?'

'My family,' the girl mumbled, 'has forgotten me, Hajoor.'

'Just tell everyone you went to meet them—if they ask.'

'My family has forgotten I was ever born.'

'Tch.' Indira held the girl's cool, clammy hands. 'I'm your mother-father, Durga. Do you know what I've done for you here? I found you a doctor, I got you a hotel room, I took the whole morning off to be with you,' she said, though this wasn't, in fact, true. She'd have to leave before long for a meeting at Vishwa Bista's cousin sister-in-law's NGO, National Network Nepal. 'You know what else I've done?' Indira said. 'I've lied to my family, Durga. Never before in my life have I lied to my family.' Neither was this true. 'I know things have been difficult for you, girl, but now you have to forget everything and move on.'

Durga just lay there like a broken doll.

'I'll get you some food.' Indira said. 'You just lie in bed and watch a movie.' She went to the TV and pressed the button, but it wouldn't turn on. She checked the lights: there was a power cut. Oof. 'Why don't you just—sleep,' she said. 'Take a nap, Durga. You need to recover your strength.'

She left.

Outside the hotel, on the main street, a taxi honked, a bicycle whizzed by, people jostled through the crossroad. It was dusty, the dry season was here, they'd have to start trucking in water to the house. On the far end of the block was a fast food place called Tandoor & Kebab. That would do.

A little boy was minding the counter while an older man cooked in the open kitchen. The menu was painted in enamel on the restaurant wall. Indira placed her order with the boy: 'One whole tandoori chicken, one dal tadka and four aloo parathas. And saag paneer, give me saag paneer, and do you have yogurt? One order yogurt. All for home packing.'

He took her payment. 'It'll take twenty minutes, auntie.'

'Twenty minutes!'

'So? You want to cancel the order?' he asked, suddenly querulous.

'No, no.'

She went to a table splattered with oil stains and waited. The scent of fried cumin arose as the man put the tadka in the dal. Indira checked her watch. She'd be late for the meeting at National Network Nepal. She didn't want to attend it at all. Why did the Canadian want to meet Vishwa Bista's cousin sister-in-law? Perhaps she had noticed irregularities in the WDS-Nepal proposal. To Indira, the entire proposal seemed to be written in red and highlighted in yellow, pointing out its own corruption. Vishwa Bista needed to get it approved, and swiftly.

She fished out her mobile phone and texted Vishwa Bista: *Family emergency pls excuse me from meeting 2day Vishwaji, So sorry Indira.*

He texted back immediately: *Very very sorry 2 hear.*

Very very sorry to have ever heard your name, Indira thought.

'Auntie!' The boy called out from the counter. 'You want sweets with your order?'

'What kind do you have?'

'Rasgullas.'

'Pack four.'

'Only four, auntie?'

'All right, six.'

'Take a dozen, auntie. What's a dozen rasgallas for a nice, rich auntie like you?'

'La, pack a dozen,' Indira said. She resigned herself to spending the morning with Durga. It was the least she could do for the girl.

Poor Durga. She was ruined now, Indira thought. Just as she herself might have been, for had she not been an idiot-fool in her day? Yes, she had. She'd given herself to Uday Sharma a fortnight before the wedding because he had said he loved her so much, he needed to show her how much. They'd gone to a dirty hotel in the tourist district, and in a dirty room she'd endured Uday Sharma's clumsy groping, mortified at the thought that other couples in the dirty hotel were doing the same dirty thing in their own dirty rooms. She should have refused, she should have saved herself. For though everything had worked out, anything might have happened, Uday Sharma might have left her; and she was only a woman. She could easily have been ruined.

'Ready, auntie!' The boy held out a plastic bag and a bill.

'But I already paid for the food!'Indira glared at him.

'Haaa, auntie, you asked for rasgullas, did you forget?' the boy sneered. 'Or did you think they were free?'

Snotty little bastard.

She paid and went back to Heaven Hotel.

Thinking: maybe Durga needn't be ruined by this—little mishap. It wasn't fair on women, really. Nepali society wasn't fair. Maybe the girl could be whole again. Was it possible? Of course. Maybe not. It would be hard, but she should try and help Durga be whole.

When she got to the girl's room, the lights—and the TV—were on. The girl was engrossed in a Hindi tele-serial.

Good.

Indira sat down on her bed. 'I hope you're hungry, girl, I hope you're really, really hungry, because I think you're really going to like what I've brought you.'

'THANKS, CLAIRE.'

'You're right to be cautious, Ava, but don't forget: when the assessment's done, you'll need to double the budget for the Five Year Outlook.'

'I won't forget,' Ava said. How could she, when Claire ended all her conversations with this reminder?

She left Claire's office. Next she had a meeting at National Network Nepal. On the way to her office to pick up her attaché case, she stopped by the washroom to freshen up. She was feeling better now that Claire had approved the assessment of WDS-Nepal. The assessment would give her an additional six weeks to pick through WDS-Nepal's proposal. She'd also use the extra time to double the Five Year Outlook. The Women's Empowerment Programme had to have an annual budget of more than four million pounds. The prospect of drawing up such a budget daunted her. She washed up, and after drying her hand poked the rubber breast in the washroom: each time, the underside felt stickier, and the lump lumpier.

Herman Banke was in her office when she got there.

Without any preliminaries, he said, 'Can you have women's empowerment without inclusion, Ava?' His face was red, his mien charged, as ever. He'd lost his appeal to have the Social Inclusion Programme reinstated. He was working on the short-term project on resilience, but spending his days lobbying to turn it into a long-term programme on inclusion.

Ava picked up her attaché case. 'I'm stepping out for a meeting.'

'Can you really empower women exclusively through employment generation, or—Herman snorted—'peacebuilding?' What is Jared going to do, build peace with the PEON, the permanent establishment of Nepal? Don't you know, Ava?' He stepped in so close Ava could feel his breath on her face. He said, 'This country is run by high-caste men, fifteen per cent of the population, who have always, historically, monopolized power, excluding all other identity groups. And don't even talk to me about women!'

'I've read your social exclusion index, Herman. I understand, but—'

'There can be no buts!' he shouted. Then he took in a deep breath and stepped back. 'I'm sorry, Ava. I have a tendency to get carried away. My wife is taking me to a meditation retreat next week, maybe it'll help.' He bared his teeth in a feral smile. 'It's just that if you were a Nepali woman, Ava, everything would be determined by your gender and caste. If your family were rich, you'd have some mobility, but otherwise—what you eat, what you wear, what you say, what you do: everything would be determined by your birth.'

Ava thought back to what the official had said, that Christmas. *Caste is unknown.* She said, 'I know inclusion is important, Herman. It's just that I have a meeting.'

'Are you going to Jared's dinner party tonight?'

'I, well—'

'He invited everyone from the office except me,' he said, sounding hurt, like a boy ostracized at school.

'Let's meet when you're back from the mediation retreat?' Ava said.

'Ten days of complete silence.' He grimaced. 'I don't know if I'll survive it.'

~

Vishwa had gone ahead to Nepal Network Nepal to debrief its director, Preety Rana, on Daphne Muirwood's implementation strategy on aid effectiveness. All of IDAF's national partners were required to comply with it.

The SUV that Ava had requisitioned was waiting at the front door. The driver took her a block along the main road and turned into an alley, steering through a narrow lane into a neighbourhood of high brick walls and tall metal gates. It turned out that National Network Nepal's office was within walking distance. They stopped at a tall gate. After the driver honked, the gate opened to reveal a second, taller gate inside. The security guard who had opened the first gate scurried to open the second one.

Past it lay a half-built highrise rising up from a construction site filled with cement sacks, oil drums, wood planks, iron rods and bricks. The highrise's front door was still unfinished. The cavernous lobby inside smelled of wet cement. By now Ava had been to several NGO offices for meetings, and they could feel rudimentary—though the provisional, thrown-together air to National Network Nepal's office was of a whole other order. There was a reception desk in the lobby, but no chairs. National Network Nepal was, according to WDS-Nepal's proposal, one of the country's leading NGOs for capacity enhancement. Its director was well-connected. 'You should know,' Vishwa had told Ava this morning,

'Preety Rana is married to the former finance minister. He's still very powerful in his party.'

A man appeared out of nowhere. His face was hidden by a grey woollen muffler. He led her to an office complex at the back of the building.

There, in an inner sanctum, in a warm, sun-drenched office complex, was Preety Rana. She was sitting at her desk, across from Vishwa. She was in her forties, and dressed in a sari. She had a polished manner and an impeccable British accent: 'I'm sorry about the state of the office, they raised the rent on our old office, so we're camped here like refugees.' She showed Ava a chair beside Vishwa. 'Will you have coffee or tea, Ms Berriden? I'd recommend our masala tea with ginger—our helper makes an excellent brew.'

'That sounds wonderful.'

She placed the order with the man in the muffler, then turned back to Ava. 'Mr Bista tells me you're from Canada. I've been there,' she said. 'To Montreal. It was beautiful—but cold!'

'You were there to study federalism,' Vishwa said.

'That's right.'

Vishwa mentioned that Preety Rana had been a member of the first constituent assembly. 'The one that was dissolved.'

'Without drafting a constitution.' Preety Rana laughed.

'Indira Sharma texted, she won't be able to make it to the meeting. I'll have to debrief her afterwards.'

Preety Rana started the meeting when the tea came. 'I've consulted on women's issues for over two decades, Ms Berriden.' She named the organizations she'd worked for—'ADB, DFID, World Bank, UNDP'—and rattled off the titles of reports she'd authored: 'Increasing Empowerment through Capacity Enhancement. Mapping the Mainstreaming of Gender: Creating a Matrix for Inclusive Development. New Measurement Paradigms for Sustainability. You can keep this copy.' She slid a hefty report across her desk. 'I wrote this for the Canadian Cooperation Office, before CIDA collapsed. It's a pity that the Canadian government has cut back its involvement in the world, isn't it? Canada has no presence left in Nepal: they even downsized their consulate. That report is out of date now, but I thought you might be interested, as a Canadian.'

'Thank you.'

'You're welcome. Now, as you know, Ms Berriden, National Network Nepal is less than a year old, but as its director I assure you, we're deeply dedicated to customizing the results logframe. We aim to partner with stakeholders at all levels, all over the country. For WDS-Nepal, we're proposing to conduct capacity enhancement workshops nationwide. In fact, I just came back from a workshop in Capetown. We trained thirteen NGOs from all over Africa, including from sub-Saharan Africa, on microfinancing.'

'On that subject,' Ava said. She took WDS-Nepal's proposal out of her attaché case and flipped to an index of community based organizations that National Network Nepal was proposing to partner with at the village level. 'Can you tell me which of these CBOs does the best work on microfinancing?'

'All of our local partners are excellent. That's why we partner with them,' Preety Rana said.

'Well, Vishwa and I are going to the field soon, and we'd like to visit some of them.'

'I'm sure Mr Bista can find you a good CBO to visit.'

'Maybe you could join us on the trip?' Ava said.

She smiled. 'Unfortunately, I'll be on assignment in Bangkok for the next two months.'

'Oh. Well, I hope we can count on you to cooperate with an assessment we'll be conducting of WDS-Nepal and its partners.'

'A what?' Vishwa said. 'Why? Is there a problem with the proposal, Ava?'

'No, I just—it's such a large grant, I wanted to—'

'You should have discussed it with me first!'

Had she breached protocol? Was she supposed to have passed the assessment by Vishwa before taking it to Claire? 'I'm sorry,' Ava said. 'It's just a routine—I didn't mean to—I'm really sorry, Vishwa. Let's talk about it after the meeting.'

Preety Rana was observing the exchange coolly. 'Of course I'll cooperate with the assessment,' she said. 'Do you know, Ms Berriden, that I've worked in all seventy-five districts of Nepal?' She slid across another report. 'Here's the proposal we submitted to WSD-Nepal.'

Ava had already read it in the WDS-Nepal proposal. She leafed through it as the other woman began to speak about deliverables, quantifiables, indexes, measurements and matrixes. Preety Rana was extremely articulate. Yet something about her needled Ava. Was it that she was too professional, too polished? That wasn't fair. 'My personal mission,' Preety Rana said, 'has always been to empower the poor with tools to uplift their socio-economic status. Over my career, I've seen the fortunes of an entire family transformed by the empowerment of a single woman. As a Nepali woman, I dream of ordinary women—mothers, wives, daughters—being agents of change. In my own family,' she said, growing passionate, 'I'm the first generation to study beyond high school. My mother was a housewife, and I'm a PhD from the University of Leeds. I really believe, Ms Berriden, that women are the ones who create change, lasting change, the kind of change that transforms society.'

~

By the time they left, Vishwa was no longer upset about the assessment. 'I know a consultant, John Barnett, he's the best—we must get him to do it,' he said.

'Would you look into it, Vishwa? That would be really helpful.'

'Sure, sure.'

They were both going to Jared's, so after stopping by the office to drop off some documents, they shared a ride over. Jared lived close to Ava, on a leafy side road at the bottom of the hill. A guard opened the gate and let them into a sprawling estate, where a crowd of expatriates—and one or two Nepalis—stood around a lawn.

There was a self-serve bar at one end of the lawn. Vishwa got them two gin and tonics, then fell into conversation with another Nepali man at the bar.

Ava went back out to the lawn and circled around, looking for Jared or anyone else from IDAF. The expatriates in Nepal came in several varieties, she observed. A few, like she, wore ordinary western clothes. Most accessorized their outfits with splashes of local colour: embroidered silks, flowing tunics, dramatic Tibetan jewellery, embroidered pashminas. Yet others came dressed in flowing silks and woollen robes finer, and more delicate, than she'd seen any Nepali wear.

There was a woman commanding the attention of a small crowd. Ava stopped to listen to her. The woman was swathed in maroon robes and her hair was shorn: were it not for a glass of red wine in her hands, she'd pass as a Buddhist nun. Or perhaps she was one. She was talking about hidden valleys.

Then, seeing Daphne Muirwood by the bar, Ava went to her.

Daphne was scowling at her cell phone.

'I need some advice,' Ava said, knowing better than to waste the other woman's time on small talk. 'I've started to draw up WEP's Five Year Outlook, and want to achieve higher performance without, well, throwing money at everything. Could I come into your office to talk, sometime, about your implementation strategy?'

Daphne nodded. 'I'm in the process of expanding its modular component,' she said, when her cell phone pinged. She scowled and checked the message, then looked back up. 'I'm aligning more closely to the principles of Accra and Busan, in particular—' Her cell phone pinged again. 'One moment. Can you give me a minute?' She typed a brief message. 'I'm sorry, where were we?'

'The modular component.'

'Yes. I'm aligning—'

The phone pinged.

Daphne's jawline tightened. 'I'm sorry. I should turn the phone off, but it's urgent—a personal matter.'

'We can talk about this in the office.'

'I'm in the middle of negotiations.' Daphne bit her lips. 'My future ex and I are working out custody for our son.' She peered at Ava, as though noticing her for the first time. 'Are you married?'

'Separated. No children.'

'You're lucky—about the no children part, I mean. Was separating hard for you?' she asked. Without waiting for an answer, she mused, 'Sometimes it feels feel like something will be unbearable, but when you go ahead and do it, it's not. For me, it was a relief to separate, but the divorce—that's thornier. My son is seven. He'll remember this time in his life: he'll remember his mother being abroad, his father being home with him.' She scowled again. 'I should have stayed in London till it was sorted out. I shouldn't have left headquarters till we'd settled.'

'It must be difficult.'

'It's what it is.' Daphne shrugged. 'Now, where were we?'

'You know,' Ava said, 'If you want to talk, I'm a very good listener. Why don't you come over for dinner sometime? I've got a nice garden, we can sit out and look at the view.'

Daphne stiffened. 'I'll have to look up my schedule and get back to you about that.' 'Oh. Of course.'

Daphne's phone pinged again. 'I'm afraid you'll have to excuse me, Ava. I really should deal with this.'

~

Ava milled about, feeling oddly out of place among the expatriates. They were, in a way, her tribe in Nepal. At the centre of the lawn, a man with a ponytail had pulled out a guitar, and was crooning Bob Dylan songs. Ava listened to his off-key rendition of 'Tangled Up in Blue'. When he started an off-key rendition of 'Lay, Lady, Lay', she decided to leave.

'Excuse me, I'm sorry.' An elderly woman in a red brocade gown passed by, trailed by the soft scent of marijuana.

Ava found Jared by the gate.

'You are already leaving, have you eaten?' he asked her.

'Yes,' she lied. 'Thanks for inviting me, that was lovely.'

'What Herman has said to you about my programme, it is not true, Ava.'

Ava's heart sank.

'Ava, poverty is this country's biggest problem, not social inclusion,' Jared said. 'I am not a Marxist, Ava, do not think I am endorsing Marxism, but it is universally acknowledged that class struggle is the primary means to human progress.'

'But I understand that some identity groups have historically—'

'That is dangerous talk, Ava, you must not listen to Herman, he is wrong.'

'Why don't we talk about it at the office?'

'It is not true that I wrote 'poor and marginalized' in my report because the government of Nepal told us to do so. Yes, the government did ask us to do so, but I agreed because I believe that 'poor and marginalized' is a more neutral category than 'excluded'.'

I don't care, Ava wanted to say.

'What Herman says about me is simply not true.'

She'd never be friends with her colleagues at IDAF.

DURGA WAS GOING to kill her, she really was. The girl was refusing to eat, saying, 'I don't like it,' as though anyone could not like tandoori chicken. Indira bought her lamb kebabs today: lamb kebabs for a servant girl! Never mind. The girl was doing better physically, but still showing little sign of recovering emotionally. When the power was on, the girl would watch Hindi tele-serials, but during the hours-long stretches of load shedding, she lay in bed staring vacantly at the ceiling, despite Indira's exhortations: 'Go for a stroll, it'll do you good.' She didn't even wash or get dressed, which was frustrating, because what more could Indira do for her? It was already two nights, three days: she couldn't keep skipping office. She'd take the girl home tomorrow, and that would be that.

She marched into Heaven Hotel, passing the unmanned lobby to reach the girl's room. The door was locked from inside. She rapped on it. 'Open, ey, Durga.' She had a one-on-one with Rick Peede this morning. She had to tell him that she'd applied to replace him as the director of WDS-Nepal. She had to ask him to support her application. WDS-Nepal had never, in its history, had a Nepali director—or a woman director. This was the twenty-first century. It was time.

She rapped again, sharply. 'I don't have all day, girl. Open the door!'

There was no reply.

Oof. She wondered if she should leave the food at the door: but then someone might steal it. Durga would have to go hungry all day. There'd be an extra key in the lobby—if only someone were there. 'Open the door, Durga!' She banged on the door. 'Open, I said!' Nothing. She jiggled the doorknob. She kicked the door: once, twice. Then a terrible thought flashed into her mind, and she hurled herself against the door.

It flew open and she tumbled in and Durga was unconscious in bed with a bottle of—what?—lying empty beside her. The whole world wobbled. The lamb kebabs went flying. Indira ran to bed and felt for the girl's pulse, but her own heart was hammering so loudly, she couldn't feel anything. She screamed.

Then a burst of energy swept through her. She ran out of the room, past the unmanned lobby, to the street. At the choked crosswalk, she yelled at three loafing men. 'You! You! You!'

'What happened, what happened?' A crowd quickly gathered around her.

'There's been an accident, come and help!'

The men swept back to the hotel with her, and carried Durga out. 'Let's go, let's go,' Indira cried. 'Someone fetch a taxi!'

A taxi arrived. The men placed Durga in the back seat, and Indira squeezed in beside her.

The driver turned on the blinkers and raced to the hospital, which was on the other side of the crosswalk. He was a wrinkled old man, but he helped Indira carry the girl into the emergency room, where an orderly laid her out on a gurney.

'Here.' Indira gave the driver a hundred rupee note.

He refused it. 'Use it for the girl's treatment, Bahini.'

The orderly wheeled Durga to a room. Indira followed behind, shouting, 'Doctor-nurse, doctor-nurse! Where's the doctor-nurse?'

'Wait here,' the orderly said, and slipped out. A nurse came in and took the girl's vital statistics. Durga was unresponsive—was she even alive? Indira hovered over her, explaining, 'She took something, Nurse. There was a bottle in her hand when I found her. Was it poison? Where would she have got it? Will she live? Will you pump her stomach, will she need medicine, shall I fetch her water, or saline for an IV drip? What should I do?'

'If you would just wait outside for a moment.'

'Tell me what to do, she's like a daughter to me, I'll do anything, anything, nurse.'

'Wait outside.'

She went reluctantly to the waiting room. Her mouth was parched: it felt as though she'd swallowed sand. She bought a bottle of mineral water and gulped half of it, but there was still sand in her mouth.

Her meeting! Oof: this world, her life. She fished out her mobile phone and called Rick Peede's secretary, her voice emerging in an ugly rasp: 'Neha, there's been—I can't come to the meeting this morning. I need to reschedule.'

'How about tomorrow, Indira ma'am?'

'Tomorrow we have a meeting at IDAF. How's this afternoon?' Indira said, wondering desperately whether she'd be able to leave the hospital at all.

'Rick sir is out most of the afternoon, ma'am, and then he has a meeting with Chandi sir.'

Why was Chandi Shrestha meeting Rick Peede? Was he applying for the director's job too? 'Schedule me before Chandi sir,' she rasped.

'I can't, ma'am, but I can fit you in tomorrow morning before the IDAF meeting.'

'No, I have to meet him before Chandi sir!'

'Sorry, ma'am, tomorrow morning is the only opening I have.'

'Lau, then.' Why was everything so hard? She hung up and took another gulp of water. The waiting room smelled of disease and disinfectant. In one corner, a large family was swarming around a pale, wilting man in one corner. A boy was sitting with his emaciated mother on another side of the room. A woman was weeping quietly beside Indira.

It was more than an hour before the doctor came out to talk to her. He was young and tall and upright, with an arrogant manner. 'So how did she get a hold of rat poison?' he demanded.

'Is she all right, Doctor Sah'b, how's she doing, will she live?' Indira asked.

'If it wasn't a suicide attempt it'll turn into a criminal case.'

'Of course it was a—!' The implication! 'I'm the one who—!' Indira cried: 'I found her and—are you saying I tried to kill her?'

'The things we see in here you wouldn't imagine,' he said drily.

'Is she, Doctor Sah'b, the girl—' Was Durga even alive? Indira couldn't even ask the question out loud.

The doctor said, 'You'll have to answer some questions before leaving.'

He put her in the hands of a nurse, who was kinder. 'The girl will be fine, don't fret,' she said. 'She just needs a good night's rest.' Then she sat Indira down and asked her some extremely unpleasant questions: who was Indira, where did she live, what was her home life like, what did her husband do, what were Durga's circumstances, had the girl ever been abused, beaten, raped?

'I'm the deputy co-director of WDS-Nepal, I work for women's empowerment!' Indira protested, handing the nurse a business card. 'The girl, well, she had a mishap, she's sad, her engagement ended, and—I've been helping her, Nurse. I'm like her mother-father.'

'We'll discharge her tomorrow unless it turns into a criminal case, in which case...' The nurse said, 'Come back first thing tomorrow morning.'

'I can't come in the morning. I have a very important meeting!'

'Then—how old is the patient?' the nurse said. 'We can discharge her into her own custody.'

'No, no, don't do that! I'll come.'

A nightmare. This was a waking nightmare. Indira staggered out of the hospital and got into a waiting taxi.

It turned out to be the same one as before. 'How's the girl?' The elderly driver asked. 'Is she all right, Bahini?'

'She'll be all right, Dai.'

'May God keep her safe.'

Indira was grateful for his gentility. 'Dai,' she said, 'I have to go Patan side.'

'Patan side?' He shook his head sadly. 'There's trouble in that area, Bahini. A demonstration. They're not letting traffic through.'

'But it's an emergency; it's a big, big emergency!' Indira said, and tears sprang to her eyes: tears of tension, exhaustion, distress.

The driver turned around, aghast. 'Don't cry. I hate it when women cry. Women are always crying in this land. I don't want you to cry.'

'But I have to go to the office! My boss will be angry! I'll lose my job! Then how will I feed-clothe-house my family?'

'My mother, in the village, she spent her whole life crying,' the driver said. 'It made me feel so helpless.' He turned back and started the engine. 'What's a few rocks hurled at a battered taxi, right, Bahini? The human heart, that's what matters. Lau, I'll get you to your destination through the back alleys. Just, I beg you: don't cry.'

THERE WAS A power cut; the lights were off. Tomás had lit up a single candle. His apartment had no heating, and Ava was freezing. She pulled up the bedcovers. Tomás's collarbone jutted, bony and satisfying, against her face.

'You believe him?' he said.

'I don't think he would lie about it.'

Gavin had written again. *It wasn't a date or anything.* He'd run into Leez Anne Williker. *We passed each other outside the bank on King Street, we didn't even stop to say hi. But it made me wonder—should I wait for you anymore, Av? Have you met someone? Is that what's going on? Do you have any intention of returning to Toronto, to our marriage?*

She'd fired back a one-line reply: *It's only fair to tell you that I'm seeing other people.*

This wasn't exactly true. Her brief romance, or one-night stand, or whatever it had been with Anthony, had petered out due to distance. And what she had with Tomás wasn't a relationship, though it did bear the marks of one. They were spending most of their weekends together, as well as some weekday nights, though out of respect for Tomás's vow of celibacy Ava never acted on any sexual impulse with him. She did feel them. Maybe he didn't feel any such impulse with her, though. It was hard to tell, with him.

'From everything you've told me, Gavin sounds boring,' Tomás said.

'He'd be happier with the woman he cheated on me with—she's an equity sales director.'

'You shouldn't drag out the divorce.' He had a bottle of red wine in his hand. He took a swig from it. 'I dragged out my annulment, it was a mistake,' he said.

'Why did you want an annulment, anyway?'

'I have a problem with intimacy. Hey, did I tell you? I'm applying for a job in Myanmar.'

'Oh.' What? 'You're leaving Nepal?' What was an intimacy problem?

'Nepal is passé.' He took another swig of wine. 'Things are changing really fast in Myanmar—you should come too. I mean, fuck IDAF, right: you hate this job.'

'Have I mentioned the size of my annual budget?'

'Fuck the aid industry, all it does is enrich the global elite,' Tomás said.

For a while they lay silent, he drinking, she musing over everything she'd read in the past months at IDAF, everything she'd written. All the meetings she'd sat in, all that had been said to her, all that she'd said. The presentations she'd listened to, the presentations she'd given. WDS-Nepal's proposal. That dinner at Indira Sharma's house. Vishwa, explaining things to her. All the meetings at IDAF. So many words.

'I'm looking forward to my trip,' she said. 'I've waited too long to get to the field.'

'You should really switch to humanitarian work, Ava, it's the only ethical intervention in poorly governed countries like this.'

'The only one?'

'There'll be lots of openings in Yangon. I'll help you find a job there. We can move there together,' he said, as though they were a couple.

Ava liked him so much. His wandering eye and dreamy expression charmed her, as did his rants about the aid industry, as doctrinaire as they could be. Tomás made her feel like she was living in a world of ideas that mattered. And he was her touchstone in Nepal, neither a lover nor just a friend, but something else, something intimate if uncategorized. It did occur to her, when she was in bed with him, that he was a married man—though they weren't having sex, so it didn't matter. Or, perhaps it did. What was Tomás's intimacy problem?

She rubbed her face against his clavicle. He smelled of warm, sweet skin. She could really use the kind of magical night she'd had with Anthony. Or even—she missed the certainties she'd had with Gavin. But at least she could talk about anything with Tomás. 'Hey, Tomás?' she said. 'What caste do you think I am? I mean—what caste was I when I was born?'

'Fuck knows. You'd have to ask a Nepali. They carry around all that useless information in their heads.'

'I kind of like not knowing my roots,' she said. She'd told him about her visit to the orphanage. She talked about it again. 'I saw a boy there. He was—I don't know—eight or nine years old. He was the only person I saw there. Otherwise it was—there was nothing there for me.'

'What were you hoping to find, my dear?'

'I don't know. It was following a kind of instinct in coming to Nepal. Maybe the instinct was wrong.'

'So come with me to Myanmar,' he said. 'IDAF is a collusion between the international and national elite.' His voice rumbled pleasantly through his chest. 'It's criminal,' he said, 'though they're all complicit.'

'All of them?'

'This country needs to take responsibility for itself,' he said. 'You know the risks. This entire region is overdue for—well, it's already a socio-political disaster. But imagine what's going to happen when the Big One strikes. All this,' he gestured, and the wine sloshed in the bottle, 'will vanish.' None of these houses, these streets, this shitty infrastructure, will remain. The only international airport will close. The government will be paralysed—I mean, even more paralysed than it already is. There'll be no water, food, shelter, medicine. People will have to fend for themselves—and the powerful, the strong, will prey on the weak and vulnerable. That's what aid should help the country prepare for, Ava: preventing the worst case scenario when—not if—disaster strikes.'

Ava shuddered at the vision.

'All of this,' he repeated, 'will vanish.'

'Shut up,' she said.

'This country's doomed.'

'Tell me about Myanmar. Tell me why I should switch to humanitarian work and move with you to Myanmar.'

'Nepal is completely doomed.'

SHE GRABBED HER purse from the security guard and rushed down IDAF's driveway. The receptionist—what was her name, she used to know it—recognized her from her visits to Catherine Christy and trilled, 'Namaste, Indira ma'am! Pat sir and the rest are already here—please go up.'

'Thank you!' She hurried up the stairway. She was half an hour late. This Durga business was really going to kill her.

Indeed, Rick Peede was in the conference hall, as were the Canadian and Vishwa Bista—and why was Chandi Shrestha at this meeting? Her rival smiled at her unctuously, as she took a seat.

'There you are, Indira,' said the Canadian, looking far too young to be IDAF's director of WEP. 'I'm sorry, we had to start, but I'll fill you in afterwards.'

'Sorry I—little emergency at home,' Indira said.

'Oh, is everything all right?'

'No—yes! Just—sorry.' Indira tried to catch Vishwa Bista's eyes, but they were hidden behind his floppy hair.

Rick Peede returned to the discussion she'd interrupted. It was on capacity enhancement. He had a way of droning, and even after all these years of working together, Indira found his accent hard to follow. In any case she was too agitated to pay attention.

She'd got Durga discharged from the hospital this morning—without incident, thank the gods—and had installed her back in Heaven Hotel. 'You have to be good, Durga,' she'd pleaded with the girl, who lay bloodless and bereft in bed. 'What more can I do for you? What will make you better? Tell me, girl. Tell me what you want.'

The girl had whispered, 'I want a life.'

What did that mean? 'Well, spend a few more days resting here, then we'll take you back home,' Indira had said. 'And don't try to kill yourself again, Durga. You know how hard it's been for me to manage this? No one at home knows anything, I've kept everything secret. And at the office I've got so much pressure right now, I don't need—' She'd had to catch herself. 'Now I'll go and get you some lamb kebabs. I'm sure you'll like it. And even if you don't, eat it, Durga. I beg you, girl: you have to be good.'

She'd rushed to Tandoor & Kebab, rushed back to the hotel, pleaded with the girl some more, and then rushed here.

Rick Peede kept droning on about capacity enhancement. Indira stared at him vacantly: that big head, the red hair. These expatriates were so unencumbered, so free. They could do anything they wanted all the time. She'd met Rick's wife Misha at office parties. She was even taller than her husband. They had three children: the youngest was two. An image came to her of Rick and Misha Peede having sex: there'd be legs everywhere.

'Wouldn't you concur, Indiraji?' Rick Peede asked her.

'Yes.' She sat up. 'Yes, Rickji, I fully concur.'

And even though no one had asked him, Chandi Shrestha said, 'As the other deputy co-director of WDS-Nepal, I also concur.'

'Ava, I can't emphasize this enough,' Rick Peede said. 'In our annual appraisal last year, WDS-Nepal identified five key areas for prioritization...' Again, he droned on.

What if Durga tried to kill herself again, Indira suddenly thought. What if the girl were taking rat poison right now?

She fidgeted with her purse, she squirmed in the chair, she wondered if she might excuse herself to go out and call Heaven Hotel. Then Rick Peede stopped talking, and everyone stood up, and Indira also shot to her feet. All her ambitions came frothing up like overheated milk: what had happened, had IDAF approved her proposal, was she going to become the next director of WDS-Nepal?

Rick Peede and Chandi Shrestha left after a round of handshakes. Vishwa Bista slunk away, muttering about a meeting. The Canadian turned to her with a smile. 'Shall we go to my office, Indira?'

'Yes, why not?'

Catherine Christy's old office used to be cozy, with family photos up on the wall. Now it was stripped of decor. *You must become the first Nepali director of WDS-Nepal.* Catherine Christy used to sit with Indira on the sofa, like a friend. The Canadian invited her to sit on a hard-backed chair across her desk. 'Would you like tea or coffee, Indira?'

'I will have tea.'

Catherine Christy used to make her a special goji berry tea: it stimulated the libido, she'd say with a wink. The Canadian brewed her a weak, watery cup of milk tea.

Then she sat at her desk. 'Before you arrived at the meeting, I was telling Pat and Chandi that IDAF is undergoing an internal exercise to enhance the implementation of the Paris Declaration on Aid Effectiveness. I've been discussing this with Claire—do you know Claire Ross-Jones?'

'Of course, many times I have met her.'

'And we've got Daphne Muirwood in from headquarters. She's innovating an internal implementation strategy for the country offices of the Asia Pacific Region.' The Canadian opened WDS-Nepal's proposal and turned to the section on the budget. 'As I said when I came over to your house for dinner, Indira, I'm new to this field. My background—I used to work on mergers and acquisitions in a corporate law firm in Toronto. And I've only ever worked with organizations in Canada, so I may be bringing in my own biases, but, well.' She frowned. 'WDS-Nepal has so many partners, and they're so very different. Some work at the village level, and others in the districts, and others seem to—I can't quite figure out what some of them do. National Network Nepal, for example.' She pointed at Vishwa Bista's cousin sister-in-law's NGO. 'It's slated to receive almost a quarter of your budget, and—well, you couldn't make it to the meeting, but I met the director, Preety Rana. Now Rick has explained that WDS-Nepal places a special emphasis on capacity enhancement, but, you see, I'm on my own mission for gender responsive budgeting at IDAF, and Claire is really hoping to highlight the Post-2015 Priority Themes going forward, so there's a lot I'm grappling with here.' She smiled apologetically. 'You'll have to bear with me, Indira. I'm wondering why you've chosen to partner with National Network Nepal. I want to know why them, specifically.'

Why them, why them. Indira's mind slid from thought to slippery thought, searching for one she could land on. 'Ava, there is a big difference among our partners,' she ventured. 'They are all different in their mandate and methodology. The work is all—different.' She pointed at another partner on the budget. 'For example,' she said, 'this NGO is not an implementing agency. It partners with NGOs who do implementation. Whereas this one'—she pointed at yet another partner—'it does direct implementation. Understand?' She said, 'National Network Nepal supports other partners, small ones, NGOs and CBOs in the field, to enhance capacity. It does not do direct implementation itself. So, it is like that, Ava.'

She studied the Canadian's face to see if this had convinced her.

The Canadian was frowning delicately. There was a drawn-out pause before she spoke. 'I'll probably see all this for myself on my upcoming field trip, but I guess the question I keep asking, Indira, is, what value do NGOs like National Network Nepal add? They should add value, right?'

Value? 'Value they add.' Now Indira was irked. How little these foreigners understood. 'Ava, there are four thousand villages in Nepal. Big international NGOs like WDS-Nepal, we cannot help every CBO in every village, that is too micro in scale, and also, our mandate is not for that. Understand?'

'Yes, of course.' The Canadian pointed, again, at National Network Nepal. 'So what will National Network Nepal be doing, other than disbursing funds to partners in the districts and villages? Because if that's mainly what it's going to do, that would be akin to, well, to sub-contracting, isn't it?'

Why the fixation on National Network Nepal? 'That one,' Indira said, 'has a sector-wise approach, Ava.'

'What's its sector?'

Was the Canadian a complete idiot? 'Capacity enhancement for the empowerment of women, of course.'

'Oh, right, I meant—that wasn't what I was asking, of course I knew that.' Now the Canadian was flustered. 'Sometimes I feel a bit dense, Indira, like I'm just not getting it. It's just that if we approve your proposal, it'll be our biggest collaboration outside of the government of Nepal. I've read everything I could find—though maybe I just need to stop reading and get out there, to see the work myself.'

'You still have not gone to the field even now?'

'Vishwa and I are going next week. We'll visit several CBOs that National Network Nepal is proposing to support, CBOs in'—she mangled all the names of the villages—'near a town called Butwal.' She pronounced the town's name butt-wall. 'So I'm going to wait to make my decision on your proposal till after I return. In the meanwhile, Claire and Daphne have allocated a special budget to conduct a review.'

A review? A review of—? 'A review of what?' Indira stammered.

'Our partnership with WDS-Nepal.' The Canadian smiled to soften the blow. 'I'm sorry, I know it's a hassle, but it'll be clarifying to me as I draw up the Five Year Outlook. Vishwa's already lined up a consultant, he says he's very good—an anthropologist, John Barnett.'

John Barnett. John Barnett! John Barnett was still in Nepal? 'I know John Barnett!' Indira cried. She had worked with him together at Help more than twenty years ago. She remembered him as a chocolatey-handsome man with bright blue eyes and eyelashes as long as a girl's. He was an intern, or no, he was writing a thesis back then. He was fluent in Newari and Tamang and several other Tibeto-Burmese languages. His thesis was on the indigenous management systems of—the Tamangs?

Or maybe the Newars. She said, 'Tell John Barnett to meet me, Ava. I will give him whatever information he may need.'

'That would be wonderful, thank you, Indira. I'll tell Vishwa to put you two in touch, Vishwa's in charge of the review.'

Of course. Vishwa Bista would handle this, Indira thought. He'd done things like this before. She felt better now. 'Is that all, Ava?'

'Thanks for your cooperation, Indira.'

They stood. Catherine Christy used to embrace her, but the Canadian reached over for a handshake, cold and impersonal. Anyone could tell, just from looking at her, that she had no special sympathy for women.

Out in the hallway, Indira tried to regain her composure. She wiped her face, patted down her hair. Would Vishwa Bista really clean up this mess? He had to—he'd created it. She turned into his office to confront him.

He was sitting on a couch with a woman in a sequinned miniskirt. 'Indiraji!' he cried, springing up as though she'd caught him doing something dirty.

Indira sprang back. 'Sorry, sorry!'

'No, no!' he said. 'Please come, meet Shakuntala Shree Shakya. You must have seen her on TV. She's sure to win the title this year. She is our future Miss Nepal.'

The future Miss Nepal smiled at Indira.

'Yes, of course, I recognize the name,' Indira lied. 'And, who wouldn't recognize the face?'

'I'm mentoring Shakuntala Shreeji to be an ambassador for women's development,' Vishwa Bista said. To the young woman he said, 'Indiraji is highly knowledgeable on the subject. You must learn from her about women's development.'

'I would like to learn about women's development,' said the future Miss Nepal.

'Come by my office any time.' Indira gave her a business card. Then, to Vishwa Bista, she said, 'About the assessment—'

'Leave all that to me.'

'Thank you, thank you!' Indira said, wondering bitterly why she was thanking him, when he'd dragged her into his filth. 'Thank you so much, Vishwaji!'

'You're welcome, Indiraji.'

She left, loathing him viscerally, and loathing herself too.

Excrement, filth.

Downstairs, the receptionist trilled, 'Namaste, Indira ma'am!'

'Namaste.' What was the receptionist's name?

Out in the driveway, Indira's thoughts returned to Durga. There was so much to do at the office, but how could she possibly work? She'd take the day off to look after the girl.

SHULINBABA WAS JUST a rock, and a misshapen one at that—he wasn't even a fine carving like the Hanuman statue beside him. Yet everyone was elbowing each other aside to kneel down before him. The temple bells were pealing, the air was thick with incense, it was hard to see. Sapana found an opening in the inner sanctum, and knelt before the rock.

She closed her eyes. Shulinbaba, she prayed, help let me make a good speech at the CBO meeting. Let me speak clearly and remember everything, Shulinbaba. The whole village was going to attend the meeting. After the speeches, there'd be a feast for the foreigners. All of the CBO's beneficiaries, including the members of the women's committee, would show the foreigners their work. The occasion would be momentous. Sapana prayed: let my words have power, Shulinbaba. Let them impress the foreigners.

'Ey, aren't you finished?' Ritu nudged her from behind. 'You're not the only one who needs a husband, you know. Namrata's getting desperate.'

'How could you speak like that in a temple?' Namrata hissed

Someone had offered marigolds to Shulinbaba. Sapana put one in her hair. Then she got up to let her friends take her place.

She had to shove through the crowd to leave the temple. Outside, the devotees' queue snaked all the way down the hill to the mad river. Women from surrounding villages came here on this day, the unmarried to ask for a groom, and the married to ask for their husband's longevity.

Rama Bhauju, who was standing in line with her brood of four, said, 'You're already done, Bahini?'

'It'll take you an hour just to get in!' Sapana said, wondering why she'd bother praying for the longevity of a husband who'd taken a second wife.

When Ritu and Namrata came out, they all ran down the hill, Ritu babbling, as always, about boys. 'Listen, girls, if we don't marry soon, all the good boys will be taken, and we'll have to settle for the leftovers. You know that monkey who lives across from my house? The other day he told me I'm too proud, I'll learn my lesson when I end up as his bride. You know what I said?' She crooked a pinkie finger, mimicking a limp penis. I said, 'Eeeeh!'

'Tchee!' Namrata giggled.

Ritu told them she'd got a marriage offer. The boy's family was

116

from the far-west, but he had an office job in Kathmandu. Her relatives were acting as go-betweens, arranging a meeting for them in the bazaar. 'I'm worried,' she said. 'What if he's not handsome—or rich?'

'Then say no. You can say no,' Namrata said.

Chandra had refused to go to the temple. She was waiting for them at the bottom of the hill, by the river. She scoffed when she saw them. 'You're done praying for a husband?' She linked arms with Sapana. 'The old widower just passed by, he said he wants to talk to you about the meeting.'

'Again? I spoke to him only this morning!'

'He just wants to look at you.' Ritu snickered. 'You know, he doesn't look so old if you look at him from behind.'

'Tchee!'

After they crossed the bridge, they parted ways. Ritu and Namrata went home. Sapana and Chandra went up through the village.

Gyanu Dai wasn't home when they got there. They waited for him at the kitchen table. They'd grown so used to having him cook for them that they just sat around, doing nothing, when he wasn't around.

He was spending less and less time at home nowadays. Sapana had thought he'd have more free time now that the land transfer was done, but he went into the bazaar every day—to make phone calls, he said. He seemed unhappy, somehow. Sometimes, Sapana saw him sitting all by himself on the ridge by Ba's plot, lost in thought. When he was home, he kept busy with tasks that he assigned himself to improve the home. Since coming back, he'd stocked the larder with expensive spices, oils, unfamiliar herbs—the whole house smelled like a garden. He'd hired a woodworker from the bazaar to replace the chipped laminate on the table and repair all the chairs. The pots and pans now sat in an orderly row on a new shelf. This week he'd finished sandpapering the doors and windows. He was going to paint the house by himself.

'Mmm.' Chandra was leafing through a book of poems. 'I like this, listen to it.' She cleared her throat and recited:

What grows in these still villages
but death. To stay is to die.
To leave is to die too.
Mother! Save me.
I'm fading.

Then she reread the poem, and frowned. 'Actually, the poet seems depressed, I've changed my mind, I don't like it at all.'

'Read me a love poem.'

'This poet doesn't know how to write love poems.'

Dusk fell. A tranquillity descended over the house. Sapana stirred, at last, turning on the Petromax so that Chandra could keep reading. Then, because she was up, she started to cook dal-bhat-tarkaari for the evening meal.

Gyanu Dai arrived when she was halfway through. He was carrying a sheaf of papers. He put them on the table and came over to help her. 'What are you making, Bahini?'

'The usual. What else do I know how to make, Dai?'

'It needs a bit more—here, let me do it.' He put down the papers and began to cook.

Sapana happily returned to sit with Chandra at the table.

The papers Gyanu Dai had brought were from the Electricity Authority. He told them that he wanted to electrify the house. 'It'll be good not to use a Petromax anymore. I meant to do it last time I came, but, well.' He told them he'd go to the bazaar tomorrow to hand in the application form and make the payment.

It struck Sapana that her brother was always looking for some task to occupy himself with. He just seemed to need to do something, always. She had an idea. 'Dai,' she said, 'at the CBO meeting, after the speeches, there'll be a feast. Maybe, you could make the food—something that foreigners would like.'

'You want me to work for Thulo Ba?' he asked.

'If we impress the foreigners, they'll give the CBO money, re,' she said.

'And will that money come to you?' His tone was suddenly angry. It took Sapana aback. He said, 'What, actually, has the CBO done for you, Bahini? You're doing all this work for the women's committee. Are they giving you a salary? No. Are they training you? No. They took you on one small study tour—and did they do it for free? Do you know how much Thulo Ba must have pocketed for that tour?'

He was being so negative. Sapana didn't want to respond.

Chandra had looked up from her book. She said, 'It's true, Sapana. Your Thulo Ba wouldn't have conducted the study tour for free.'

'Yes, but the women's committee is doing good work.' Sapana refused to give in to negativity. 'You know that, Chandra. Your own Muwa is a member. And Dai, you'd be surprised. I've talked to all the members, and—we saw so many cooperatives on our study tour, we're thinking of opening one here.'

'And is that enough?' Gyanu Dai left the stove and came to them. 'A cooperative. That's really enough, Bahini?' He sounded puzzled now.

'The main thing is to find a market,' Sapana explained. 'Everything they've done out east, we can do here.'

Chandra looked from one sibling to the other, and moderated, 'The women's committee is good, Gyanu Dai. It's not going to create a revolution, but having it is better than not having it, I guess.'

Gyanu Dai took this in with a nod. 'It's just that I worry.'

'You love us, that's why you worry about us, Dai.' Sapana took his hand. 'But we're not like other girls, we don't want to have the lives of our mothers, we want to be modern, Dai, really and truly modern. The world has advanced so much. We want to advance too.' To make her point, she borrowed a few lines from her speech. 'If we don't make things better here, who will? We're the youth, we're the future, we're the hope of the nation. If we work together, there's nothing we can't do.'

Gyanu Dai still looked sceptical, or maybe conflicted. It was always difficult for him to say what was on his mind. Finally, he confessed. 'It's just that I won't be here much longer, Bahini.'

Ey. That was it. He was leaving. Sapana let go of his hand.

'I have to go to Kathmandu to talk to some manpowers,' he said. 'I lost my old job in the desert, I'm looking for a new one.' He asked Sapana, 'Will you really be all right living here by yourselves?'

Sapana didn't reply.

Chandra answered for her. 'We'll look after each other, Dai. We'll be fine.'

But Gyanu Dai wanted Sapana to say so too. He wanted her permission to leave. He kept looking at her, but she refused to say what he wanted to hear.

'Now that the land is in your name,' he said, 'your rights are secure, Bahini.'

Her rights. She didn't know why this upset her so much. '*My* rights?' she said. 'What about *your* rights, Dai? What are you, a stranger to this house?' She didn't hold back: 'You worry about me, but maybe I should worry about you, Dai. You wander the world as though you're homeless; you come back here only to perform last rites; you feel as though you don't belong, Dai. But aren't I your sister? Aren't you and I of the same blood?'

Gyanu Dai hung his head.

'Isn't this your home too?' she cried.

He took out a photograph from his wallet and placed it on the table. It was of a woman with a soft face and a trusting expression. She was sitting on a bench beside a river, or maybe the sea. She was dressed in tunic and jeans. She was smiling. He said, 'I'm going to marry her, Bahini.'

Sapana picked up the photograph and looked at the woman.

Her brother explained that he'd met her in the desert. She worked there. She was from a country called the Philippines. She was a widow. She had a young son. His name was Crisanto Balana and hers was Maleah.

Why had he kept this from her, all these months? Why was Gyanu Dai so private, so unknowable? Why was he a stranger to his own family? Looking at the woman, Sapana was struck by an unfamiliar emotion—resentment, or maybe jealousy. What about me, she wanted to say. You're leaving me. Of course I have Chandra, but don't you love me, Dai? You're my only family.

Gyanu Dai said, 'I don't know where we'll end up, but I'll follow Maleah anywhere. That's why I have to leave, Bahini.'

This wasn't true, Sapana thought. He was leaving because he'd always felt himself an outsider here. Otherwise why not marry this woman and bring her and her son here? Gyanu Dai's life from before Ma married Ba seemed to haunt him somehow. It had driven him out of the village at a young age, and it kept him away after his studies, even though all of them—Ma, Ba, she—had always made him feel wanted here. When he came back for Ba's funeral, he'd never intended to stay on. He'd transferred the land to her name, and had made improvements to the home, so that he could leave with a free conscience.

Gyanu Dai was still waiting for her to say something conciliatory. 'I'll stay for your speech,' he said. 'I know it's important to you, I'll talk to Thulo Ba, I'll help with the feast.'

Sapana couldn't get herself to say anything. The sadness that she'd refused to feel after Ba's death swelled up inside her. She wished she could reverse time, she wished she could have Ba and Ma back, she wished their family would return to being whole again. With difficulty she reached for Gyanu Dai's hand. It was warm, he was here, but she already missed him. This was the end of her childhood. She wished she could have it back.

HE DIPPED THE brush in the paint, scraped off the excess, and drew its bristles evenly over the post. The deep sea green brought back those endless days of childhood—Ba reading out loud, Ma listening with baby Sapana slung on her back. Family happiness, precious and fleeting. The fulfilment Ma and Ba had found together, the fulfilment they'd shared with him.

He painted the doorpost, using broad strokes at the centre of the post, taking care at the corners. When the post was done, he started on the jamb. He'd already painted the rest of the house. Only this door, which opened onto Ma and Ba's room, remained. The house looked almost proud as it used to, once. It satisfied Gyanu, in some deep physical way, to restore it; and the diversion helped quell his anxieties.

Sapana was still angry at him, she wasn't talking to him. She was right to be angry. For he wasn't simply leaving; he was leaving her. He understood the betrayal, but he had to get back to Maleah while he still could.

Maleah and her room-mate Susanna had gone to Jojo's agent. The only jobs on offer in Germany were for certified child minders. The agency did offer certification. Susanna was going to train for it, but Maleah was uncertain. She had renewed her contract at the gift shop for another year. 'Come soon, mahal,' she'd said. 'I do not want to lose you, ever. Come back, and let us marry.'

After painting the outside of the door, Gyanu entered Ma and Ba's room. He hadn't been here since Ba's passing, and neither had Sapana nor Chandra. Through some unspoken agreement they'd avoided the room as a way of evading their grief.

The air was stale inside. The bed lay stripped bare in the corner. There was a film of dust on the table, and on the two framed photographs on it. One was a black-and-white of Ma and Ba, taken at a studio in the bazaar on the year of their marriage. Ma was young in that photograph, and beautiful. Ba was serene, holding Gyanu's hand as he, in red shorts, stood in front of them staring wide-eyed at the camera.

The other photograph, faded and sepia-toned, was of the entire family in the same studio several years later. Gyanu was seven years old. Sapana was a newborn, swaddled in cloth in Ma's arms. Gyanu remembered going to the bazaar to take this photograph. It had been a festive day, a family celebration, a private triumph for Ba and Ma.

After taking the photograph, they'd eaten samosas at a tea shop. Ba had bought Gyanu jalebis. He remembered how complete they'd felt as a family on that day.

Above the table, on the wall, hung a small mirror. It too was covered with dust. Looking into it Gyanu saw his reflection, and behind him, Sapana. He turned. It wasn't Sapana: it was Ma. She placed a hand on his face the way she used to. Her hand was soft, a wisp. Gyanu felt her presence. Through all the difficult choices she'd made, he felt her tenderness for him.

I couldn't even give you your own identity.

She'd said that to him on her deathbed. She'd also said what she told him now: *You had to give up your past so I could live.*

He'd replied to her, 'You gave me my whole life, Ma.'

After a while he couldn't feel Ma any more. He turned away from the mirror. And in the dark edges of his memory he located a few lost shards of the past.

He saw a large, open yard with a date tree.

He smelled dust, heat, tar.

There was a house with a chicken coop.

He saw himself racing past the coop, through the yard, to the front door of the house. He heard the bellow of man's voice, he heard a woman's cry. He felt his own panic. He saw himself turning around and racing back across the yard to hide in the chicken coop.

~

To change anything in this room felt, to Gyanu, like an erasure of Ma and Ba. He decided not to paint the rest of the door.

When he stepped out, there was a visitor in the kitchen. It was Kisne, sitting at the table with a girl—from the resemblance between them, clearly his daughter. Gyanu put down the can of paint and brush and wiped his hands on his pants. 'I didn't hear you come in.'

'I came for the number of the manpower.' Kisne grinned. To his daughter, he said, 'Chhori, say namaste to Gyanu Kaka.'

The girl was about three, and shy. She hung her head and didn't say anything.

'Where are your manners?' her father said, prodding her. 'Say namaste.'

'Let it be.' Gyanu went to the stove. 'I'll get you the number, but first, let's have tea.'

'Sure, let's try the tea of a five-star hotel.' Kisne laughed. 'Hai,

Chhori?' He scooped up the girl in his arms. She squealed. 'Let's see what five-star hotel tea is like, hai, Chhori?' The girl giggled. 'Hai? Hai?' He began to tickle the girl.

She squealed. 'Stop, Baba, stop! Don't tickle—stop!'

'Hai?'

They made a sweet picture, father and daughter. Kisne, tickling the girl. 'Hai, hai, hai?' The girl, squealing: 'No tickling, Baba, stop, stop, stop!' The whole house rang with the girl's laughter. 'Stop, Baba, no tickling! Stop, Baba! Baba, stop!'

IN HER STUDY, Ava clutched the newspaper, reading the story over and over. The words slipped and slid, they were impossible to take in.

The director of the Bal Mandir Orphanage, as well as another official, had been arrested the day before, and charged with multiple counts of rape.

~

She read:

The officials were accused of organizing 'wedding parties' at the orphanage on Saturdays.

They gave alcohol to autistic girls, they showed them pornography.

They dressed them as brides, in red saris, and made them dance.

They sprayed them with water, forcing them to undress.

They took them to bars and trained them as prostitutes.

~

She reread the story.

~

The arrested officials were proclaiming their innocence.

~

The words slipped and slid.
She reread the story, shuddering.

~

She reread the story again.

THEIR HOTEL WAS damp, with a hint of mildew in its dark, clammy corners. It was a relief to step into the daylight. Ava moved slowly, feeling shaky, as though something might give and she'd tumble.

She'd known, of course, that conditions were poor in the orphanage. And she knew that life was cheap in Nepal. Everything she'd learned at IDAF underscored this truth, and she'd felt it instinctively, in the bones, since that Christmas. After joining IDAF, she'd come to understand that Nepal's girls and women were especially vulnerable; and yet the news about the orphanage had struck her with a force that gutted her, made it hard to breathe.

The hotel's front gate opened onto the town, which was smaller than she'd expected. Outside its central core, it had the sleepy air of a village. Or perhaps the hotel was in a quiet residential part of town. She walked down to the main road.

Driving into town last evening, she'd seen that the residents were moderately well off, or at least not abjectly poor. Now, too, she noticed new, westernized clothes on a man passing by, and sturdy shoes on the feet of two girls who were playing marbles by the side of the road. A woman in a nightdress strolled by. She had a thin gold chain around her neck. Ava observed her own relief at these tokens of prosperity, and wondered what she was doing: looking for signs that not all Nepalis were suffering? Allaying her guilt for having survived this society, for having thrived in Canada.

Past a row of empty lots, she entered a busier part of town. There were small businesses here: shops, banks, boutiques. Six headless mannequins in bright red saris stood in the window of a shop called New Nepal Fashions. Those were bridal saris: the sequins glinted, stabbing the air with light. They brought to mind the wedding parties at the orphanage.

A horn blared at a nearby bus station. A conductor was yelling to attract passengers to a departing bus. On the other side of a row of parked vehicles was a river. She'd seen it yesterday, driving in. She walked to the bridge over the river. She stood at the centre of the bridge, looking down. The slow-moving river was wide and clear. The water looked clean. She wondered whether people swam in the rivers in Nepal. There was no swimming in Kathmandu's befouled Bagmati River. Yesterday, on the highway, they'd driven alongside two rivers: one large and wild, its water crashing down massive boulders, and the other one narrow, with swift, deep rapids. There'd been no one on the banks, perhaps because the water was dangerous, or too cold. Here, below the bridge, she saw a man ambling along the pebbly bank. A woman was washing clothes at the water's edge. A flock of birds—starlings, perhaps—swooped down from the far shore and glided back up into the sky.

She was glad for a chance to be alone. Vishwa had talked non-stop throughout the drive yesterday. 'Finally, the real Nepal,' he'd said as they drove out of Kathmandu Valley, launching into tales about every single town, every single village, they passed: 'Now this area, Ava, is very inspiring. They've had a successful open defecation free movement. It's set a real example for the rest of Nepal.'

'There's a big Hindu temple nearby here, Ava.'

'This area is famous for organic farming. They've banned all pesticides.'

He was only being helpful, and Ava hated to be uncharitable in her thoughts, but she was in shock over the news about orphanage. She would have given anything to take in the countryside in silence.

'That village, up on the hill? It's where my ancestors are from. Now, if we were to continue on this road? We'd get to Pokhara. You must go to Pokhara sometime, Ava. It's much nicer than Kathmandu.'

The countryside was astonishing: the land was riven with cliffs and canyons and gorges, breathtaking, and utterly unworkable. Ava had stared at lone huts high up in the hills: how would they ever get electricity or drinking water? Why would anyone choose to live in such isolation? The thought—it could have been me—had recurred like a nightmare she couldn't shake off. Nodding politely at whatever Vishwa was saying, she'd thought: I could have been born in any of these huts.

I could have been one of those girls in the orphanage.

The high mountains had eventually given way to hills. The highway had followed the course of the second river, then, after a confluence, broken through to the southern plains. They'd driven along a stretch of low blue hills overlooking flatlands.

'Now in this area, Ava, IDAF supported many peacebuilding initiatives during the Maoist conflict.'

By the time they reached Butwal, Ava was exhausted.

On the bridge, from behind her, came a burst of laughter. She turned to see four young women walking by, holding hands. They were dressed in grey-and-pink tunics: school uniforms, or—how old were they?—perhaps college uniforms. They looked so confident in their youthfulness, their beauty, their intelligence. One woman said, 'Namaste!'

and then they walked on, following the course of their lives.

Ava remained on the course of her life. She remained very much on the course of her life, her life of—she cringed at the word, it was strident, unsubtle—privilege. It had been impossible, on yesterday's drive, not to see how shielded she was from the country of her birth. She'd been shielded by family love, by Mom and Dad's financial stability, by everything that came with a childhood in Overwood: an education, healthcare, and things she'd never even thought about not having, like running water and electricity. She'd been shielded by her law degree, even by her marriage, and by the heft, the solidity, of Peckham and Poole. Being in Nepal threw her privilege into stark relief: her salary at IDAF afforded her a mansion, three household staff, trifles and luxuries. How much ought a person have to buffet themselves against—others? The poor. Reality. Bleakly, she thought: here she was, at last, in the real Nepal, completely fortified against it.

'Ava, Ava, there you are, Ava!'

A lasting fatigue washed over her.

Vishwa strode up to the bridge. 'I've been looking for you everywhere.' He'd dressed for the trip in outdoor gear: a tangerine North Face jacket, a wide-brimmed hat, new Merrell boots. Ava had dressed, as always, in a suit. She was carrying her attaché case. She felt conspicuously foreign.

'How are you this morning, Ava?'

'I'm fine, Vishwa.'

'Did you sleep well? Did you have breakfast? Should we get you something to eat?'

'I'm fine.'

'Nice, isn't it?' With a toss of his hair, Vishwa looked out at the river and made a sweeping gesture with his hands. 'This is called the Tinau River. Did you get a chance to look around this morning? There's a strong industrial economy in Butwal, though of course there's still poverty among the marginalized. See there, across the river?' He pointed to a few mud huts on the shore. 'Sometimes, I really feel helpless, Ava. After decades of aid, well, there's been progress for sure, but there's so much left to do. You'll see what I mean when we get to the villages. Are you ready? The driver's waiting. It's an hour's drive to the first CBO.'

THE SKY WAS silver-grey and the birds were chirping outside the window. She rolled over and shook Chandra. 'Ey, get up!'

Chandra groaned.

'The sun's already out,' Sapana lied.

'Let me be.' Chandra drew the quilt over her head. She'd stayed up late reading a thick book on social science, and she'd have trouble waking up.

'Sleep all day, then,' Sapana said.

She went out to wash, and afterwards, came back and changed into the kurta that Gyanu Dai had bought her. She'd been saving it for a special occasion. She checked herself in the mirror. The blue stripes really suited her. Chandra was snoring underneath the quilt. Some revolutionary she'd make! Sapana went and shook her. 'Ey, don't I look pretty?'

Chandra groaned. 'I said, let me be.'

'I look really good.'

'Stop being so vain.' Reluctantly, Chandra opened her eyes. 'You always look good.' She yawned, stretched, sat up. 'Lau, I know it's your big day, I'll go and make you something to eat.' She straggled out of bed, her hair tangled and her nightdress crumpled.

Sapana went back to the mirror, combing her hair back in a tidy braid, lining her eyes with gaajal and placing a black tika between her brows. She had to look mature and responsible today. She'd been feeling mature and responsible: she'd have to take on all family duties after Gyanu Dai left. She could: she and Chandra had been doing so anyway. Gyanu Dai could leave. They'd be fine.

Out in the kitchen, Chandra had made tea, and also Sapana's favourite: spiced potatoes and roti. 'Eat.' She put a plate on the table. 'Gyanu Dai's already gone to prepare the feast,' she said, sitting beside her. 'You know what he said? The CBO bought a gas cylinder at an inflated price, re. Your Thulo Ba's taking a cut off the gas, the loose tea and milk, sugar, even bottled water.' She sat back and became philosophical. 'That's how it is with the feudal classes. They capture all the resources, ey, Sapana. That's what this book on social science says. We need a revolution to overthrow your Thulo Ba.' She laughed. 'Though look at the Maoist revolution: even that didn't dislodge him, hai? You know the poet I was reading? The depressed one? Sometimes I think he's right.'

Sapana wasn't paying attention. 'Make sure your Muwa's ready to meet the foreigners, Chandra.'

'You're really going to show them her stupid pickles?'

'I should go and make sure everyone's ready.' She got up.

'But you hardly ate anything.'

Sapana was already out the door. 'Come soon, hai, Chandra, come and find me wherever I am!'

~

The season of morning mists had given way to incandescent springtime. The bottlebrush trees were red with flower. The sun was blazing, the breeze was sweet. On days like this, even life's biggest challenges seemed like light refracted through crystal: and the whole world glittered with colour.

Sapana went to Naina di's house first, because it was the closest. Naina di was in the kitchen. Her sari was stained and her face was smeared with dirt. 'Di, your face!' Sapana cried.

Naina di laughed, wiping dirt off with the end of her sari. 'I spent all morning cleaning the stall, the goats look better than me.'

It was true: in the stall behind her house, her goats were lustrous and lively. Naina di squatted down to pet a frisky kid. 'They're a mix of khari and jamunapari, but I hear that boers breed faster,' she said. 'A group of us should get boers, Bahini. That cooperative you've been talking about? Let's make it a goat farm.'

'I'll talk about cooperatives in my speech, Di. Now make yourself as clean as your goats, or the foreigners will think you're a jungly animal.'

As Sapana left Naina di's house, she saw Chandra ahead of her. Chandra hadn't changed out of her nightdress or even combed her hair: what a slob! Little Tara was scampering behind, trying to keep up. They turned past the bottlebrush trees and went into their Muwa Buwa's house.

Jethi Didi lived in one of the concrete houses by the fields. She was on the front porch chatting with Rama Bhauju, who lived next door. 'Bahini, you have to convince Rama,' Jethi Didi said when she saw Sapana. 'I've been telling her to forget about her Jersey cow and plant an orange orchard instead.'

Rama Bhauju laughed. 'All I want is to go on another study tour. Remember the fun we had, Jethi?'

'How we sang on the bus ride back.'

'I can still taste the yogurt we had on the last day.'

Sapana asked if they were ready to meet the foreigners.

Rama Bhauju laughed. 'Haaa, stop worrying, Bahini. I'll show them my Jersey, Jethi will show them her orange trees. Everyone else knows what to do too.'

'Really?'

'You go, go and practise your speech.'

Sapana had memorized her speech, but she was eager to see the preparations. 'Lau, hai, I'm counting on you!' She ran off.

The lower part of the village looked festive today. Thulo Ba's house looked like a fairground. A multi-coloured tent had gone up in the front yard. There was a wooden stage in the front half of the tent. Political workers were strutting about, barking out orders to one another. Some were setting up a podium on the stage, others were carrying over a sofa from Thulo Ba's house. One worker was wiring up a microphone. Jeevan Bhatta was supervising them.

'Sapana Nani,' he called out. 'Go up to the stage, let's see if everything's in the right spot.'

She did as he said, standing behind the podium. Jeevan Bhatta walked from side to side, staring at her, ostensibly to assess the placement of the podium. The poor old widower. It was mean the way Ritu joked about him, but she was right: he looked at her a lot. 'The podium's all right where it is,' he said at last, 'but move the sofa forward, ey, boys. And make sure there are enough plastic chairs on the side for all the board members.'

Sapana remained behind the podium, imagining herself making a speech. Everyone in the tent would be able to see her, even from the back. And everyone would hear her because of the microphone. She mustn't be nervous. Shulinbaba, she prayed: give my words force.

From the podium, she saw a makeshift kitchen at the back of the tent, and went there. Gyanu Dai was stacking plates on a table where he'd serve the feast. He was subdued. She felt a pang of guilt, making him work for Thulo Ba's CBO. He despised Thulo Ba. And she'd been cold to him. Wanting to make up, she helped lay out cups and saucers. 'The women are ready,' she said, 'but I don't know about the men, Dai.'

'The men are always ready to make money.'

She tried to leaven his mood. 'Did the CBO really make a profit off the gas cylinder, Dai?'

'Would Thulo Ba let go of the chance?'

She wished he weren't always so negative about everything. 'He let go of Ba's property,' she said.

'I lost my job waiting for him to do that, Bahini.'

She gave up, and they set up the table in silence.

At the end, Gyanu Dai said, 'Did you see Chandra? She was here, looking for you. Has she told you?' He frowned. 'Surya sent a letter from India.'

Sapana didn't understand. 'What?' Had she misheard him? 'Surya Di's—she's alive?'

He pointed towards the front of the tent. 'Chandra went that way. She's very upset.'

Surya Di was alive! This was good: it was great! Why then was Chandra upset?

Sapana ran off to find Chandra. The villagers had begun to gather. The crowd was thickening in the tent. 'Ey, Sapana Nani, are you ready to make your speech?' someone called out to her. She saw Chandra on the other side of the tent—her hair was still tangled, she was still in her nightdress. Just then, someone yelled, 'They're here! The foreigners are here!' and the crowd surged.

Sapana was shoved out of the tent. Across the mad river, a jeep was racing up from the highway, kicking up a cloud of dust. 'Make way, make way!' A commotion ensued as Thulo Ba, dressed in a crisp, ironed labeda sural, muscled his way through the crowd. The CBO's board members followed, carrying marigold garlands. The board consisted of Jeevan Bhatta and other party workers, as well as Thulo Ba's youngest daughter-in-law. Sapana turned back to look for Chandra, but couldn't see her from here.

She turned back, craning her neck to watch as the jeep halted by the bridge. Three people got out. The driver stayed behind and the other two crossed the bridge, where Thulo Ba and the board members were standing in a row to greet them. The crowd strained to watch as they offered the foreigners garlands.

Thulo Ba then led them up to the tent. There was a charge in the air. To Sapana, everything suddenly felt like a show, a play, that she too had a part in. As he passed by, Jeevan Bhatta grabbed her arm and led her onto the stage, sitting her down on a plastic chair. Only after the foreigners were seated did Sapana realize that one of them was a woman.

She was wearing pants, that's why she looked like a man. And her hair was short like a man's. She was small and dark, with black eyes:

you could tell she was foreign only because of her bearing, which was not at all Nepali. Sapana had expected white Americans with yellow hair and blue eyes, but even the foreign man wasn't like that. Then she heard him speaking to Thulo Ba—'How long will this take? We have two other villages to visit'—and she realized he was Nepali.

Was the woman Nepali too? Now she was confused.

Thulo Ba sat with the guests on the sofa as Jeevan Bhatta rushed around, seating everyone else. 'Here.' He placed Thulo Ba's daughter-in-law beside Sapana.

The crowd in the tent quieted when Jeevan Bhatta went to the podium. Leaning over the microphone, he cleared his throat.

An enormous crackle burst out of the speakers. Everyone gasped.

'Forgive me!' He turned away and cleared his throat before beginning his speech: 'Respectable international as well as national visitors, honourable CBO Chairmanjyu, distinguished board members and esteemed assembled residents of the village, it is my great honour, as the secretary of our great CBO, to welcome you to this august gathering.'

~

The man's voice thundered through the mic, insistent and declarative. Ava had no idea what he was saying. She didn't even know who he was: no one had bothered to introduce him. The only introduction she'd got was to the traditionally costumed Chairman of the CBO, whose air of authority intimidated her. He was like a relic of some ancient way of life that was inaccessible to her. He didn't speak English. Did anyone here do so? Vishwa, seated beside her on the sofa, was nodding in agreement with the speaker, who was saying—what? Asking for funding. Begging, Ava thought. And who was she to say yes or no?

The stuffing in the sofa was flabby. She was low to the ground, her knees stuck up. Everyone else was seated in plastic chairs, presumably signalling that they were of lower status. The formality of the event—the formality of all the Nepali events—was mind-numbing. The garlands prickled her neck. The crowd was gawking at her, as though they'd never seen a foreigner before: though how could that be? A coil spring chafed against her thigh. She squirmed.

The man thundered on and on with his speech. How many more speeches would she have to sit through? There were only two other women on the stage: a teenage girl and a middle-aged woman. Otherwise it was all men—of which caste? She'd have to run the CBO's board members' names past Herman Banke when she got back.

She looked from person to person, trying to read them. From the Chairman's costume, and his demeanour, he seemed well off. The rest of the crowd looked distinctly less so, perhaps because they were farmers, or peasants. The women's faces were chapped. The men looked worn down. At the edge of the tent was a group of children with flyblown hair. Why weren't they in school? Was there a school in the village? The tent blocked the view of everything but an electric pink house. Was that the CBO's office?

When the speaker finally finished, the crowd clapped, and the Chairman took his turn at the podium.

He spoke commandingly, in a voice that boomed over the tent. The crowd sat at attention. Ava squirmed. Why, she wondered, was she expected to sit here, uncomprehending, as everyone talked in Nepali? Why was this considered reasonable? How was she to figure out whether IDAF should fund WDS-Nepal, so that it could fund National Network Nepal, so that it could in turn fund this CBO, if she couldn't understand what the speakers were saying?

She leaned in to Vishwa and asked, 'What's he saying?'

'He's talking about the CBO's work in the village.'

'And who was the first man, Vishwa?'

'The secretary of the CBO.'

'Did he say anything interesting?'

He waved vaguely. 'He said the CBO had done a lot of work and can do even more if they get more funding.'

That was all the secretary had said? She persisted: 'And what's the Chairman saying now?'

'He's saying that the productivity of people's fields have doubled with a new variety of seeds that the CBO has promoted.'

After a while, the Chairman's voice rose into a crescendo.

'What's he saying now?' Ava said.

Irritation flickered, like a shadow, over Vishwa's face. 'He's saying that the CBO cured a man who was going blind, Ava.'

'You're kidding, right?'

He shrugged. 'It was at a health camp that the CBO organized. There was a man who was going blind, he was cured.'

'Is that true?'

'Why would he say it if it weren't?'

The Chairman spoke on, shaking a fist. He wagged a finger, thumped the podium, punched the air. This was, Ava saw, a performance. It was in keeping with the theatrical nature of so many of her dealings in Nepal. Nepalis seemed to adhere primarily to form: content was secondary. What the Chairman was communicating wasn't as important as the need to communicate it properly, in this case by making a fiery speech.

A long-winded, fiery speech. Ava sat, growing increasingly uncomfortable. Even Vishwa glanced at his watch. The coil spring in the sofa chafed. The Chairman thundered on—till, with a flourish, he stopped.

There was another burst of applause.

Then the teenage girl came up to the podium.

She, Ava wanted to hear from. She shifted to the front of the sofa so that she wasn't sinking down so low. Maybe the girl wasn't a teenager; maybe she was an undernourished woman. Ava couldn't tell. The young woman reached the podium and turned to Ava with an earnest, determined expression. Ava asked Vishwa, 'I'm really sorry, would you mind translating? Not just the gist. I want to know exactly what she's saying.'

'You want me to be your interpreter?'

Was that an imposition? 'Would you? I'm sorry,' she said.

'Sure, sure. I can interpret. If it'll help you understand. Of course.'

~

Sapana felt light, as though her body weighed nothing, and she were afloat on the stage. The foreign woman had a sympathetic face. She really wanted to impress her. The microphone was high. She lifted her head to speak. And saw Chandra at the back of the tent with little Tara.

Chandra's arms were crossed, her face was dark, her eyes were red. She was crying.

Sapana forgot her speech. In confusion, she turned to the foreign woman. She was looking straight at her, as was Thulo Ba. Jeevan Bhatta nodded, indicating that she should begin. The whole crowd was waiting for her.

She said, 'Namaste to my elders.' She felt weak, her knees trembled. From the corner of her eyes, she saw the Nepali man whispering to the foreign woman. He was translating her speech into English. At this, her nervousness dissipated. The speech she'd memorized came back to her. She told the foreign woman about everything: the funds the women's committee had collected, the loans it had given, the profit its members had earned and the few losses they had incurred. She told the foreign woman about the dreams the women had seen on the study tour, and their vision to develop Nepal. 'We want to form a cooperative,' she said, and the microphone echoed, giving her words a certain poetry. 'We're young, we have the energy and the determination to develop our country,' she said. 'Everyone says there's no hope for our country. Everyone wants to give up, everyone wants to go abroad to work in foreign lands. But if we, the youth, don't build our own house, who will? We are the future of this nation,' she said. For emphasis she repeated the line: 'We are the future of this nation. Believe in us. If you help us, we can work together and develop Nepal and make it rich, like America.'

At the end, she ran out of breath. Everyone clapped. The foreign woman was smiling, as was the man who'd translated her words. Sapana was pleased at how she'd spoken; but now she had to go to Chandra.

Instead of sitting down, she left the stage. 'You spoke well,' someone in the audience said to her. Someone else patted her on the back. She left the tent and went to the other side, to Chandra and little Tara.

'Gyanu Dai told me.' Sapana led them to an open patch of grass so they could talk.

Chandra was carrying Surya Di's letter. She gave it to Sapana, and began to cry—in relief, and in grief for all those years of thinking her sister dead.

'Don't cry, Di,' little Tara said; and then she, too, began to cry.

Sapana read the letter carefully.

Surya Di lived in a town called Ghaziabad, near India's capital, Delhi. This was where the middleman had taken her, right at the start. She worked as a maidservant in the house of a wealthy master. Over the years, she'd worked for other masters too. Her present masters paid her modestly, but didn't work her too hard.

Sapana read every sentence carefully.

One of the other girls who'd gone with her had been unlucky, Surya Di had written. She'd also found work as a maidservant, but she'd got pregnant by a fellow Nepali, a doorman at the same house. The doorman already had a wife back in the village. Their masters kicked them out when they found out. The middleman took the girl to another town to work. She'd fallen out of touch after that.

Surya Di was still in contact with the third girl, who worked in as a maidservant in another part of Ghaziabad. On Saturdays they met at a park and reminisced.

'All these years, Surya Di was sending us letters,' Chandra said. The middleman threw them away, believing that she'd want to come back if she were in touch with her family. This time, Surya Di met a Nepali who was coming directly to Butwal Bazaar. He'd left the letter with a shopkeeper, who'd sent it to Chandra's Muwa Buwa in the hands of a customer from the village.

When Sapana was halfway through the letter, Chandra took it back from her. She folded it and tucked it away in her nightdress. 'She wants me to come, Sapana. She says she can find work for me.'

'As a maidservant?' Sapana said.

Chandra looked down. A loose strand of hair fell over her face. She tucked it behind her ears. When she looked up it was clear that she had made up her mind. She said, 'Surya Di's given us her master's telephone number. Little Tara and I are going to go to the bazaar to call her.'

'I'll go with you,' Sapana said.

'To India?'

'No, to—' Was Chandra really going to go to India? 'I'll go with you to the bazaar,' Sapana said, her emotions churning. 'I meant I'll go with you to the bazaar to call Surya Di.'

Chandra nodded.

Little Tara, who was still crying, said, 'When I grow up I'll also go to India!'

'Be quiet,' her sister hissed.

This only made little Tara cry harder.

'Tch.' Chandra gathered her sister into her arms. 'I didn't mean it. Don't cry, little one. Forgive me, I shouldn't have said that, that was wrong of me.'

They were still consoling little Tara when Jeevan Bhatta came rushing out of the tent. 'This is no time to sit around gossiping with friends,' he said to Sapana. 'The speeches are almost done. Come at once!'

Sapana took Chandra by the hand. 'Come with me.'

'I haven't even changed. I'm still in my nightdress.'

'You can't leave me, Chandra.'

Chandra looked at her. 'Come with me, Sapana, let's go to India together.'

THE YOUNG WOMAN had spoken in tones so rousing that Ava's speech was bound to be flat by comparison. Not that anyone understood what she was saying. Feeling futile, she spoke about IDAF's mission in Nepal, the Millennium Development Goals and the Post-2015 Priority Themes. She might as well have been lecturing the village on rocket science. She'd meant to highlight IDAF's partnership with WDS-Nepal and National Network Nepal, but she skipped over those parts, and indeed over most of her speech, rushing to the conclusion. 'This is my first field trip since coming to Nepal. I'm very pleased to get a chance, today, to see the work that IDAF hopes to support through its national partners. Thank you very much.'

People were kind. They clapped for her, as they had for the previous speakers.

Then the Chairman stood, and everyone else on the stage scrummed up to the sofa. A hand guided Ava as the Chairman and the rest of the board members herded her off the stage. The crowd parted, letting them through. She'd assumed that they'd go to see the CBO's work, but they led her to a table laid out with kebabs and rotis and crisps and patties and puddings and what appeared to be a baklava: a thin roll with nuts.

Smiling nervously, the middle-aged woman on the board offered Ava a plate.

Vishwa produced hand sanitizer from his pocket. 'Want some?'

Ava baulked. 'We're eating?'

'The Chairman has organized a feast in our honour. We'll have to eat quickly, we're already running behind schedule.'

What? 'I'd rather skip the meal and see some work,' Ava said.

'That would be very rude, Ava.' Vishwa glanced at the Chairman, who was waiting for Ava to serve herself. 'We can interact with some beneficiaries as we eat.'

'No.' Ava insisted, 'I'd like to see some work, Vishwa.'

'Ava—'

'I mean it, Vishwa. I didn't come here to eat, I came to work.'

Vishwa checked his watch. 'But we have two more CBOs to get to today.'

Jesus. Feeling helpless now, Ava pleaded, 'At the very least, let's see what the women's committee has done.'

'Let me ask.' He turned to the Chairman, and they got into a protracted conversation full of questioning, hemming and hawing, declaring. What was there to discuss at such length? Nepalis talked so much. In response to what they were saying, a man at the buffet table began to put away the food, covering some dishes and moving others to a room at the back of the electric pink house. The man's expression jarred her. His eyes were turned down, his lips were pursed. He was barely concealing his contempt.

At the end of the discussion, the Chairman issued an order. The Secretary stepped up with the young woman who'd made the speech. She was holding hands with two other girls, one tall, with a shock of uncombed hair, the other one younger, nine or ten years old. The two girls looked different—racially, or in terms of caste, or identity—from the first young woman. All of them looked distressed: had they been crying?

After another lengthy discussion, the Chairman and the Secretary announced that they'd show them the work of the women's committee.

Only at this point was the young woman introduced to Ava. She was the treasurer of the women's committee. With a refreshing lack of diffidence she reached out to shake hands with Ava. Her hands were small and hard and rough: a worker's hands. Her name was Sapana—Car Key?

'Car Key?' Ava asked Vishwa.

'K-a-r-k-i.'

~

Ava felt more in control once they left the tent. Past the electric pink house, the crowd fell away. The village came into view. It was beautiful, with all the romance that the idea of a village could evoke. The path in veered away from the river, along a stretch of terraced fields. There were hills on the horizon. The air was sweet. There were electric poles along the side of the path, though not all the houses were connected to the line. Ava remembered, from all her background reading, that less than five per cent of rural Nepal was electrified.

Sapana led the group to a concrete house that looked neither rich nor poor, but decidedly middle-class by Nepali standards. Their arrival threw the residents into a flurry of bowing and scraping. They laid straw mats for them in the courtyard. Following some intricate hierarchy, the Chairman sat on one mat, and Ava, Vishwa and the secretary on another. Sapana and the other girls sat with the woman of the house on a third, more tattered, mat.

The woman of the house was dressed in a cotton sari and wore a gold ring in her nose. Ava couldn't even begin to guess how old she was. Upon Sapana's prompting, she began to talk, mainly addressing the Chairman.

Ava asked Vishwa if he would mind translating.

'Sure,' he said coolly, making it clear that he minded, but would oblige her. After listening to the woman, he started:

'When I came to this village as a bride of sixteen, I knew this area was famous for its oranges. That's what I'd heard, ever since I was a little girl, in my village. Of course, not everything you hear is accurate, but everyone always said—'

The secretary cut in. The woman stopped talking. Then Sapana said something. The Chairman replied to her. A sharp exchange followed. Ava asked Vishwa what was going on.

'The secretary told her to hurry up and get to the point.'

'Tell her to take her time. We're here to listen to her.'

When Vishwa conveyed this, the woman swallowed hard, and, glancing from the Chairman to Ava and back, continued. Vishwa translated for her:

'As a new bride, I missed my mother and father, I missed my brothers and sisters. My husband and his family were strangers: I cried every day for six months. But how long can a woman cry? It's our lot, when we marry, we move to an unknown house and have no choice but to adjust.

'There were orange trees in my neighbour's house. When I had my firstborn, I cut a sapling and planted it in the yard. The oranges were juicy, with a fine skin and very few seeds, not like the oranges that you get in the bazaar. My family loved them. So when the women's committee began to give out loans, I thought: why not plant an orchard? The land behind our house is lying fallow. My husband said, "Do it, I'll talk to the Sahuji in the bazaar to help sell them." I planted sixty saplings.'

Behind the house was the first orange tree she'd planted. Beyond it was a field with smaller trees, spaced evenly in rows. She showed them the oranges, which were still green. She'd dug an irrigation canal to keep the roots watered. The first year the trees had borne fruit, she'd earned more than twenty thousand rupees.

Ava asked Vishwa, 'Did she really get married at sixteen?'

Vishwa translated the question.

The woman covered her mouth with her hands and laughed.

Vishwa translated her answer: 'I was fifteen-going-on-sixteen. I had my first son at seventeen, and four children after that.'

At twenty-eight, she was younger than Ava.

~

From there they went next door, to another concrete house, though this one was smaller, older, grubbier. Ava would have liked to go inside, to see what the living conditions were like, but it didn't seem to be the village way to invite guests into the house. Here, too, they sat on straw mats in the courtyard.

The woman of this house spoke as though making a speech, though her voice quavered throughout. Vishwa translated for her:

'I come to this village from Bhairahava town, from a well to-do family. My family sold milk to the dairy, so I grew up knowing it's profitable work. I never thought of doing it here, though, till the CBO set up the women's committee. The loan I got wasn't big enough, so I added my own money and bought a Jersey cow. It just birthed. I've been selling milk to friends and neighbours. It's been helpful. I'm raising four children all by myself.'

As she spoke, a girl came out of the house and served everyone glasses of milk. Ava took a sip. The milk was warm, and it tasted—not unpleasant, but too creamy.

The cowshed was beside the house. Tethered to a post, her cow was chewing impassively on cud. Its calf cowered behind, looking out at them with wide, startled eyes. With the birth, milk production had increased, and the woman would repay her loan at last. She was, she confessed, more than six months late.

'But I don't want you to think badly of the committee.' Vishwa translated for her. 'I'm the only member who hasn't repaid the loan on time. I told the chairperson to fine me, but she said, No. But I insisted: I'm the secretary of the committee, you have to fine me, otherwise everyone else will also be tardy. So the chairperson said, All right, I'll fine you; but she hasn't set the fine yet.'

Sapana told them that the committee would set the fine at the next meeting.

Then the Chairman announced that the board members were waiting for them, they had to go back for the feast.

'But we've only just started,' Ava said, turning to Vishwa.

He said, 'It'll all be like this, Ava. You get the general idea.'

It took her a moment to realize that she disliked him. 'No,' she said. 'I'd like to continue, Vishwa.'

He sighed. 'If you'd wanted to spend this much time at each site, you should have scheduled a week for the trip, not three days, Ava.'

After a discussion with the Chairman, they decided that the Chairman would go back to the tent. 'We can fit in just one more house,' Vishwa said.

'Okay,' Ava said, wondering why he got to decide, when she was, in effect, his boss.

As they set off, Sapana and the secretary got into a discussion, which soon escalated into an argument. Vishwa explained that the entire women's committee was hoping to meet them. 'They don't know what to show us: there's goat rearing, there's chicken farming, there's vegetable farming, there are lots of other things. Is there anything in particular you want to see, Ava?'

She didn't even have to think about it. 'I'd like to see what the poorest member of the committee has done with her loan.'

~

Further up the village, the houses grew raggedy. Concrete gave way to mud, tin roofs gave way to thatch. A hut lay rotting by the side of the road. The atmosphere here was moribund. They turned by a copse of tall, willowy trees with bristly red flowers. Beside it was a hut, or a hovel: its walls were flimsy, of bamboo-and-mud, and the thatch on the roof was bald.

Sapana's friends went in and brought out an emaciated woman. It was obvious from the resemblance between them that she was their mother. A blind man also emerged from the hovel. He squatted at the door as the mother and daughters laid out mats.

Sitting down in their yard, Ava felt unforgiveably wealthy. She wished, especially here, that she could go into the house. These were the poorest people she'd ever met.

The woman laid out a row of jars, big and small. When she began to speak, her face scored with wrinkles. Her voice was low. All the girls leaned in to hear her.

'My family, we're unfortunate, we've suffered.' Vishwa again. 'My husband lost his sight as a young man, and I, unlucky woman, couldn't give birth to a son. Of course, nowadays they say it's the same thing, daughters and sons are the same, and I love my daughters, but it's not the same thing at all. My elder daughter went to India to work. These others'—she pointed at her two daughters—'they'll go too, otherwise how will they survive?'

The effort of talking seemed to drain her. She wiped her face with the back of her hand before continuing.

'When the women's committee formed, I didn't even know what it was for, or why we should pay a monthly due. A hundred rupees is a lot of money for a wretch like me. But then I thought: how long can I support my family working in the fields of rich landlords?

'I waited to take a loan. I watched what the others did with theirs. Some made good investments, others didn't. I kept looking for my best option. I don't have enough land for a goat stall or cowshed: I don't even have enough land for a chicken coop. What I have are some rich relatives in the bazaar. They have a shop: they sell everything in that shop. Now everyone in the village knows I make tasty pickles. Everyone says my pickles are delicious. So I asked my relatives if they would sell them in their store. They said, all right, but it's not enough to make tasty pickles, you have to put them in jars so they don't get mouldy, you have to stick bright labels on them so that people will want to buy them. I said, give me a few jars, but they said, no, you have to buy your own jars. I bought a hundred glass jars with my loan. Then I went to my relatives and said, here, here are the jars. Now teach me the rest.'

She laughed feebly, and continued.

'Rich folks—why would they help us? But I pestered them: they had to give in. I began making pickles last winter, with dried cauliflower and fermented greens. When it became warmer, I used cucumber and fruit. Then I made other pickles, with lemon, fenugreek, mustard seeds, chilli, and green mango. Some sold, others didn't, but I earned enough to repay my loan. My relatives told me to make only three or four of the bestselling pickles. That's what I'm doing now.'

With that, she held out a jar of her bestselling pickle as a gift for Ava. Ava took it, feeling a pang of guilt: surely she should be the one giving, not the one receiving.

Sapana turned to her. 'Madam,' she said, and to Ava's surprise, she broke into English: 'What is country from where you are?'

'Canada,' Ava said. The other two girls were listening closely: they clearly understood a little English. 'Do you know where Canada is?' Ava asked them.

They shook her heads no.

'We should go now,' Vishwa said.

Ava ignored him. 'Do you know where America is?' she asked the girls. They all nodded. 'Canada's north of it,' she said. 'It's a big country, it goes all the way up to the Arctic. I'm from—have you ever heard of the city of Toronto?'

Sapana said, 'No, madam.'

'It's on Lake Ontario. Do you know about the Great Lakes?' She didn't.

Vishwa said, 'We really have to go now, Ava.'

But then Sapana reached for her with her hard, rough hands, and began to talk in Nepali. Begrudgingly, Vishwa translated for her:

'The women's committee wants to do so much more than we're doing, madam. The CBO has helped us, and we're grateful, but we can do these things—making pickles, rearing cows, starting an orange orchard—by ourselves, using the money from our monthly dues. We want your help doing bigger things, madam. As I said in my speech, we want to open a cooperative. Teach us how. I'm saying this on behalf of the entire women's committee. Believe in us. We'll prove ourselves to you. If we work together, there's nothing we can't do.'

With that, Vishwa stood. 'Okay, we absolutely have to go now.'

Ava couldn't hold him off any longer.

After they said their goodbyes, Sapana and her friends lingered behind as they left. Ava was sorry to leave their company.

~

Back at the tent, the Chairman and the CBO's board members were waiting by the buffet table. The woman board member set about serving them. Ava didn't want to be subjected, right now, to this particular form of Nepali hospitality. She excused herself and slipped away to an outhouse behind the electric pink house.

The reek of urine assaulted her before she could even close the door. She held her breath, scanning the under-lit room in alarm. To one side was a squatting commode, or not even that: a hole. A tap was dripping beside it. The floor was slippery. She stayed till her breath ran out.

She didn't want to go back to the Chairman, she didn't want to eat, she didn't want to hear about all the good work the CBO had done. Behind the outhouse was a ledge facing out, towards the river and hills. She went there.

It was a relief to have a moment's silence. From the ledge, she could see a few houses: they were large, like this one. Their residents were prosperous, or if not exactly prosperous, upper middle-class by Nepali standards. She thought of the woman in the last house: the hovel. How emaciated she was. She thought of her blind husband and her daughters, bound for India. How much could the woman possibly make selling pickles? Nepal's poverty level was defined as an income of less than a dollar a day.

She heard a movement beside her, and realized that there was someone else on the ledge. A man had been watching her, waiting for her to notice him. It was the man who'd put away the buffet earlier.

'Oh, I—I was just.' Ava felt as though she'd been caught playing hooky. She pointed behind her, at the electric pink house. 'Is this the office of the CBO?'

'It is house of Chairman.' The man's English was simple but clear. 'You like to go in, sister?'

'No, I was just taking a break.' Ava tried to explain. 'We went to see some of the CBO's work, it gave me a lot to think about.'

He nodded. 'You like the CBO?' he asked, pointedly.

Ava had to think about her reply. 'I'm impressed by the women's committee,' she said. 'The treasurer—Sapana?—took us to three homes.'

He nodded. 'Sapana is my sister. She is very idle. Always she is wanting to do big things.'

He must have meant ideal; or idealistic. 'Is she all right?' Ava asked. 'She looked upset at the beginning. She and her friends looked like they'd been crying.'

The man's face hardened. He seemed to want to say something, but held back. 'Just it is life,' he said. 'For girls, for women, life is not easy in Nepal.'

He was being circumspect. It made Ava want to draw him out. 'Well, to answer your original question,' she said, 'yes, I do like the CBO.' She was intrigued to see him grimace. 'Why? Isn't it doing good work?' she asked.

He looked away, towards the hills. For a while he didn't speak, but when he did, it was with a strange vehemence. 'Will the women become rich with one-two cows, sister? Will that make big change in their life?' he said. 'What help the CBO gives, really? Where all the money goes?' He scoffed. 'You are coming today, so everything is nice, sister. It is just for show.'

Ava recoiled. 'Are you saying that everything I saw today was a lie?'

He studied her, as though assessing whether or not to be honest with her.

'Tell me,' she said. 'How will I know if you don't tell me?'

But she could almost see him deciding to hold back. After a pause, he said, 'No, everything is not just for show. Sorry for saying,' he said. 'Don't mind.'

Was that how he truly felt? Or was he tempering his outburst out of consideration for his sister? 'Well,' Ava said, 'I was certainly impressed by your sister. Please tell her that.'

The man nodded.

Ava went back to the tent, feeling ill.

AFTER THE VISITORS left, the crowd dispersed and the farce ended. Thulo Ba's lackeys pulled down the tent, disassembled the stage and swarmed, like carrion, over the leftovers of the feast.

Gyanu walked to the highway and waved down a bus to the bazaar, finding a seat beside an elderly man and his middle-aged son. The letter from Surya had rattled him. Surya was two years younger than he. He remembered her as a feisty girl, like Chandra, but even more independent. He knew, from the letters that Nepali brothers and sisters sent back from the desert, that their letters could conceal the truth. He tried not to think about what Surya may have been through in Ghaziabad. How she must have cried over the years. There was something about Nepal, he thought desperately: this land made its women cry. Ma had cried in her day. Chandra was crying now. And if Chandra were to go to India and he to the desert, Sapana, too, would cry.

The thought tore at him inside.

Come soon, mahal, Maleah had said over Skype. *I do not want to lose you,* she'd said. She'd said, *Come back, and let us marry.*

Halfway to the bazaar, his mobile phone caught a signal, and he got off the bus. He stood by the side of the highway and placed a call: 'Jairus, all I need are some permit papers—I'll do any kind of work to get back there.'

A truck roared by in a haze of diesel.

Jairus said, 'Gyanu, are you all right? You sound too worried, hey.'

'If I don't come back soon—' His voice caught. 'Help me, Jairus. I'll do anything to come back.'

'Gyanu? I'll see what I can find. God will look out for you.'

After they hung up, Gyanu walked to the bazaar. A private car sped by, blaring its horn. A truck roared past him, and another. He stopped at the bridge over the Tinau. Maleah would be at the gift shop right now. She'd be free in an hour. He sent her a message: *Skype, meri maya?*

After a while, she replied: *I am free tomorrow morning only mahal.*

He remained on the bridge, looking out at the water, clinging to Jairus's words for courage. *God will look out for you.* He ought to leave for Kathmandu in a few days to meet the manpower agent. Sapana would have to move into Thulo Ba's house: there'd be no alternative if Chandra were to go to India. From there, Sapana would have to find her own way forward. He had to believe she could do it. He did believe it. Ma had done it: she'd left one family and started another. She'd been strong enough to do so. He thought of Ba's love for Ma, and Ba's acceptance of a stranger's son as his own. There was good in this society. Sapana would have to find it, or create it. She was strong, like Ma, or she'd have to become so now. He wasn't his sister's guardian: he couldn't be.

He closed his eyes and saw Maleah as he'd first seen her, in church: the white lace, her bowed head. He heard her whispered prayer. *Our father who art in heaven.* She'd saved him with the miracle, the mercy, of love.

He saw his earlier life: the large, open yard, the date tree. The house, the chicken coop. The dust, heat, tar. He heard the bellowing of a man and a woman crying. That was all he'd had before Maleah: an origin he could never get back to. A memory of loss.

'Our father,' he murmured, standing on the bridge. 'Our father.'

'MADAM DEPUTY CO-DIRECTOR of WDS-Nepal, Indira Sharmaji.'

It was him, it really was him, it was John Barnett, after all these years. His body had thickened and his hair had thinned, but his eyes were still bright blue and his eyelashes as long as a girl's.

'Johnji!' Indira was aflutter at her desk.

He took her hands and held them to his heart, as a boyfriend would. 'I always knew you would go places, Indiraji.'

Flattered, pleased, embarrassed, Indira withdrew her hand. 'What would you like, Johnji—coffee or tea?'

'Pukka Nepali tea with milk and sugar, the way we used to have it at Help—remember?'

She remembered, yes, she remembered it now. 'Of course.' She put in the order, and they sat looking at each other fondly.

John Barnett shook his head. 'Can I make a confession? I always wanted to say something to you, Indiraji. I hope you won't take offense.'

'Please say.'

'I was head over heels in love with you at Help.'

'So long ago.' Indira hardly knew where to look. That was a few years before she got married. A fancy passed through her mind, a thought of what might have been...

'But I was also terrified of you!' John Barnett laughed. 'I was afraid to even talk to you. Every day I'd tell myself: say something to her, but I couldn't. You were such a proper, pukka Nepali girl!'

'You know how things were,' Indira murmured. 'Everything was strict, not like now.'

'True: I didn't know a single Nepali girl before I met my beautiful wife, Vidya. Ah, Indiraji. Tell me,' he said, 'what have you been up to?'

Then he launched into the story of his life.

At the end of his internship at Help, he'd stayed on in the country, researching his PhD thesis on the indigenous natural resource management systems of the Newars of Bhaktapur. He'd met his wife, a Newar from Bhaktapur, during this period. 'Oh, how her family objected! A queeray, a white man—the dishonour!' He laughed the full, throaty laugh of a man whose troubles were far behind him. After winning her family over, they'd had a traditional Newari wedding. Their eldest child was in her first year at Oxford. The other two were studying at the British school here.

A reedy boy—a new peon?—came in with the tea. When he left, John Barnett resumed his life story. Indira mused over the life choices we make.

John Barnett's wife didn't work. 'Vidya's a simple woman, a woman with a good heart, but, well, she's not like you, Indiraji. She has nothing outside of the family,' he said. 'For her, we are God.' They lived in an old-fashioned brick house on his wife's ancestral property. 'You must visit us, Indiraji. Vidya will be so happy to meet you.'

'And you must meet—' Indira said. Nepali womanly decorousness prevented her from uttering her husband's name in public. 'He is under-secretary at the Ministry of Works and Physical Planning.'

'A lucky man! And children? You must have children. Tell me about your children, Indiraji. Tell me everything, everything.'

It wasn't possible, of course, to tell John Barnett everything. After mentioning Aakriti and Aakaash, Indira steered the conversation towards work. 'You know what it's like, Johnji, for Nepali women. How we have to struggle at work, how we have to struggle at home.' She pushed forward a stack of reports that she'd compiled for him. 'Do you remember Ramila Singh from Help?'

'Wasn't she the only other woman on staff?'

'She had to stop working after marriage. Her mother-in-law-father-in-law wouldn't allow it.'

'Isn't that terrible? Oh, that makes me so mad, Indiraji. Ramila was a rising star!'

'My mother-in-law is also a very strict lady.' Indira handed him a business card. 'But this is the reality for all Nepali women, even we highly modern, highly professional, highly successful Nepali women, isn't that so, Johnji? Ki garne: what to do? Now, about the assessment, if you need any further information, or if you'd like to interview me or other staff, please call.'

'I'll definitely call,' he said. 'Oh, there's so much to catch up on, Indiraji. We'll have you over to our home very soon,' he said. Then he stayed on for another hour and reminisced about old times:

'Whatever happened to Raju Sharma? Remember him? He was always cracking jokes.'

'He is in the UN now, in Addis Ababa.'

'And—who was the one in Social Mobilization? The fat one.'

'Jeewan Khadka. He won the green card lottery. He is in America now, in Queens.'

'Wow.' He blinked; or maybe he winked; his eyes suddenly twinkled. 'Just now, Indiraji, when you were speaking, you looked exactly like you used to. I can hardly believe it. You're as stunning as ever.'

'Johnji.' She blushed like a little girl.

'It's true.'

Leaving, he again held her hands to his heart.

Afterwards, Indira could hardly stop smiling like an idiot-fool. What was wrong with her? She chided herself. Was it so rare to be admired by a man, a chocolatey-handsome man? All John Barnett had had to do was look at her with those bright blue eyes, and... tchee. She smiled.

She was feeling better now, better than she had in days, weeks, months. If she could manipulate—no, guide—John Barnett into giving WDS-Nepal a good assessment, things would be all right at work. Yes. If she could guide John Barnett, and if Vishwa Bista could guide the Canadian director of WEP at IDAF, then: definitely. Maybe. Maybe not, too, but hopefully: hopefully things would be all right.

At home, too, things were improving gradually. Durga had come back, and she'd promised not to try to kill herself again. Every morning, before setting out to the office, Indira spent time with the girl, talking to her, pepping up her spirit, boosting her morale: 'What happened, Durga? That was nothing.'

'Nothing, Hajoor?'

'Nothing.'

She slipped extra money to the girl so she could buy new kurtas and make-up and trinkets. Durga was rallying day by day: she was almost back to normal. And this restored normalcy to Indira's life. Which was crucial, because she'd told Rick Peede that she expected him to support her bid to succeed him. He'd assured her that if IDAF were to accept her proposal, no one could stop her from becoming the next director of WDS-Nepal.

The new peon came in to clear away the tea cups. He was a clean-cut, good-looking boy, a bit reedy, though that would change with age. 'What's your name, Babu?' Indira asked.

He snapped to attention. 'Hira, sir. My name is Hira.'

Sir. How sweet. She watched him place the empty cups on the tray. 'Hira,' she said; the tray rattled, and the cups clinked. 'When did you join WDS-Nepal, Babu?'

'Sir,' he said, and coughed. 'It will be two weeks tomorrow.'

'Two weeks. And how has it been? Have you enjoyed working

with us, Babu?'

The fear on the boy's face was endearing. 'I'm enjoying working at WSD-Nepal very much, sir.' He added, 'Sir, it fills me with great pride to be working for an organization that helps so many poor brothers and sisters in—in this great nation of ours. It is very big work, sir, and though I'm just a peon, it fills me with great pride.'

His answer genuinely moved her. 'You can't be very old,' she observed.

'I'm going on twenty, sir.'

'And is this your first job?'

'In an office, yes, sir. Before this—' He lost his breath and had to pause. 'Sir, I've worked since I was a boy. In the village I worked on the landlord's fields, and in the city—I've done everything.'

'And how did you find this job, Babu?' she asked, curious.

'My uncle—my uncle.' The boy stammered. 'I was—I was working at a shopping complex, sir, and my uncle, he's a driver here, he drives the car of the big white sir, the sir with red hair? He told me the office was hiring a peon. He helped me apply.'

So his uncle was Rick Peede's driver. 'Narayan is your very own uncle?' Indira asked. 'Do you have a lot of relatives in the city, Babu?'

By now the poor boy was so nervous he was shifting from foot to foot, desperate to bolt. 'My uncle and aunt are all I've got here, sir.'

'And in the village? Who's left in the village?'

His face brightened. 'Everyone's there, sir. My mother and father, my sisters and brothers... we're seven children altogether. I'm the oldest. The youngest is two years old.'

Yes, she could see it now. The loving but poor family in the village. The dutiful eldest son in the city. 'So you're living with your uncle and aunt?' she said. He'd be sharing a corner of their rented rooms, no doubt.

'Yes, sir.'

'Very well.' Indira dismissed the boy and watched him scuttle out the door.

Men. She smiled. Men were so... And yet... Her thoughts wandered back to John Barnett. She saw him as he'd been: young, chocolatey-handsome. *You're as stunning as ever.* He'd flirted with her today—hadn't he? A little bit. He'd even winked, or blinked. There was nothing wrong with flirting—a little bit—as long as it was innocent. It had been innocent. John Barnett was happily married, she was happily married: there was nothing wrong here. Romance was a part of life, after all. It was natural, and necessary, even. It was a basic human right, or at least it was nice to have.

You're as stunning as ever.

Johnji.

It's true!

There was nothing wrong.

You're as stunning as ever, you're so stunning, you're truly stunning.

Oh, Johnji, you're just saying that.

It's true, Indiraji, I mean it, can I confess? I hope you don't mind. I love you.

THE TREES SHOOK violently in the blustery springtime winds as Sapana rang the temple bell once, twice, thrice—and again. Again. Again. The peals echoed against the hillsides. She kept ringing the bell again. Again. Again. Till the peals echoed up to the sky.

She tossed away her slippers and stormed in. There was no one in the inner sanctum today, no devotees, not even a bird or an insect or a worm. She knelt before the deity, fulminating: Shulinbaba, make everything right, you'd better make everything right, or else!

Or else, what?

Shulinbaba was just a misshapen rock, and Chandra was leaving, and there was nothing she could do.

All the energy drained out of her, as though there were water, not blood, in her veins. Her stomach churned, her body ached, her heart hurt.

Yesterday, she'd gone with Chandra, little Tara and their Muwa to the bazaar. At the grain store, they'd dialled Surya Di's telephone number, and suddenly her voice was on the line, after all these years: 'Hello?'

The entire family had wailed.

'Ey, Muwa, ey—ey!' On the line, Surya Di had wailed; and in the grain store her Muwa and sisters had wailed: 'Eeeey!' Their emotions flooded like the mad river at monsoon time, a froth of white rage decimating everything in its path, including the pact that Chandra and she had made to live together forever.

'Muwa!'

'Eeeey! Chhori!'

'Muwa!'

'Eeeey! Eeeey!'

It was a long time before they were able to talk.

When they did so, Surya Di repeated what she'd written in her letter: Chandra should come to her in Ghaziabad. She'd find work for her there. 'It'll just be housework, but you wouldn't be idle, you'll earn, you'll stand on your own two feet,' Surya Di had said. 'How long can you depend on Muwa Buwa, Bahini? You're not a child anymore.'

Chandra had hung her head, listening, not saying yes, but also not saying no. Sapana knew what she was thinking. Her Muwa Buwa needed her to earn. Of course she'd go.

And it hurt, Shulinbaba, it really hurt. It felt to Sapana as though a part of her were being ripped out of her, leaving her amputated, bleeding.

153

Afterwards, returning to the village, no one had said anything: the family had exhausted all their emotions. Only Sapana had been in tumult: Chandra would go, and: would she be all right in India, would she be safe?

Shulinbaba, she prayed: look after her, don't let any harm come over her in that foreign land, keep her safe. Keep her safe, or else...

Or else, nothing.

Everything would change for Chandra now; and everything would change for Sapana too. Gyanu Dai hadn't said it because he was too much of a coward to ever talk about anything directly, but she wouldn't be able to live by herself at home. She'd have to move in with Thulo Ba and Thuli ma, and what did they care about her future? They'd force her to marry, and maybe there'd be no choice, maybe she'd have to marry, because that's what all girls did, in the end. Everything she and Chandra used to talk about—they were dreams, they were childish delusions.

She felt like curling up on the floor and crying forever. But then she felt a familiar trickle of warmth between her legs. She shot up, cursing. Everything was hellish, this whole world was hellish. She ran out of the temple into the blustery winds, cursing the universe.

'WHAT IF ANYTHING were to happen, Jairus?'

'Nothing will happen, hey, Gyanu. Women have an inner power, na. Never underestimate them: they're stronger than us menfolk.'

'I'm betraying her. She's angry. She's won't even talk to me properly.'

Jairus sighed. 'In life there's only so much you can do for others, Gyanu. And how can you help your sister if you're weak? You have to make yourself strong first.'

Gyanu nodded: he understood, but couldn't agree.

'Now listen, friend, this isn't a fancy five-star hotel, it's a small place behind the spice bazaar. The restaurant is called Zafran. Irani food: chelo, kebab, polo, khoresht. The owners want someone who'll stay for at least two years. This is the fastest way back.'

'I'll go to Kathmandu to get the permit,' Gyanu said.

'The owners are good people. You can marry your love, na. And I miss your cooking, hey.' Jairus laughed. 'When you come back, you'll see how thin I've got, friend. You can look for better options once you're here. You know, Gyanu, I want to leave too. You and Maleah, me and my wife, let's all go somewhere else,' he said. 'I have a cousin in Australia, he's a chartered accountant, he lives in a little brick house. We can go to Australia and live in little brick houses.'

His patter was soothing. 'Jairus?' Gyanu said. 'I'm grateful.'

'Why such formality, friend?'

'I'm just grateful.'

Jairus laughed. 'Remember one thing, Gyanu. The world needs people like you. You're a trained chef from a country that everyone loves. Me? I'm a driver from Pakistan, but you know what? The world needs me too. The world needs all good people, Gyanu. Remember that. Now, go, Skype your love. She said she'd wait for you at the cyber café.'

~

'Luke?'

'Big Sis, is that you? The line's kind of bad. Hold on? There's this really loud punk rock band.'

'Is this a bad time?' Ava shouted into her cell phone. 'I can call later.'

'No, no. Okay, that's better. What's up? How are things going out there in your imaginary homeland?'

'Luke, you're right, I made a mistake,' she said.

'What was that?' he said. 'Sorry, Ava. I'm at a club and there's this band, it's fantastic, but—I'll step outside.'

'Never mind, I'll be back in Kathmandu tonight, we can talk then,' Ava said.

'No, hold on, I've got news for you too. Shit. Let me cross the road, it'll be quieter there.'

Ava waited on the bridge, looking down at the pebbly shore. There was no one by the river this morning, only a dog. It sniffed a rock, stopped to pee, trotted on. The river felt desolate. Everything felt bleak. This field trip—her entire time at IDAF, her decision to come to Nepal—had been a colossal mistake.

Yesterday, after the first village, she and Vishwa had gone on to two more villages. At both, they'd been subjected to speeches so formal and empty that Ava had stopped asking for translations. There had been tea and snacks at both villages, but no time to see any work. The worst part was: Vishwa kept reminding her that it was her fault. And he was right. She hadn't realized, when she'd planned the field trip, that the villages were so far apart. They'd sat right next to each other on the map. Neither had she realized they'd be spending two full days driving from and back to Kathmandu. She should have asked Vishwa for help. She should have scheduled a whole week for the trip. She didn't know what she was doing—at IDAF, in Nepal, in life.

'Right.' Luke came back on the line. 'Is this any better?'

Ava blurted out, 'Remember, in Miami, at the beach, you said I was coming here because these do-gooder Canadians rescued me and I wanted to repay my debt?'

'Oh, God, I was just saying that, I didn't actually mean it, Big Sis.' There was some rustling on the line. He whispered to someone, then said, 'Are you okay out there? What's going on with you?'

She sighed. 'I'll be back in Kathmandu tonight, let's talk then.'

'Yeah, cause I have something to tell you,' he said. Then he whooped. 'We're pregnant! We're going to have a baby, Big Sis, a baby!'

What? 'Oh, my God, Luke! You and—?' The heavily-pierced performance artist?

'Revolution Mary! We literally just found out!' He whooped again. 'We're out celebrating.'

At a nightclub? 'That's amazing,' Ava said. 'Oh, my God.'

'I know, I know! Auntie Ava! I'm going to be a dad, can you

believe it?'

She couldn't quite. She said, 'I want to hear more. Let's definitely FaceTime: how's my tonight, your tomorrow morning?'

'Don't make it too early. Oh, hey, Anthony's here. Want to rekindle your romance with him? Hey, Anthony! Anthony! It's Ava, she's in Nepal, she wants to say hi.'

'No, Luke, hey—'

But before she could protest, he put Anthony on. 'Hi, there.'

'Anthony! Hey. Hi.' Ava cast about for something to say. 'How are you doing?'

'I'd be a lot better if you were in Miami.'

'Me too, actually.' She laughed.

'You heard the news?'

'About Luke and, um, Revolution Mary? Yeah. Great news, huh?'

'You think your brother's ready for fatherhood?'

'Jesus. I guess he'll have to learn on the job.'

'Hey,' Anthony said, 'Where are you right now? What are you looking at? What's directly in front of you?'

'I'm looking at a dog on a river bank.'

'I'm looking at a man in a dog collar. Coincidence?'

They laughed.

He said, 'It's nice talking to you, Ava.'

'And to you, Anthony.'

'Come and visit.'

'I may just.'

After they hung up, Ava felt lost. She wanted her old life back.

She and Vishwa were going to head back to Kathmandu in an hour. She already dreaded all the talking he'd do on the drive: the constant explaining of Nepal. The Mansplaining. Or Nepalsplaining. The weary combination of the two.

The stray dog was still trotting along the shore. There was a trail near the bus stop that seemed to lead down to the river. She decided to follow it.

~

The bus to the village wasn't in. A newspaper lay crumpled on a bench. He picked it up and scanned through the usual grim news of strikes and closures, blockades and impasses, grandstanding among the political parties. There was no sign of the constitution ever being drafted. Half the paper was filled with pictures of starlets. In a corner he saw an article about artificial intelligence, but most of it had been ripped out.

He tossed the paper aside in disgust, and, looking around, saw the woman from yesterday: the foreigner. Her suit and briefcase made her stand out. She had stopped at the top of a goat path down to the river, staring in consternation at the litter around her feet. This was where the neighbourhood threw its garbage.

He went to help her. 'Sister.'

'Oh.' Her face lit up when she recognized him. Then, perhaps remembering their exchange, she stiffened. 'Hello, there.' For a while she stood awkwardly. Then she said, 'I wanted to go to the river, not to swim, but—would it be okay, I don't know, culturally, to dip my feet in the water, do you think?'

'It is no problem, sister.'

'Please just call me Ava,' she said. 'I'm sorry, I didn't catch your name yesterday.'

Gyanu introduced himself, then explained that there was a better path down to the river. 'I will show,' he said.

She didn't say much as he led her down the main path. She seemed tense, though she appeared to relax a little when they reached the water's edge. She crouched down on her knees and dipped in a hand. 'Oh, that's gorgeous.' She sat down on the shore and rolled up her trousers. After taking off her shoes, she dipped her feet in the water. 'That feels incredible.'

She became more sociable after that. 'How's your sister doing?' she said. 'Sapana, isn't that her name?'

'She is fine, sister—Ava.'

'Yesterday, her friend...I didn't catch her name. Her mother makes pickles?'

'It is Chandra.'

'She seemed very upset. Both she and her—I think that was her younger sister? I kept thinking about it later on. What were they upset about?'

Gyanu wasn't sure how to explain it in English. 'Chandra has one older sister. Many years before, she—she went to India. They think she is dead,' he said. Seeing the alarm on Ava's face, he quickly added, 'She is alive. Just: they are worried.'

'Oh. Her sister's all right, then?'

'She is all right.'

Ava frowned. 'This is a high-risk area for trafficking, isn't it? I saw that in National Network Nepal's report. I really can't get my head around it: more than ten thousand Nepali girls trafficked annually.' Her tone grew introspective, as though she were talking to herself more than to him. 'They were so poor, Chandra's family. Later on, after we left the village, I kept wondering how they could live like that. I mean, they had nothing.'

This struck Gyanu as naïve. 'They do little bit everything,' he said. 'Little labour, little farming, little business. In the village, everybody does little bit everything.'

She looked at him. 'What do you do, Gyanu?'

'I—I do not live here. I am chef in Dubai. Just I am visiting my sister.'

'Oh.' She studied his face, examining him for signs of—what? 'Yesterday,' she said, 'you told me that the CBO's work was a lie.'

He demurred.

'Did the women's committee really do all the work they showed me?' she asked.

Gyanu had to calibrate his response. 'The women's committee is good.'

'But?' She kept looking at him. 'What's the catch? What are you holding back, Gyanu? How will I understand if you don't tell me?'

He returned her gaze, trying to assess whether she wanted to know the truth. He decided to risk it. He said, 'The CBO: what money they are getting, what money they are spending, what cut they are taking?' He hesitated. 'The Chairman—if he cannot take the cut, he won't have the CBO, he won't have the women's committee, he won't do any works. Maybe ten per cent of budget is going to programmes. The rest?' he said. 'To the Chairman.'

Ava looked pained, as if he'd landed her a blow.

'It is okay,' he said, surprised at her reaction.

She began to blink back tears.

'Also the rich have to make money, yes? If no, why they will do any works for the poor?' He repeated, 'It is okay, Ava.'

'No, it's not okay,' she said. 'It's not okay at all, Gyanu. Jesus! It's not okay.' She turned away and cursed under her breath: 'Fuck, fuck, fuck!' When she turned back, her expression was tormented. 'Can I tell you a secret, Gyanu? I came here—' She paused. 'I was born in Nepal,' she said. 'I was adopted by a Canadian family when I was a few months old. What I'm doing here isn't just a job for me, Gyanu. I could have been born in your village—and you know what? I don't think I would have survived.'

Why was she telling him this? Now Gyanu felt sorry for her. 'You did see, yesterday, how people survive,' he said.

'I didn't see anything! I was hoping I'd really understand everything on this field trip, but there's been so little time, all I've seen is the surface.' She let out a bitter laugh. 'Even when I went to the homes of the women's committee members with Sapana, everyone was so open, they were telling me all these things, but—it's silly—I kept wanting to go into their homes, to see how they live.'

What did she want to see? Something related to work, or something more personal? 'I can show,' Gyanu said. 'I invite you to my home.'

She looked at him. 'The car's leaving for Kathmandu soon.' She bit her lips. 'Maybe, I could hire a car to go back?'

'You can take the bus.'

'Is it safe?'

'There is tourist bus, that is safer.'

'I'll have to tell my colleague. There's a ton of work I have to get to this weekend. What time would the bus get me into Kathmandu, do you think? Will I get there by tonight?'

'You will get there tomorrow morning time.'

She mulled it over, then said, 'Fuck it,' and punched in a message on her mobile phone.

She couldn't bear to listen to Chandra's Muwa Buwa urging her to go to India. She got up and ran out.

'Sapana, ey!' Chandra rushed to her feet and followed her. 'Stop, listen!'

'I don't want to hear anything you have to say!'

'Just stop for a moment, ey.'

'Leave me alone!' Sapana ran through the courtyard and turned past the bottlebrush trees. Chandra was faster than she was. She'd almost caught up to her by the time she reached home. The two of them burst into the kitchen to find Gyanu Dai sitting at the table with the foreign woman from the day before.

Sapana stopped, suprised. Chandra collided into her. They both stood at the door, panting and out of breath.

The foreign woman stood to greet them. She had a notebook open in front of her. Gyanu Dai explained that she was here to find out more about the women's committee. 'She wants to meet the rest of the committee members,' he said.

'They won't be prepared,' Sapana said, 'but—of course, Dai.'

'Come and sit.' He got up and made a round of tea.

The four of them spent the morning in the kitchen. The foreign woman—Ava madam—had been dissatisfied by how little time she'd had here the day before. She asked Sapana about the committee, about the prospects of a cooperative in the village, about the CBO, and even about Thulo Ba.

Sapana answered her questions faithfully.

Gyanu Dai translated between them, switching effortlessly between Nepali and English.

Sapana knew her brother spoke English in the desert, but she'd never heard him speak English before. With her rudimentary school learning, she couldn't fully follow what he was saying, but she did catch a few words and phrases. At one point, Ava madam said something that made Gyanu Dai smile. Sapana couldn't understand what she had said. Then they spoke among themselves. Watching them, Sapana found Gyanu Dai different, all of a sudden. He was open with the foreign woman. He was at ease. He didn't have his usual unhappy expression. It was as though he were a different man in her company. It made Sapana wonder how well she knew her brother. Or—she knew him in the role he played in her life, as her brother, but this stranger speaking English to a foreign woman: this was Gyanu Dai too.

He threw together a fragrant noodle soup for their morning meal. Then they took Ava madam to meet the committee members, going right into their houses. Some of the members were home, others were out. Ava madam was interested in everyone's stories. She took copious notes, filling page after page. She spent the entire day asking questions, listening to the answers and writing them down.

At the end, back at home over a cup of tea, Ava madam turned her attention to Chandra. When was she going to India? she asked. What was her sister doing there?

Chandra glanced at Sapana before responding. 'Tell her, Gyanu Dai: she met my Muwa Buwa yesterday, she saw how poor we are. How can I not go? I'm not a child any more. Shouldn't I earn?'

Her words were clearly intended for Sapana.

Ava madam asked Chandra: Was it risky to go? Was Surya Di safe? Had she been under any coercion while talking on the phone?

She and Gyanu Dai and Chandra parsed over the matter, and by the end of the day, came up with a plan:

Ava madam knew some NGOs in Kathmandu that rescued women who'd been trafficked to India. She'd ask one of them to check in on Surya Di. If Surya Di were in any danger, or if she changed her mind about staying on in India, the NGO would bring her home. But if she wanted to stay, and if Chandra wanted to join her, Ava madam would help Chandra get to Ghaziabad safely.

'If you want to go, you should go, Bahini,' Gyanu Dai explained to Chandra. 'Her intention isn't to stop you, just to make sure you and Surya Bahini are safe.'

Chandra kept glancing at Sapana for approval, but Sapana wouldn't give it.

Gyanu Dai would stay on in the village till Chandra's plans were finalized. 'After that, I'll have to leave,' he said.

These words, too, were intended for Sapana.

Towards the end, it was mostly Gyanu Dai and Ava madam talking among themselves again. Sapana watched them—they were attentive, animated—and an unfamiliar emotion, resentment, bloomed inside her like a strange dark flower. She knew she should be grateful to Ava madam. She'd help Chandra. She'd help the women's committee. And she'd help Sapana too. But the foreign woman's presence in the house heralded a change that she wasn't prepared for. It angered her. The more she watched Gyanu Dai talking to Ava madam, the more clearly Sapana saw how narrow the horizon to her life had been. From a young age, Gyanu Dai had had an independence that she'd never even thought to have. Now that she thought about it, she wanted that independence too. She wanted the same broad horizon he'd had.

At dusk, Gyanu Dai said he'd take Ava madam to the bazaar to catch a bus to Kathamndu. Saying farewell to Sapana and Chandra, Ava madam became emotional. She embraced them, and thanked them for letting her into their home. Gyanu Dai translated for her: 'I learned so much today, it's been very important to me. I'll always be grateful to you for what you've given me today.'

It was a little surprising.

Sapana and Chandra stood at the door, watching Gyanu Dai and Ava madam leave. The sky was growing dark, darkness was engulfing the corners of the village. Gyanu Dai and Ava madam disappeared into that darkness.

Chandra put an arm around her.

Sapana slapped it off.

For a while Chandra was silent, rebuked. Then she said, 'You know you'll be all right, Sapana.'

'Be quiet!'

'You should enrol in the Plus Two. You and I aren't in the same situation. I would have never been able to afford it, but you should study, you should—'

'Don't tell me what I should do!'

'Listen.' Chandra put an arm around her again.

Again, Sapana slapped it off.

'This woman will help you, Sapana. She'll help you start a cooperative in the village. You know the change, the progress, the revolution we dream of? It'll happen. You'll make it happen. You can do it, you can—'

'You don't love me, no one loves me, you're all getting on with your own lives and forgetting about me!' Sapana cried.

ALL THE WAY across the house she heard a screech, a bellow, the clatter of a pan flung across the kitchen. 'What's happening?' Indira rushed out of the bedroom. A cloud of myrrh was swirling out of Muwa's bedroom door, which was ajar. Her room was empty. The sitting room was empty too. The old witch was nowhere to be seen.

In the kitchen, Durga was crouched on the floor, sobbing into her hands, shaking like a bud in a storm. Her hair was tousled, lipstick was smeared over her face, the gaajal on her eyes was running. The back door was open. From the telltale scent of myrrh, Indira deduced that Muwa had slipped out of there into the backyard. The old witch had given the girl a pummelling.

'I should die,' Durga sobbed. 'I should just die, Hajoor. I should take poison and die.'

'Tch, tch, tch. What are you saying?' Indira crouched down beside the girl. 'Don't ever say that, Durga, don't ever say anything like that.'

A squeal emerged from the girl's mouth. 'You told Muwa!'

'I never! I would never! I gave you my word!'

'She came in.' Durga gasped for breath. 'I was putting on lipstick. She grabbed my hair and called me a—a—a—'

'Tch, tch, tch, tch, tch.' The girl had been doing so well, the last thing she needed was a setback. 'Forget Muwa,' Indira said, wiping the lipstick and gaajal off her face. 'Muwa's insane. She's losing her mind. She's been crazy from the day I married into this family, actually.' What was she going to do about the old witch? 'Remember,' Indira said, to comfort the girl, 'what you said to me at the hotel? I've been thinking about it, Durga, and you're right. You need a life.'

The girl looked up at her with sad, doubting eyes.

'I know what you're thinking, Durga. You're thinking. I'm just a servant girl, brought to Kathmandu by a father who couldn't feed-clothe-house her; what kind of life can I have? But have I ever let you down? No, I've never let you down. I give you my word. I'll give you a life.'

The girl sniffled. 'Will you raise my salary, Hajoor?'

What?

'Hajoor,' Durga said, 'You have to pay me minimum wage. I heard in the bazaar. It's the law, re.'

Oof. The girl was right. Indira should have done this years ago. She'd been meaning to, in fact, she'd simply forgotten. 'All right, la,' she said. 'But don't tell Muwa, or she'll kick you out.'

The girl sat up a little. 'I also want a day off, Hajoor.'

What was going on? Indira looked at the girl: and she looked back expectantly, all her hopes laid bare on her face.

'Lau, you can take Tuesdays off. I'll tell Muwa you're fasting for Lord Ganesh.'

The girl smiled through her tears.

'Now, be happy.' Indira helped her get to her feet. 'Look, Durga, I know Muwa's difficult, but what can I do? I'm just a daughter-in-law in this family, there's nothing I can do. Just avoid her for a few days and it'll pass. Now.' Indira issued the instructions for the day. 'Don't forget to open the windows after Muwa's puja, I don't want the house stinking of myrrh. And what's in season in the bazaar? Buy pumpkin greens. Don't forget to make fresh yogurt—yesterday's batch was sour. Do you have enough money for the shopping?'

'I have enough left over from yesterday.'

'Good. Now I'm off to office.' She patted the girl on the back. 'And you, you're already in your office, Durga. We, professional women, our work is never done, isn't that so?'

Oof.

Avoiding Muwa, she went out from the front door. Uday Sharma, who always absented himself from family crises, was waiting by his ministry car with Aakaash and Aakriti. 'Is everything all right?' he asked.

Cowardly man. 'There's no problem at all!' Indira declared loudly, for the benefit of the children. 'You-all get going, now. Aakaash, Aakriti, be good at school. We'll have pumpkin greens for dinner.'

Aakaash groaned. 'I hate those!'

'They're my favourite!' Aaktriti beamed.

After herding her family into the ministry car, Indira's thoughts turned towards work. Rick Peede was picking her up on the way to a seminar on Post-2015 Priority Themes for the MDGs. After the seminar, they'd return together to WDS-Nepal to conduct a multi-sectoral briefing on sustainability. On both rides, she'd be able to reassure him about John Barnett's assessment. She was sure—or at least hopeful—that his assessment would be positive. Yes, it would be positive. Most definitely, yes.

With a honk, a Pajero arrived at the front gate, but instead of Rick Peede, Chandi Shrestha was inside. 'Rickji said he'd walk, you know how he hates sitting in traffic. I'm getting a lift to ActionAid,' he said.

Indira got in.

'Drop me off first, ey, Narayan,' Chandi Shrestha instructed the driver, before turning back to Indira. 'Vishwa Bista from IDAF told me there was some problem with your proposal?'

Vishwa Bista was talking to him about her proposal? 'No, there's no problem,' she said. 'It's a routine assessment, Chandiji.'

'He said IDAF's new director of WEP has some very strange ideas.' He jeered. 'He called me from the field, he said she has no idea what she's doing.'

'Vishwa Bista called you from the field?'

'He was calling about something else, this just—came up,' he said, suddenly growing discreet.

'Of course, you're free to talk about my proposal,' Indira said. 'Women's empowerment shouldn't concern only women; men should care about it too. Indeed, I wish more men shared my passion for women's empowerment, Chandiji!'

'You're so right, Indiraji, women's empowerment is for all of us, men and women. In fact, as the father of two daughters, I feel that women's empowerment is more important for us men than for you women. We're the ones who are holding you back.'

That male glibness: Indira had heard it all her life. Men were always patronizing her, talking down to her, telling her that of course she was superior, but also letting her know—through connotation, inference, signs and body language—that they were in charge. All these glib men were always letting her know: I have a penis.

I have a penis, and you don't.

'Anyway,' Chandi Shrestha went on, 'Vishwaji was telling me that the assessment will come in soon. He said the meeting with IDAF is next Friday?'

'I know that,' Indira snapped, and immediately began to fret. A few days after their first meeting, John Barnett had called her. For an hour he had talked about himself, his charmed life, his beautiful wife, their brilliant children. 'I meant it when I said I'd like to have you over, Indiraji,' he'd said at the end. 'I can't wait for our families to meet. I'll call.'

But he hadn't called.

He hadn't called, and now that Chandi Shrestha had brought it up, it was impossible not to fear the worst. John Barnett was giving WDS-Nepal a poor assessment. He'd found out about the bribe. Or worse: Vishwa Bista had told him about it. Or even worse than that: Vishwa

Bista had conspired—with Chandi Shrestha, yes, of course, with her rival—to expose her as a giver of bribes, and get her fired.

The entire conspiracy fell horribly into place.

In fact, Chandi Shrestha must have put Vishwa Bista up to all this. He must have offered Vishwa Bista a bribe even bigger than hers. They must have met—they were men, they could meet anywhere—and hatched a plot to sideline her. Why else would Vishwa Bista phone him from the field? It had been a plot all along, a male place to sideline her: for she was just a woman, in the end.

She didn't have a penis and never would.

Indira sank into the seat like a deflated balloon.

Chandi Shrestha would replace Rick Peede as the director of WDS-Nepal.

Traffic thickened. Outside the window, the city was a vision of the kaliyug: an age of destruction. This government was widening the road in this neighbourhood. The houses on the sides had been ripped open, their rooms gaped open like the soft, exposed innards of freshly slaughtered animals. The traffic was kicking up dust. There was a snarl up ahead. The car was barely moving.

'What's the problem?' Chandi Shrestha demanded of the driver.

He said, 'Sir, there's a demonstration, sir.'

'Then why did you take this route? Turn off and take the bridge, the bridge is faster, take that!'

'Sir, it's blocked in every direction, sir. That's what they were saying on the radio. There's a demonstration, sir, it's like this everywhere.'

'Tch.' Chandi Shrestha looked at his watch. 'I'm close enough, I'll walk from here. Lau, Indiraji, sorry to leave you in this jam: best of luck getting to your meeting on time.' He hopped out.

Indira sat dispirited, as the car lurched and halted, lurched and halted. All was lost. Her dream was over.

At the centre of the traffic jam, protesters were waving banners and flags. 'What do they want?' she asked, more to herself than to the driver. 'These people, always demonstrating—for what?'

The driver replied, 'Madam, they want a constitution, madam. They're protesting the delay, madam.'

'The constitution, always.' She scoffed. 'Always, the constitution.'

'Madam, the political parties, all they do is blame each other for the delay. I shouldn't say it, it isn't my place, but everything that's gone wrong with our nation? Is because of our political parties, madam.'

The driver seemed like a sensible man. Indira looked at him in the rear-view mirror. 'Narayan,' she said, 'we've never really talked, have we?'

'Madam, why would a driver like me talk to a boss like you, madam?'

'Well, I'm glad we're getting a chance today. I want to ask you about that nephew of yours, Hira.' She sat up to get a better view of his face in the rear-view mirror. What, she wondered, was Narayan's caste? 'Hira seems like a good boy,' she said.

'He is a good boy, madam.'

'The other day, he told me about his family in the village, and I've been thinking.' Indira felt re-energized by the thought that was forming in her mind even as she spoke. 'I'd like to help him establish himself in the city. It would be good to see a young man like him flourish, wouldn't it, Narayan?'

The driver glanced at her in the mirror.

She went on, 'Our youth are the hope of the nation, after all. That's why I want to know, Narayan, what are your nephew's plans, ambitions, dreams? He told me he's twenty years old, and I'm wondering: is he by any chance hunting for a pretty young bride?'

SHE FELL ASLEEP despite the jouncing of the bus, her head constricted by a spiky metal bar. When the bus halted with a screech, she awoke with a crick in the neck. It was dark, and the air was dewy. The woman in the seat beside her was asleep, breathing loudly through her mouth, a fine trickle of drool leaking from her lower lip. Ava checked her cell phone. It was five in the morning. For a while she couldn't tell where they were, but then she recognized the checkpost at the border of Kathmandu valley.

When the bus started up, the woman beside her awoke and started to chant—prayers?—under her breath.

On the descent into the valley, Ava looked at the concrete maze, feeling completely alert in an underslept, unhinged way. In her somnolent vision, the concrete maze looked sheltering and secure instead of squalid. Kathmandu was where Nepal's countryside came to look for fortunes, she thought. The countryside came here to rally resources, to move out into the world. If the city was ugly, it was because people spent most of what they had on personal advancement. They couldn't spare much for aesthetics.

The roads were still congested at this hour, though less so than usual. There was less dust, the air was mostly clean. The houses were still, and with only a few lights on. Kathmandu at dawn felt like a city of huddled dreams and sleeping ambitions.

The eastern horizon was glimmering to blue when the bus drew into a vast bus stop. The city was wide awake here. Horns blared, people swarmed, all transactions teemed with urgency. 'Taxi, madam?' The familiar refrain started up when she disembarked from the bus. 'Taxi, taxi.' 'Taxi, sister, taxi, you want taxi?'

She got into the nearest cab and gave directions. The driver started the engine wordlessly. She sat back, her mind ablaze.

All these months in Kathmandu, this was what she'd been missing: the connections she'd forged yesterday. The time in Gyanu's home, the time in the homes of the women's committee members. It helped her—it healed her—to know she could do something for a girl like Chandra. It wasn't, of course, Ava's job as the director of IDAF's Women's Empowerment Programme to help individuals. This scale was micro, or even smaller than micro: it was personal. But it was clear, now, that this was why she'd come to Nepal.

The driver turned into her neighbourhood and drove up the hill, stopping at the gate. Ava added a hundred rupee tip to the fare. He pocketed it silently, and left.

She pressed the buzzer to the gate. There was no reply from inside. She checked to see if she could open it, but it was locked from inside. She knocked on the metal, and then banged, but there still was no reply. Harihar was probably asleep.

She waited, wondering if she should call the landlady. But then Mrs Thapa would scream at Harihar. She didn't want that. She scoped the compound wall. It attached to the neighbour's wall, which was low. She climbed it without difficulty. Their dog began to bark. An Alsatian raced out of the house. She clambered up, out of reach, onto the adjoining compound wall. The dog started baying as she made her way from there to the wall of her own house. After lowering her attaché case, she jumped, landing with a thud on the other side.

The neighbour's dog kept baying. Harihar never woke up. She let herself into the house.

John Barnett's assessment of WDS-Nepal had arrived in her absence. It sat on the desk in the study. She'd have to read it this weekend, ahead of the final meeting with WDS-Nepal.

There was another package on the desk. She tore off the wrapping. It was the sculpture she'd bought at the Academy of Art: not a portrait of the artist's mother, but her imagination about her, whatever that meant. The artist had taped her business card at the bottom of the clay figure. Ava read her name out loud.

After making coffee, she carried the sculpture from room to room, trying to figure out where it should go. It was too small for the study or the living room. The dining room was so large that the sculpture disappeared into it. And she didn't want it in the bedroom. The house was too big, the sculpture didn't look right anywhere. She gave up and placed it back in its wrapping.

The sun rose. At her laptop, she scanned through a few work emails: several memos and a reply-all conversation that had gone on for days.

Congratulation!

Hearty congratulations to all on the team!

Another laudable IDAF success!

Hats off to all of us!

Anthony had written immediately after their phone conversation. *Hey, any chance you're going to be in Toronto this May? My film's premiering at Hot Docs.*

There was also a new email from Gavin. It was curt. *I haven't heard from you in forever, Ava. Wondering if you got my last email. I wanted you to know that Leez Anne and I are seeing each other. We should talk sometime.*

He'd written Ava, not Av.

Av and Gav.

Leez Anne and Gavin.

She shut the laptop and went out to the garden with John Barnett's assessment.

Spring had unloosed itself on the garden. The acacia and crepe myrtle trees had only just started to bud a few days ago. They were suddenly dense with colour, a riot of pinks and reds and greens, effusive and unrestrained, right up to the jasmine hedge, which was an eye-dazzling yellow. Ganesh Himal was visible beyond: the morning sun casting it as hard edges and light.

The Himalayas. She'd be up there, soon, in Langtang, trekking with Tomás. She thought about calling him, but didn't.

She spent the morning reading the assessment, rereading WDS-Nepal's proposal, looking up NGOs working on trafficking, and placing a series of calls on her cell phone, starting with one to Claire Ross-Jones:

'Hello Claire? It's Ava. Sorry to call you on a Saturday, but I need to meet you and Daphne Muirwood urgently about the Paris Declaration. Monday after the briefing would be great, thanks.'

'Hi Shova, it's Ava. Could we meet this week about microfinance and cooperatives?'

'Herman, it's Ava. Could we meet soon to discuss social inclusion?'

'Andrew, it's Ava. I need your advice on donor shopping.'

'Jared? Can we talk about peacebuilding?'

Vishwa called mid-morning. She let it ring, and when it stopped, she sent him a message saying she'd see him on Monday.

By noon, Ganesh Himal had disappeared in the usual fug of Kathmandu. She got up to get something to eat, and saw Harihar at the gate, staring at her slack-jawed, as though he'd seen a ghost. She waved to put him at ease. The landlady, too, was staring at her from the balcony. Ava waved at her too.

There was leftover dal-bhat in the fridge. She ate it cold.

Then she returned to the study, and without letting herself think twice, wrote: *Dear Gavin.*

Steady.

I guess we should file for divorce.

I'm sorry, she wanted to write. I love you, I'll always love you, she wanted to write. She didn't. She pressed the send button and sat, stunned.

She spent the rest of the day napping, falling in and out of sleep, caught up in a dream in which the villages she'd been to, and Butwal, Kathmandu, Miami, Toronto, Overwood and Georgian Bay all came together in a massice, unmade jigsaw puzzle.

In the evening she awoke clear-headed. She poured herself a glass of wine and FaceTimed her brother. 'Oh, Luke, I still can't believe you're having a kid!'

'Neither can I, Auntie Ava!'

Revolution Mary was with him. She was radiant on the screen. 'Hey, babes, don't you think Luke's going to make a great father?'

'Tell me more,' Ava said. 'I want to hear more.'

'Mom and Dad are freaked out!' Luke laughed. 'They're not ready to be grandparents at all. We're discussing names,' he said. 'We haven't found a girl's name, but if it's a boy we're going to name him Baby Jesus.'

THE RECEPTIONIST TRILLED, 'Namaste, Indira ma'am.'

'Namaste,' she called back—what was her name?

It didn't matter. Focus, Indira Sharma. All was not lost, all couldn't be lost, she told herself. Vishwa Bista and Chandi Shrestha mustn't defeat her. She'd fight back. And she'd win.

Her confidence collapsed as she entered the conference hall, because there was Chandi Shrestha: I have a penis. Why was he always, always at her meetings? Rick Peede was sitting with him, across from the Canadian and Vishwa Bista. All three of them looked somber.

Only the Canadian was collected. 'There you are, Indira,' she said, her usual girlishness replaced by cool authority. She seemed older today, in her mid-thirties, maybe because she was wearing a pinstripe suit.

She waited for Indira to sit before speaking. 'I'm going to voice my concerns very clearly,' she said. 'I've seen significant leakage in IDAF's work, and it's built into the way our funding is structured. We fund our partner INGOs, they fund their partner NGOs in Kathmandu, and they in turn fund their partner NGOs and CBOs in the districts and villages.' She looked from person to person to make sure they were paying attention. They were. 'I understand,' she went on, 'that neither we nor you can implement projects at the micro level, but in light of an IDAF headquarters directive to innovate an internal implementation strategy for the Paris Declaration, I've decided to demand a higher level of transparency.'

Indira's mind went blank.

The Canadian was clearly expecting a reply. Rick Peede offered one. 'As you know, Ava, WDS-Nepal itself initiated the Transparency Matrix over two decades ago,' he said in his droning way. 'It has since been adopted by over two hundred NGOs in Nepal. All our national partners are required to sign it as a precondition to funding. And we've always observed the highest level of compliance in reporting, though of course we'd be happy to address your concerns.'

The Canadian said, 'Our assessment revealed that some of your partners have a thin presence on the ground. Our consultant, John Barnett, confirmed my own misgivings when I met with'—she consulted her notes—'Preety Rana of National Network Nepal. Now Vishwa has pointed out to me that Ms Rana has an impressive CV, but her organization is new.' She turned to Indira. 'To be frank, I'm puzzled that you chose National Network Nepal as your largest partner.'

Indira glanced at Vishwa Bista for help, and caught him, with his smug face, exchanging glances with Chandi Shrestha.

Penises!

Indira said, 'You see, Ava, in the past,' and had to swallow. 'There were some'—her voice caught—'irregularities with our old partners. Not big irregularities, just: failure to comply with the transparency matrix due to an inability to customize the results logframe.' Her heart was beating wildly, like a trapped animal's. 'So we thought...' She said, 'Preety Rana is very good, Ava.'

At this point, Chandi Shrestha had the gall to contradict her: 'But the previous partners were better, Indiraji. To be honest, I am also surprised.'

Penis!

The Canadian leafed through her notes. 'Talking about irregularities,' she said.

Indira had to stop her before she could go on. 'I want to say one thing!' she cried.

Everyone looked at her, startled. Even Vishwa Bista was looking at her now. He was glaring at her from behind his floppy hair. She glared back at him with venom.

'I want to say one thing!' she repeated. But in truth, there was nothing to say. She'd offered Vishwa Bista a bribe. Chandi Shrestha had outsmarted her. He'd obviously offered a bigger bribe. He'd replace Rick Peede. She was done.

A roar burst out of her mouth and ricocheted off the walls. She couldn't stop. She roared once again. Then, mortified, she stumbled out of the hall. Outside, she gasped for breath. Oh, Mother Earth, open up and take me in, as you did the goddess Sita in the Ramayan! Humiliated, she reeled into the women's washroom, where a rubber breast was sticking out of the wall. Disgusting! She locked herself inside a stall and wept.

'What do you want to do when you grow up?' her elders used to ask when she was a little girl.

'I want to develop Nepal and make it prosperous,' she used to say.

In the stall, she wept hopelessly, helplessly, till she ran out of tears; and then she wept some more. Her mind looped over the same thought: she was corrupt. That's what she'd become. Look at her. Just look at this excrement, filth.

It took a while for her to stop weeping. It took ages before she felt ready to leave the stall. She did so despondently, and saw, to her horror, that the Canadian had come into the washroom. She was standing by the wall, poking at the rubber breast.

'Oh! There you are, Indira,' she said. 'I was worried. Are you all right?'

'Yes, I...sorry.' What was there to say? 'I am having a little problem.' She tried to come up with a plausible explanation: 'At home, there is a girl. The girl who served the dinner when you came? She has... problems, Ava, I am worried about her. I am experiencing too much tension at home.'

'We've rescheduled for next week, everyone's gone.' The Canadian was back to being her usual girlish self. 'Why don't I make you a cup of tea?'

In her office, she invited Indira to sit on the sofa. 'You take your tea with milk and sugar, right?' she said. 'I don't want to pry, Indira, but if you ever want to talk—not that you have to, at all—I'm a good listener.'

'Oh, it is too much a bother, Ava.'

'It would be no bother at all.'

So then—why not? Over a cup of weak, watery milk tea, Indira told her about Durga's misadventures. 'She is a young girl, Ava, a village girl, very innocent. I am her guardian—I am her mother-father, her only family. Ava, the problem in Nepal is—women are idiot-fools. We give men everything, and these men: what do they do? Life is too hard for Nepali women.'

'It really is, isn't it?'

'You don't know! You see me, a leading gender expert of Nepal. I am modern, I am independent, but how do I live at home? Do you know, Ava, how many rules I must follow as a daughter-in-law? Like when you came for dinner: can I drink a glass of wine in my own house? And at work—am I equal? How much I have to struggle every day, just to be respected by my men colleagues. These men, in public they say: you are equal to us; but in reality? Always, in small things, in big things, they dominate us!'

'I've come to realize this.' The Canadian nodded. 'On my field trip I saw—and in Kathmandu, too—the gender balance is incredibly skewed.' She thought for a while, then said, 'It's hard for me to accept, given the way I grew up. I'd find it impossible to be a Nepali woman.'

'Oh, it is too impossible!'

'Can I be honest with you?' she said. 'I don't think I'd be able to do what you do, Indira. On my field trip I met these women, these incredible, strong, resilient women, they were so inspiring. And, I mean, some of them were so poor.' To Indira's surprise, the Canadian's eyes began to moisten. She said, 'I kept thinking—if I were them, I don't know how I would have survived.' She blinked back tears. 'I'm sorry. I don't mean to be emotional. I just wanted to say—I don't know how you, all of you, Nepali women, do it. I really admire you.'

Something tender, something warm, stirred inside Indira. This Canadian, this Ava Berriden, wasn't hard-hearted after all. 'Ava, you are also a woman, you are also strong,' she said in a big-sisterly tone, a tone of woman-to-woman camaraderie. 'All of us women are survivors,' she said, and as an afterthought, added, 'The important thing is, we must support each other against men.'

'Well, that's what I'm hoping you'll do with my pilot project. But we can discuss it another time.' Ava smiled. 'I'd hate to force you to think about work in the middle of a personal crisis.'

'No, tell me. Tell me right now. I must know!' Indira insisted.

So Ava filled her in on what she'd told the others at the meeting. IDAF was going to launch a pilot project to increase aid effectiveness, a project that Ava was designing jointly with a consultant from IDAF headquarters in London. 'I'm hoping to partner with you on this, Indira,' she said. The pilot project contained a direct implementation component, which would allow Ava to get to the field regularly. All she needed from Indira were a few amendments to the WDS-Nepal proposal. 'I've had to work hard to convince everyone at IDAF—and between you and me, I've had to fight Vishwa in particular,' she said. 'He's completely against the pilot project. From today's meeting, it seems Chandi's not in favour of it either, though Rick's open to it. So I'm really counting on your support.'

Not only did Ava want to approve WDS-Nepal's proposal, she wanted to increase the budget so that WDS-Nepal could hire two full-time consultants to work with her on it. One of the consultants would be John Barnett.

Ava said, 'In his assessment, John Barnett suggested that we cut out the middleman—National Network Nepal—and work directly with CBOs at the village level. That's what I'm hoping to do in the direct implementation component. I want to go directly to the women and support them—not just to bypass men, but also that,' she said, becoming thoughtful. 'Also to bypass men. Because they're everywhere, aren't they? Everywhere you look in Nepal, there are men.'

'Always, men are there!'

'I've been lucky with the timing.' Ava smiled. 'I came in just as IDAF was drawing up its Five Year Outlook. IDAF headquarters has already given me a go-ahead. Daphne and Claire—I can never remember, do you know Claire Ross-Jones?'

'Of course, of course, I know her, of course.'

'They're both very supportive of the pilot project.'

'Me too, I'm also very supportive, Ava, I will back you fully on this pilot project,' Indira said.

'Oh, thank goodness!' Ava looked so relieved, it was odd. She didn't seem to know that she had the power to dictate the terms to WDS-Nepal. 'I'm really looking forward to working together on this. Maybe you could—why don't you come over to my place for dinner one of these days? We'll sit out in the garden and talk about everything over a glass of wine.'

The two of them, sipping wine in Catherine Christy's old house. 'Yes, why not?' Indira said.

'Wonderful.' Ava got up. 'Thanks for your cooperation.' Unexpectedly, she hugged Indira.

'No, no, thank you, thank you,' Indira said, hugging her back.

'I'll call Rick now, and let him know what we've agreed on.'

'Thank you so much, Ava, you don't know how much,' Indira said, hugging her again.

She strode out of the office, vindicated. Victory was hers in the end!

As it should be, as it always should be. With Ava's help, she'd triumphed over men. As was only just, and fair, and right.

Women always helped other women, didn't they? They really did. All her life, she'd helped women, women all over the country, and also women at home: women like Durga. Durga, who was now getting a life—for after some cajoling and a financial inducement of two lakh rupees, Hira had agreed to marry the girl. At first, Durga had hesitated: 'I don't want to marry an office peon, Hajoor, I want to be one.' Silly girl. Indira had had to talk sense into her: 'Which office will hire a class three dropout like you? Hira's a good boy, Durga. He has two lakh rupees in the bank. I'll build a new servants' quarters for you, you can live there together. You'll work for us, he'll work for the office, it'll be perfect.'

'Perfect, Hajoor?'

'Perfect.'

The girl had eventually come around.

And now—and now! It was Indira's time to rise with the help of this—Ava Berriden. Who would have thought that this young, dark, twiggy Canadian would help her rise? And rise.

Downstairs, in the lobby, the receptionist trilled, 'Namaste, Indira ma'am!'

'Namaste,' Indira said. Then on a whim, she stopped at her desk. 'Remind me, dear. What's your name?'

'Indira, ma'am.'

'No, I mean what's your name, dear?'

The receptionist smiled. 'Ma'am, my name is also Indira, though my friends call me Indu.'

'Ey, your name is also Indira!' Indira said. Yes, yes, how could she have forgotten? She remembered now. She said, 'Like India's famous prime minister, right? We Indiras, we're powerful women, aren't we, Indira?'

'Yes, ma'am.'

'Lau ta, Indira, namaste to you,' Indira said.

'And namaste to you, Indira ma'am.'

THEIR LAST DAYS together were full of defiance. Sapana moved her clothes to a room in Thulo Ba's house and prepared to lock up the family home. She refused to feel sad, and in any case there was no time to feel sad, because everything was happening so fast.

A few days after reaching Kathmandu, Ava Madam had got an NGO to locate Surya Di. She telephoned Gyanu Dai to confirm that Surya Di was safe in Ghaziabad, and that it was all right for Chandra to go to her. Gyanu Dai and Chandra were going to take a bus to Bhairahava town tomorrow to meet a woman NGO employee who'd agreed to escort Chandra through the Sunaili border post, to Ghaziabad. Gyanu Dai would go on from there to Kathmandu to obtain a permit for his new job in the desert. He'd stay at Ava madam's house till the permit came through.

Gyanu Dai clearly felt bad about leaving. He kept asking Sapana, 'Will you be all right, Bahini?' and she always said, 'Of course, Dai,' refusing to show any weakness.

Because she'd also be doing something, something important. Ava madam was starting a project in the bazaar. It would teach the members of the women's committee—here in the village, and also in surrounding villages—how to form cooperatives. Ava madam would come to the village herself to discuss it with the committee. She'd said so to Gyanu Dai over the phone. 'I'll tell you more after I meet her in Kathmandu,' Gyanu Dai had said to Sapana; though she didn't believe he'd give it much attention. He was already turned away, towards his future with the Filipina woman in the desert.

Gyanu Dai spent his last day in the village taking leave of friends and relatives.

This was also Sapana's last full day with Chandra. She and Chandra woke up, washed, and ate their morning meal together, not wanting to spend a single moment of the day without each other. After the meal, Sapana helped Chandra pack. Chandra was uncharacteristically indecisive, fussing over every detail: 'Will I need a sweater? Isn't it hot in India? What do you think, Sapana?'

'Take one, just in case.'

'I'll leave the rest for little Tara, she's growing so fast, it'll fit her next year. Look after her, hai?'

'Do you have to ask?'

'And my Muwa Buwa.'

'Don't even ask.'

'Maybe I should take two sweaters. What if it's cold there? I'll take two.' Chandra's thoughts were racing to the adventures ahead. 'Gyanu Dai said it's an overnight journey. I wonder if we'll take a bus or a train. It would be fun to ride in a train, hai. I hope we take a train.'

~

They took the rest of Chandra's clothes to her Muwa Buwa's house. The families of the other girls who'd gone to India with Surya di came by. They were hungry for news. They asked about what had happened to Surya Di, and what had happened to their daughters. The mother of the girl who was still in Ghaziabad gave Chandra a letter for her daughter. The parents of the girl who was no longer in contact sifted over every detail, examining it, searching for possibility and hope. 'Send word if you hear anything, Chandra Nani. Send word immediately.'

Chandra promised to find the middleman and ask him what happened.

'We just want to know that she's alive,' they said.

In the afternoon, Ritu and Namrata dropped by to say goodbye. Both of them were somber today. Even Ritu didn't joke around. 'India's a big country, careful you don't get lost,' she said. Her own plans were set. She'd met the boy from the far-west. They'd liked each other. Their families were finalizing the wedding plans. 'We'll live in Kathmandu. I'll only have to see my in-laws once in a while. What about you, ey, Namrata? What are you going to do?'

'I don't know. Maybe—I don't know. Should I join the women's committee?'

'Won't the foreign woman's project help girls pass out of school, Sapana?'

'I don't know,' Sapana said.

'I should have studied harder when I had a chance,' Namrata said.

Chandra was mostly quiet, but at one point, she quoted the depressed poet: 'What grows in these still villages but death.' She repeated the line, and then recited the rest of the poem:

What grows in these still villages
but death. To stay is to die.
To leave is to die too.

Mother! Save me.
I'm fading.

'Tchee, what a horrible poem.' Little Tara made a face.
'The poet won a national award.'
'So? It's still a horrible poem, never recite it again.'

~

The sun was still above the horizon when Sapana and Chandra went home. 'You shouldn't go away looking so jungly,' Sapana said. She laid a straw mat on the porch, and brought out a comb and a bottle of coconut oil. Sitting behind Chandra, she unclipped her friend's hair.

It tumbled down in thick shocks onto her shoulders. Sapana combed through it carefully, easing out the tangles, and then parting it to apply oil to the scalp.

The sunlight bore down, warm and golden. A crow cawed. The rich scent of coconut filled the air. Chandra closed her eyes. Sapana kept parting her hair and applying oil till her entire scalp glistened. Then she massaged her head, kneading the forehead, the temples, the jawbone, the neck. Chandra sighed.

Afterwards, Chandra turned around and took the oil and comb. It was her turn to oil Sapana's hair and make her sigh.

For the evening meal, Sapana cooked Gyanu Dai's favourite dishes, the same dal-bhat-tarkaari she'd made after the thirteen days of austerities for Ba: rice, black dal, potatoes and cauliflower.

When he came home, they sat at the table and ate.

'This is the best meal in the world, Bahini.'

He was just saying so to ease his guilt. Sapana said, 'It's not as good as the food you cook, Dai.'

'It's better.'

Liar.

He spoke a little bit about his new job. 'It's a small restaurant, it won't pay as well, but I'll look for something better once I get there.' He said, 'I'll send money transfers, like before, Bahini. Don't tell Thulo Ba or Thuli ma about the money, keep it to yourself.' Then, as though admitting to a crime, he said, 'We'll marry soon, Maleah and I. I—I don't know how long I'll stay in the desert,' he said. 'We might move to another country. We want to live with her son, as a family, somewhere.'

Somewhere that wasn't home, Sapana thought.

Chandra asked, 'Will we ever get to meet Maleah Bhauju?'

'One day, I hope. I hope we can all come here for a visit one day.' Sapana didn't believe him at all.

They all cleaned up together, putting away the pots and pans for the last time. After that, Gyanu Dai went to his room and Chandra and Sapana went to theirs.

They changed into their nightdresses, turned off the Petromax, got into bed. And in the darkness they reached for each other. When would they share a bed again? Attached by love, by need, by desire, they held on to each other. In the morning they'd have to let go. Tonight they held on.

'Don't forget me, ey, girl,' Chandra whispered.

'Don't be an idiot.' Sapana tried not to cry.

'Tomorrow?' Chandra said. 'Let's be strong, Sapana. Let's not cry, hai.'

'Let's never cry.'

They lay awake for a long time in the darkness, holding each other, thinking their separate thoughts. Chandra drifted off first. Her grip loosened. Her leg twitched. Sapana listened to her steady, even breathing. Every moment felt precious, she wanted to gather each last memory and store it away for when Chandra wouldn't be here. She didn't want to sleep at all.

~

A harsh morning light clattered in from the window. Chandra's arms were still around her when Sapana's eyes opened. She could tell from Chandra's breathing that she was awake, too, but she also lay still, not wanting the moment to end.

But then the neighbour's cock crowed, and Chandra stirred, and Sapana also had to stir. There was no stopping time. Soon they were out by the tap.

After a quick round of tea, it was time for Gyanu Dai and Chandra to go.

There were no family elders to take leave from: there was no ritual to follow. Though he was the one leaving and she the one staying, Gyanu Dai put tika on Sapana because he was older. 'May you go as far as your heart desires, Bahini,' he said.

'You too, Dai.' She put tika on him. 'Whatever you want—may you get it.'

Then Gyanu Dai put tika on Chandra. 'Be safe, Bahini. Telephone me as soon as you get to Suyra di.'

Sapana also put tika on Chandra. 'Don't ever forget where you're from, girl.'

Gyanu Dai and Chandra carried their bags out. Sapana locked the front door with a Chinese padlock she'd bought in the bazaar. Its key was tied to a silver chain, which she slipped around her neck.

They were beside Chandra's Muwa Buwa's house when they saw a stranger marching up the path. He had a heavy bag strapped to his chest. He stopped in front of the rotting brick house and called out: 'Where's the house with the lines to be connected?' The man's forehead was beaded with sweat. 'I'm from the Electricity Authority,' he said. 'There was an application from this village.'

'Eh, sir.' Gyanu Dai went up to him. 'There's been a change of plans.' He'd forgotten to cancel the application. He explained the mistake to the man. 'We don't need to connect the lines any more,' he said.

'But I came all the way!' The man unstrapped the bag and hurled it onto the ground. 'I've brought all the wires, all the equipment!'

'It's my mistake, sir. I completely forgot.'

'Do you know how long it took? I had to wait an hour for the bus, I had to walk all the way from the highway, I had to walk up this village path in the hot sun!'

'Forgive me, sir.'

'You wasted half a day's work!'

The man calmed down only after Gyanu Dai paid him off. 'You went through so much trouble, we're grateful,' he said, tucking several hundred rupee notes into his hands.

'You should have cancelled!' The man picked up his bag.

'The mistake is entirely mine.'

~

Chandra's Muwa Buwa were waiting for them in the house, with little Tara. They'd packed food for the journey. They put it into Chandra's bag, along with a new kurta for her, and another one for Surya Di. Chandra's Muwa slipped her an envelope with some money. Then both parents put tika on Chandra, offering her their blessings: 'Prosper, daughter. Like your older sister, find your own path forward. May the gods keep you safe.'

When Chandra knelt down and bowed at her parents's feet, little Tara began to cry.

'Don't cry, little one. Don't cry.' Chandra held her sister for a long time, then released her to their Muwa Buwa's arms.

Sapana escorted them to the bazaar. She would have gone all the way to the India border if she could have. On the bus ride, she and Chandra held hands. They got off in the bazaar still holding hands.

The bus to Bhairahava was already there. The driver was honking; the conductor was yelling to attract passengers; there was no time to linger. Gyanu Dai and Chandra scrambled on. Sapana watched from outside as they found seats at the back. When the bus started with a groan, Sapana's heart leaped. She looked at Chandra, and Chandra looked at her.

The bus began to roll away. Gyanu Dai called out, 'I'll telephone from Kathmandu, Bahini!' Chandra also said something, but her words were lost in the roar of the engine.

Sapana tried to be strong, but tears sprang to her eyes, she couldn't help it. She should have gone with Chandra, she should have gone to India, it was stupid to stay here—*what grows in these still villages but death?*

The bus rolled out of the park and turned onto the highway. When it vanished, a sharp pain seared through Sapana. She fumbled at her neck, pulled out the chain with the key. She had no home to go back to.

The pain seared through her again. She gasped. The world was on fire. There was a bench nearby. She collapsed onto it, wailing.

'Sapana Bahini.' She heard a voice.

She couldn't stop wailing. It hurt so much.

'Sapana Bahini, what's wrong, Sapana Bahini?' The voice kept talking, calling out her name, saying things. 'Sapana Bahini, what's wrong, Sapana Bahini.' The voice wouldn't leave her alone.

When, with difficulty, she looked up, there was a man standing over her. The sun was behind him, she couldn't see who it was. He said, 'Why are you crying, Sapana Bahini?'

She squinted, shielding her eyes from the sun. It was Rudra sir. He was wearing a blue shirt: he always wore blue shirts on Mondays. She remembered this through her grief.

He sat down beside her on the bench. 'Why are you crying like this, Bahini? Here, take this.' He produced an embroidered handkerchief. 'Your tears are staining your beauty,' he said, looking at her sadly with his golden-brown eyes. 'Tell me what happened, Sapana Bahini. You know I've always helped you, you know I always will. All I want, right now, is to help you stop crying,' he said. 'Tell me what I can do for you today.'

SHE CRADLED THE phone in her hands, speaking into the receiver in low, subdued tones. 'What's it like, girl? Your masters' house.'

'It's huge, it's as big as a palace, it's really grand, Sapana.' Chandra's voice always came out muffled over the line. She didn't sound like herself on the phone. 'The floors are made of white marble,' she said, 'and the furniture's so fine I'm afraid to touch anything.' She laughed. 'There's a carpet in the main room, all I want to do is lie on it, it's so soft. It has a really pretty pattern, with flowers.' She paused, then asked, 'Are Muwa Buwa all right? Have they repaired the house? Where's little Tara staying?'

'I told you, everything's fine. The wall's been patched up, little Tara's back in your old room. Don't worry about anyone here.'

'What about your house? Have the cracks in the wall been repaired?'

'No one lives there anyway. Tell me more about your life there.'

Her friend indulged her. 'The other night, the master and mistress had a huge party. The people who came were sophisticated; they talked about politics, philosophy, art. Ey, did I tell you, Sapana, the government here issues ration cards?' Everything about India was new, and interesting, to Chandra. 'Rich people like the masters don't need them, but Surya Di has one, and everyone else has one too. It's for buying rice and sugar and kerosene: essentials. I think our government should also issue ration cards, don't you? Surya Di says she'll help me get one after a few months.'

'That's good,' Sapana said. She was at the grain store, trying to hold on to her own sense of self. Only a few months had passed, but so much had happened. The springtime earthquake had shaken up everything. This part of the country had been spared, but the news from elsewhere was terrifying. There were still aftershocks every other day. When the earth trembled, all of the certainties of the universe seemed to tremble: and this seemed to change everything. When she and Chandra met next time, would things be the same between them?

Chandra went on, 'I don't like the master, he's a bit arrogant, but the mistress is all right. The children are spoiled. Ey, they bought a television the other day, it's the size of an almirah, Sapana. When everyone's out I watch the news. It's all in Hindi, I don't understand it, but it's interesting.' She paused. 'Have you heard from Gyanu Dai?'

'He got married.'

Chandra didn't say anything about this. Neither did Sapana. There must have been so much that Chandra couldn't convey over the phone. Sapana, too, couldn't talk about everything. It just wasn't possible—there was too much.

After the earthquake, Thulo Ba and Thuli ma began to pressure her to marry. With false, overweening concern, Thuli ma told her, 'Who knows when another earthquake will take us all, Nani? We won't always be here. Let us find you a groom before it's too late.' Thulo Ba even tried to push Jeevan Bhatta on her. 'He's old but he'll take care of you, Nani.' It infuriated Sapana. She hadn't told Chandra about this.

Neither had she told her about her secret rebellion.

Maybe it was wrong, maybe she shouldn't have done it. *I've always helped you, I always will.* Rudra sir was a husband and father. She shouldn't have met him for tea, she shouldn't have gone on outings with him, she shouldn't have walked with him on the shores of the Tinau River. But when he held her hands, when he touched her and kissed her and told her how beautiful she was, she felt as though she were breaking through to some fierce freedom.

She didn't even know how to talk to Chandra about this.

She told her, instead, about Ava madam's project: 'It's big, Chandra. Ava madam will come back to the bazaar in a month re, that's what Jeevan Bhatta told me. She's going to organize a meeting with the Department of Cooperatives.'

'Will Namrata join the committee?'

'She's already paying the monthly dues. I'll be enrolled in the Plus Two by then, Chandra. I can't wait for it to start. I'll escape from Thulo Ba and Thuli ma's house, and move to a girl's hostel in the bazaar.'

'And Ritu's married now.' Chandra said, 'We've all gone our own ways, hai?'

We needn't have, Sapana wanted to say. Come back, she wanted to say. You can still come back, Chandra, we can live together. She knew it was futile to say so. Chandra was satisfied with where she was right now. When they last spoke, she'd told Sapana how good it felt to earn a monthly salary: 'I'll open a bank account with it, a bank account of my own.' After the earthquake, Surya Di sent money to Sapana, who gave it to their Muwa Buwa. Chandra wanted to work for a few years in India: 'After that, who knows what the future holds?'

'Ey, wait hai.' There was a rustling on the line, and then Chandra said, 'The children are back from school, I have to go.'

'I'll call you next week, Chandra.'

'Call earlier in the day, we'll be able to talk for a longer time.'

'I'll call an hour earlier.'

'Call, hai, Sapana, call me next week for sure.'

After Chandra hung up, Sapana kept the phone to her ear, listening to the silence on the line.

She wasn't sure what to do now. She knew what Rudra sir wanted her to do.

'Come with me,' he'd said this morning, at the bank. He'd booked a room in a hotel at the edge of the bazaar. 'I'll take care of everything,' he'd said. 'I won't let anything bad happen to you.' He'd looked at her with longing, he'd sighed, he'd been sentimental. 'You're everything to me. You've got to believe that. You're all I have in this world.'

He'd told her that his marriage had been arranged against his will. He didn't love his wife. Sapana wasn't stupid, she knew that married men kept girls like her off to one side, reserving the centre of their lives for their families. Yet she was tempted to go to to the hotel with him, because if she were to ruin herself, then maybe no one would want to marry her, and she'd always be free.

She put down the receiver reluctantly. Everything in her life felt unfinished, unmade. She didn't even recognize it anymore. It was no longer what it used to be, and hadn't yet become something else; and maybe it never would. Maybe this was all there'd ever be, she thought: her asking questions to the universe, and receiving no answers at all.

Nepal gets New Charter—Nepal News Service
20 September 2015

Nepal promulgated a new constitution on Sunday amid heightened security and curfews in the southern Tarai-Madhes region, where a bandh, or general strike, has been in place. More than forty people, including eight policemen and two children, have been killed here in recent weeks.

The constitution was eight years in the drafting, following a peace process and a decade-long conflict that claimed more than 19,000 lives.

Critics say that the new charter favours the country's high-caste political class in the demarcation of provincial boundaries and electorates. They also fault the constitution for denying equal citizenship rights to women.

The new constitution is the sixth national charter since the country's founding in 1768. It was long delayed and much anticipated. It was voted on by a majority of a 601-member Constituent Assembly and promulgated by President Ram Baran Yadav.

Celebrating outside the Assembly building, college student Bikash Woli says it's a historic day for Nepal. 'Today I am proud to be Nepali,' he said, though elsewhere in the country the constitution has been burned as a mark of protest.

The polarization over the new charter is set to increase in the coming days. The country is yet to recover from a devastating earthquake in April 2015, which claimed up to 9,000 lives and destroyed over 800,000 homes. Over four billion dollars pledged to earthquake reconstruction by international donors remain unspent amid the ongoing unrest.

A WOMAN BOARDS a bus, a plane flies overhead, elsewhere in the world people embark on journeys of their own—in boats, in trains, in cars. Sapana takes a seat by the window and lets the wind fly through her hair. A year has passed, an age has passed. The earth keeps shuddering. Life will not be tranquil again.

The sun, the moon, the stars move in their orbits. It's night, it's day again, and the night will return. The morning is warm today, the day will be hot. After they pass Bhairahava bazaar, the bus groans, halts, and starts up again. Is this the border? Sapana jumps off with the bus still at a roll.

Chandra, I'm here.

The other passengers who have disembarked, scatter. The crowd parts. She stands on the side of the road. Around her, Sunauli bazaar is in motion: people move on foot, in cars, buses and vans, on motorcycles and horse-drawn carts. It's hot, the air smells of petrol. There's a check post, and a large gateway made out of concrete: is that the border? Some of the people who got off the bus walk towards it. Others duck into shops, hotels, restaurants. A few catch buses to other parts of the country. Sapana is the only one with nowhere to go.

She's come to the border to see what Chandra saw when she came here with Gyanu Dai a year ago. A horse-drawn cart clatters by on the road, the passengers at the back clutching each other for balance. A middle-aged woman sails by on a bicycle, trilling the bell. Sapana has never seen a grown woman riding a bicycle. The woman's back is straight, her posture is dignified. Sapana stares at the woman.

She's told Chandra she's coming to the border. They don't talk as frequently as they used to, but every month or so, Sapana still calls Chandra on a mobile phone she bought with money that Gyanu Dai sent. The last time they spoke, Chandra boasted about being able to speak Hindi. 'I still mix in a few Nepali words by mistake, and people laugh, but they understand me. I can go to the market by myself now. And you, girl? Did you move into the hostel? What are the girls like?'

'I'm sharing a room with three girls, they're from faraway villages.'

'Are you studying hard?'

'There's a lady professor, Urmila madam, who's kind. She never loses patience: no matter how many questions you ask, she answers. But the others...I hate the sir who teaches maths.' She said, 'I think, after I pass out of the Plus Two programme, Ava madam's project might give me a scholarship to go to college.' She added, 'You can also get a scholarship, Chandra, if you come back.'

Chandra laughed off the suggestion.

That's how she is nowadays. She's evasive, or maybe distracted. Her mind is on other matters. The important thing—Sapana has to remind herself—is that Chandra isn't unhappy. She isn't unhappy, and yet... How can she be happy in India? She never even talks about coming home any more. All she said, this time, was: 'I hope Ava madam's project lasts long enough to put little Tara through college.'

A minivan careens towards the check post at top speed.

Little Tara is no longer little. She's grown, all of a sudden, in the past year. She's almost as tall as Sapana now. She'll soon catch up with her sisters. Ava madam's project has a component dedicated to something called capacity enhancement. That component will help girls like her pass out of school, enrol in the Plus Two, and then enter college.

College. Sapana never imagined she'd go to college one day. There's a commerce campus in the bazaar, she'll enrol there. Or that's what she thinks right now. She wants to study business, or maybe accounting. When she graduates she'll find a job, or start a business of her own. Or maybe she'll study something else, a subject she doesn't even know about yet.

Namrata has also got a scholarship. She's back in school, studying for the final exams, but her family is looking for a boy. They say she's too old to stay at home much longer—she'll be a spinster if she waits.

Ritu is living with her in-laws in the far-west. Her husband's apartment in Kathmandu was destroyed in the earthquake, so they moved to his family home after the wedding. She's had a child, a son. She no longer keeps in touch with Sapana or Namrata, but they get news of her from her parents.

~

Indira steps on the sidewalk gingerly, her heels catching on the cobbles, her feet sore. But she's determined to keep going. It's so pretty. The air is clean, the streets tidy, the trees on the sidewalk clipped. She stops to admire a fountain in the middle of a pond, and abutting it, a castle-like structure: the Binnenhof, parliament house.

The Hague is better than Amsterdam, she decides. In Amsterdam, when she snuck out in between sessions at the Sustainability and

Gender Summit, the city felt crowded, and even grubby, perhaps because marijuana and prostitution were legal in the Netherlands. The youth looked wanton and wild-eyed. One morning, she even saw a young man asleep by a splatter of his own vomit outside a coffee shop.

There's no such disgrace in sight in the Hague. The royal family lives here, that's why. Or maybe the Hague is just a superior city. She passes through an arch that looks like the entrance to the Binnenhof. It opens onto an enclosed courtyard, a courtyard not unlike those in the Newari parts of Kathmandu, but, well, more European. Bigger. With big windows, big doors, and no doubt, big rooms inside, to accommodate big Europeans.

A man in red pants rides into the courtyard on a bicycle. There's a little boy on the back seat. Indira reaches the end of the courtyard. The Binnenhof is small. She wonders, in passing, how many parliamentarians the Netherlands has. It can't be many if they all fit in here.

A cool breeze sweeps through the courtyard and pleasure sweeps through her. She's come to the Hague upon the instigation of Kadri Pütsep, who was at the summit in Amsterdam. Formidable Kadri Pütsep. It was six years since they last met, but they reconnected instantly. 'My sister Indira!' Kadri cried upon seeing her, and Indira cried back: 'My sister Kadri!'

'My sister!'

'My sister!'

Kadri is retired—so young!—but she's consulting with the Estonian government on women's rights, even though Estonian women must have equal rights? 'You must come to visit me in Tallinn!' Kadri said to her. 'We must have solidarity, we women.'

'Of course, of course!' Indira said, though she's no longer just a woman, is she? She's WDS-Nepal's first Nepali director—who also happens to be a woman. The distinction is extremely important. After working on women-shwomen, gender-shender all her life, Indira has become a whole person at last.

Still, she was moved by Kadri's sisterly spirit, and when Kadri said, 'You must see the Hague, it is beautiful,' she took her advice and extended her trip by two days. Never before has Indira tacked a holiday onto the end of her duty travels. It didn't feel affordable till she began to earn a dollar salary. Yesterday's train ride took less than an hour. She caught a taxi to her hotel in a fishing village by the North Sea, and walked on the windy beach, and had dinner at an Italian restaurant.

She has all of today to see the rest of the Hague.

Beyond the Binnenhof's courtyard is a plaza full of open-air restaurants. A statue stands in the centre of the plaza, a statue of a king, a prince, a nobleman. It has needles on top of its head.

Needles! These Europeans think of everything. Indira marvels. Someone in a government office somewhere decided that statues must be protected from birds. A consultant recommended needles—a city planner or a public works specialist. Budgets were drawn, contracts were signed, funds were disbursed and the needles were placed... Tch. When would such a day come in Nepal?

No, no, no. There's no comparing and contrasting. Nepal is Nepal.

She turns away from the statue. At the open-air restaurants, people are drinking coffee, people are drinking wine. She too wants to be a person drinking coffee, a person drinking wine at an open-air restaurant in the Hague. She selects what looks like a good restaurant and takes a table beside a potted plant. The menu is printed on a paper placemat. She decides to order coffee, but when a lean, lank waiter comes to her table, she points at what a blonde woman at the next table is having. 'I will have a red wine.'

Why not? She deserves to relax on holiday. After all, she's the boss of everyone now, everyone at work, and everyone at home too—except for Muwa. No one can ever be the boss of Muwa.

The waiter brings the wine, a swirl of ruby in an elegant stemmed glass. She lifts it and makes a toast to... Nothing comes to mind. She takes a small sip. The wine is light, earthy, fragrant, not at all like the inky wine she had...was that with Ava Berriden? Nowadays she goes to Ava's house every few weeks for dal-bhat and wine—expensive, high quality wine. No, the inky wine must have been from the wedding party. Yes, that was when she must have had it. This wine—she takes another sip—is much better than that wine. It floods her with ease.

~

With a wave to the dock manager Ned, she starts the engine to the old skiff. She steers out of the dock, gliding cautiously through the marina as she passes the narrow outlet past Gord Shaw's sailboat. A red sloop at the end of the dock looks like it hasn't been out all year. Most of the other boats look well used. The Leworskis are on their weekender, unfurling the mast. 'Gorgeous day!' they call out as Ava glides by.

'Isn't it?'

'The best we've had all year!'

Beyond the marina, the bay is calm, but out on the big water, the wind whips up in short, sudden gusts, rippling up cats' paws. The gnarled white pines of Franklin Island come into view as Ava rounds the bay. There's a kayak on a whaleback boulder buffeting the island. A couple is having lunch there. They watch her go by.

She's been alone at the cottage for six days.

'Are you sure you want to be by yourself, honey?' Mom asked in Overwood on the way up. 'Now, do you have everything you need? Don't forget: the Healies sell fresh perch from their house, and they might have frozen pickerel in stock. Oh, I really hope the Fortins aren't at their cottage. Did I tell you, they added another room, out on the western side? You can't even call it a cottage any more, it's a monster house.'

'See you in a week, Mom.'

'We'll bring Aunt Edie's peach pie when we come!'

A sailboat overtakes her as she steers west from Franklin. She watches it zip along, propelled by the wind: soon, it's far ahead of her, a distant speck on the horizon. On the other side of the island, near the rental cottages, is a wind shadow. She steers easily along a calm, glassy stretch. This is her last day to herself. Mom and Dad will arrive in the late afternoon, with Luke and Revolution Mary and Baby Jesus: BJ. The family will spend a week together at the cottage. Mom will get everyone to back her group that's sponsoring Syrian refugees. Dad will fish. Luke and Revolution Mary will teach BJ to swim. Dad has said that if the weather's good, he'll take Ava out on the sailboat past the outer islands.

After steering through a stretch of open water, she comes up to the cottage, Mom's old handmade STOP THE DROP! sign draped over the exposed granite. Ava cuts the engine and glides into the dock, avoiding the sharp rocks near the shore. She hops off, ties the boat, takes out the perch she's bought from Jane Healie.

The rest of the day follows the unhurried routine of the previous days. By noon, she's at the far side of the island, which is hidden from sight from the Fortins' cottage. She tosses off her clothes, and from the granite rock that juts out above the water, dives into the electric cold water, plunging into the rich blue-black depths, into life itself.

She wishes she could have this in Nepal. Georgian Bay unlocks her earliest memories of joy. She swims to the depths and comes up to the surface, enjoying the heaviness of her body in fresh water.

Later in the morning, she swims out to her favourite spot, a whalerock that rises out of the lake, from where she can look out at the far end of Georgian Bay. She and Luke spent entire days on this rock as kids. She lies down on its hard surface, taking warmth from its sun-baked curves. The wind prickles her skin, raising goosebumps that the heat of the sun eases away.

This isn't just life itself; it is, specifically, her life, her alternative life: a life not dissimilar from her old one, but also utterly different.

After they filed for divorce, Gavin didn't speak to her—till the earthquake struck. He got back in touch then, and they've stayed in touch, remaining amicable throughout the legal proceedings. A month ago, he emailed, announcing that he moved to a condo near Wychwood. He got a promotion at the bank. *A corner office!* He wrote: *I'm doing okay, Ava. I didn't think it would be possible, but I'm okay.*

In Overwood, when Ava asked about Leez Anne Williker, Mom was discreet. 'An equity sales director—she's a bit, well, she's not you, honey, but it's good to see Gavin happy.'

Gavin had written: *Your parents said you'll be here this summer. Let's meet if you have time.*

Maybe. Ava skipped Toronto on the way up, taking a rental straight up from Pearson, but on the way back she's booked two nights at the Gladstone. Lester Prease and his wife Ruth have invited her for dinner one evening. The girls at Peckham and Poole—Lori Schiff, Jenna Deans—are clamouring for a girls' night out, though she also wants to go to Kabob House—perhaps with Anthony? Anthony wrote a few days ago, saying he'll fly up if she's free. *A second date might be in order, what do you think?*

Anthony Watson.

She wrote back: *I think it's a very fine idea.*

After sunning herself thoroughly, she gets up and plunges back into the water. There's clarity to every sensation. She can't remember, anymore, the fog she used to live in. She tumbles in the water, goes down to the depths, comes up towards the light, feels a tickle against her thigh: a hydrilla oscillating in the currents. She takes a breath and plunges back in, seeking out that hydrilla, seeking out life. For this is life: to be here in fresh water under the sun, on a perfect summer's day. She's seen, in Nepal, how fragile life can be. It's all we have, it's all she has. A chance to be fully alive.

~

In the journey of life this is where he is now, in a cramped kitchen with a rickety ventilator overwhelmed by the heat rising off the stove. He wipes up around the sink, puts away the towels. The soap bottle needs refilling. He does so, and looks around. 'Everything is all right, Amram?'

'Everything's all right, Gyanu.'

'Tomorrow I will come early,' he says.

'No problem, man.' Amram is preparing a fresh batch of keema. Above the stove, his face glistens with sweat. 'I'll stay with my brother tonight. You—you have fun,' he says.

Gyanu nods in thanks.

'And don't forget: tomorrow morning's trash pickup,' Amram says.

'I will take the bin out.'

When Gyanu leaves by the back door, the smell of hot oil trails him out. The air outside is cool. He shivers. Behind the restaurant is an empty parking lot where weeds grow in the cracks. The ventilator whirs, emitting the smell of oil as he passes the window. A squirrel darts across his path. He's unused to squirrels. He watches it scamper across the parking lot into the back alley, and follows it out.

He draws his jacket around him. Amram teases him about wearing a jacket in the summertime, but he, acclimatized to the desert, feels a tinge of winter to even the hottest days here. It surprises him.

As does the drabness of the city. Canada is a wealthy country, but it lacks the glitz of Dubai. Or maybe it's glitzy in other parts. He hasn't had a chance to look around much. After landing, he moved in with Amram, and started working at Kabob House a few days later. On his days off, he has to run errands, applying for a social insurance number, obtaining a photo card, switching to a cheaper health insurance policy. At Maleah's urging, he's enrolled in an English class for new immigrants. He has yet to meet the lawyer Ava hired for him, the one who helped him with the application for express entry. The lawyer, a woman, had instructed him to obtain police clearances from Dubai, Abu Dhabi, Sharjah and Nepal; take a health test; pass an English proficiency test. She had also transferred funds from Ava to Gyanu's bank account for the application. She'd transferred the funds back afterwards. Gyanu is supposed to meet the lawyer to discuss the future. Her office is downtown. She's told him to call her in a few weeks.

At the main street, he stops and sends a message to Jairus: *I m going 2 get her.*

With its bright red façade, Kabob House stands out on the street. The rest of the buildings house small, tumbledown businesses: a dusty curio shop, an airless sports bar, a shop that sells yarn and knitting supplies. Kabob House is the only thriving business on this street, with a small but loyal following. It's just Amram and Gyanu in the kitchen. The workload is heavy and the pay is minimum, but Gyanu is grateful for the job.

His phone pings with a reply: *Now be happy, friend.*

Jairus is the one who urged him to try for Canada. In the desert, as Gyanu worked at Zafran and Maleah at the gift shop, Jairus counselled them about their new life together. He got in touch with his cousin, the chartered accountant, in Australia, but the cousin was of no help. So he put Gyanu in touch with a Somali friend who used to work as a driver at his tour company. Ghedi Mahmoud had migrated to Canada. He drove a taxi in Alberta. He gave Gyanu the number of an employment agency in Alberta. In the meanwhile, Jairus suggested that Gyanu talk to Ava. 'Your foreigner from Nepal, she's a lawyer, na? Canada has the same kind of immigration policy as Australia, friend. Maybe you and Maleah and the boy can settle there. Ask your foreigner for help.'

Gyanu was reluctant at first. Ava had helped Chandra, and she was doing so much for Sapana and the other members of the women's committee in the village. And he knew she felt like an equal: like a sister rather than a patron. He didn't want to alter their friendship by acknowledging the power imbalance between them. But he overcame his reluctance; and Ava was gracious. She helped him the rest of the way.

Let me get in touch with some lawyer friends and see what they'd advise, she emailed from Kathmandu, signing off: *xoxoA.*

Curious soul.

~

Her stomach growls. She didn't eat before the ride, and is hungry. There's a food cart not far from where she got off the bus. She goes up to it and looks at the offerings of rotis, cooked vegetables, samosas, spiced soyabeans. A woman in her twenties is minding the cart. Sapana asks her, 'How much are the samosas, Di?'

'You want a piece or a full plate?' the woman asks. Her Nepali is inflected with Maithili.

'One piece, and a cup of tea.'

'It'll be twenty-five rupees.' The woman pulls out a stool for her to sit on. 'Are you going to the other side?'

'No, I'm only going this far.'

The samosa is fresh and spicy, and the tea hot. Sapana feels much better after eating. She pays the woman and then wanders around, not sure what to do next. Should she catch a bus back home? She doesn't want to, just yet. She stops to look at a clothes shop, just to pass time. All around her are signboards, billboards, hoarding boards. She walks past a row of shops and crosses the road, heading towards the gateway.

What kind of threshold did Chandra cross here? What kind of threshold keeps her away now? Sapana sees minivans going through the gateway, and private cars too, and rickshaws. She watches a few people cross over on foot. She knows Chandra went over on foot. The NGO worker and she caught an Indian government bus on the other side.

Beside the gateway, men are loading a lorry with large, heavy sacks of—what? Maybe rice. Sapana watches them work.

Being here makes her feel lonely; but lonely is how she wants to feel: it's honest. She is alone. She stopped seeing Rudra sir after a few months of meeting surreptiously at the hotel. Now that she's moved into a hostel in the bazaar, she no longer meets Thulo Ba and Thuli ma much either. She still goes to the village to tend to the orange trees she's planted on the family fields, but it makes her sad to see the family house: the side wall, which cracked in the earthquake, has never been repaired. All the work Gyanu Dai put into restoring the house has been wasted. She won't ever live there again. Her brother certainly won't: he's across the world. And Chandra won't, either. The house has lost its soul.

A buffalo ambles up to her. Children chase each other near the check post, squealing and laughing, playing a game of catch. The scent of petrol wafts up from the road. It's unbearably hot. Sapana wipes her brow. A policeman waves a van across the border. Why do so many people go to work in India? She'll never do so, she thinks: there's so much to do in Nepal.

Ava Madam's project is keeping the women's committee members busy. At the start, Ava madam spent weeks in the village just talking to them. Then she came back with a foreign expert from Kathmandu, a white sir with blue eyes and yellow hair. They organized a meeting in the bazaar, it was held in a small hotel. The expert lectured the members of the women's committee on cooperatives, and asked if they wanted to open one. The members said yes, and so Ava madam took them to Kathmandu, to the Department of Cooperatives.

Sapana went on that trip. It was a thrill, an adventure—her first time in the nation's capital. They stayed in a five-storeyed hotel, they ate in restaurants, they even went to the Pashupatinath and Swayambhunath temples in their free time. There was some confusion in the women's committee about what kind of cooperative to open. Jethi Didi wanted everyone to plant oranges for an orchard, but Rama Bhauju felt that a dairy would be easier to manage. After several debates and a few heated quarrels, the committee voted for oranges, because Jethi Didi already had a buyer, and the market for oranges was good.

There'll be other cooperatives in the future; and in time, these cooperatives will form a federation. For now, the committee is concentrating on making the orange cooperative more profitable.

It's a lot of work. There's constant training and retraining, there are scholarships and meetings and study tours. Ava madam's project is spending so much money in the village, in the bazaar, in Kathmandu: it's astonishing. All the funding for the women's committee comes through the CBO, so Thulo Ba and Jeevan Bhatta also get a cut. They've hired half of Thulo Ba's political lackeys as CBO staff. The project pleases Thulo Ba. It pleases everyone. It's a fine project. It's doing good.

Why did you leave, Chandra, when you could have stayed right here and done good?

~

Truly, Nepal is changing, not fast enough, of course, but things aren't as bad it used to be, which is something. Indira takes a sip of wine. She sits back, remembering the wedding party: the swarm of guests, the clangour of a brass band, the swirl of saris—beaded, embroidered, sequinned and mirror-worked. The excitement of new beginnings. She, of course, was at the centre of the festivities, a many-armed goddess orchestrating everything. 'Have more,' she said to a guest who was tucking into the biryani, enjoying it, as well as he should, for Indira had hired the caterer at no small expense. She ordered every dish, every drink for the feast; and not just that. She saw to the thousand finicky arrangements that went into planning a Hindu wedding. She found a modern-minded priest to convince Muwa that there could be flexibility on caste differences in this day and age. She drew up the guest list herself. She hired a brass band and a photographer too. She even splurged on a gold-embroidered wedding sari for Durga, and on a twenty-two carat gold necklace-earring-ring set with zircona diamonds.

The girl looked pretty as a bride. She sat on a sofa with the groom, receiving congratulations, her head bowed, her expression demure. She couldn't smile, that would be inappropriate for a Hindu bride, but she was happy, Indira thinks. Or happy enough. Nepal isn't the developed world, she thinks; all we get, as Nepalis, is to be happy enough; and Durga was happy enough on her wedding day.

Hira also looked handsome as a groom, dressed in a smart white labeda-sural. There were no guests from the bride's side, but the groom's side was there in force: the driver Narayan brought Hira's entire family from the village. Everyone from WDS-Nepal was there, all the drivers and peons, all the secretaries and receptionists, everyone up the hierarchy to Chandi Shrestha and Rick Peede, only a few months before his departure from Nepal.

Rick Peede drank a whole bottle of wine by himself: 'Indira! Isn't this marvellous! I love Nepali weddings!' His face was red from drink, redder, even, than his hair. 'Look at my wife! Isn't she ravishing?'

Tall Misha Peede, dressed in a red bridal sari, was grinding her hips, Bollywood-style, to the din of the brass band. The guests gathered around to watch, thoroughly entertained. Ava was watching on from the side. Everyone was enjoying the spectacle.

Indira was gracious to them all, even to her now-defeated rival. 'Chandiji, have some food, please. It's not too oily or spicy. I made sure the caterers used the best ingredients.'

'But I've already eaten, Indiraji. It was good. The biryani was the best.'

No, Chandiji: I am the best.

The servers served food, the guests ate, the brass band played, Misha Peede danced and the bride and groom sat on the sofa, receiving congratulations and gifts.

'Madam director.' John Barnett also came to the wedding. 'Madam director,' he said, holding her hand to his heart. 'Please meet the love of my life.'

His wife, Vidya Barnett, wasn't just beautiful, she was stunning: she practically glowed, like a full moon in a classical love poem. She was also endlessly well-mannered. 'It's inspiring to meet professional women like you,' she said to Indira. 'I'm just a simple woman, I feel so humbled to be in your presence.'

'No, no!' Indira laughed. 'No, no, no.' She said, 'Welcome to my home, please. Johnji, will you have wine?' She flagged down a server. 'And Vidyaji, can I get you some fruit juice?'

'I'll have a glass of wine too.'

Of course. As a Newar, she wasn't barred from drink, like Indira.

'What's a wedding without some alcohol?' John Barnett said. 'Here's to weddings.' He raised his glass.

His wife raised her glass.

They clearly expected Indira, too, to take a glass: the server was standing by with the tray. She glanced around. Muwa was out of sight. 'Yes, here's to weddings,' she said, and picked up a glass; but even as she took the first inky sip, she caught a telltale whiff of myrrh. 'To the bride and groom,' she said, putting the glass down again.

Yes, to them, Indira thinks now, taking a sip of the light, earthy, fragrant wine in the open-air restaurant in the Hague. After the wedding, Durga and Hira moved into the newly constructed servants' quarters in the backyard, and nine months later Durga gave birth to a baby, a baby girl. Both parents were crestfallen. Indira scolded them: 'Boys and girls are equal nowadays!' They've come to accept this now, for a baby is a baby—and a life is a life. Durga has a life.

~

After a lunch of smoked fish, she sits on the porch and reads Herman Banke's report, 'Resilience: Vulnerability Index Nepal'. Herman is a changed man. He returned from the ten-day meditation retreat at peace with the world. After the earthquake, he developed a new passion for his project on resilience: 'The socially excluded are intensely vulnerable; only if we increase their resilience can we prevent a natural disaster from turning into a full-blown social-political-humanitarian disaster, Ava.' Since then, he's persuaded IDAF headquarters to upgrade his project into a two-year programme. With the promulgation of the new constitution, the peacebuilding programme came to an end. Jared Lukkinson has left IDAF. Herman's resilience programme is so well funded now that he's having trouble with disbursement. In their last meeting, he pleaded with Ava: 'Women are so vulnerable in Nepal, the women's empowerment programme must focus on increasing women's resilience, it's the only way, you have to help me.'

She's open to it. She still wonders, some days, if there's something wrong at IDAF, especially when Vishwa behaves badly: he's struck up an antagonism with her. But for the most part, she feels good about what she's getting done in Nepal.

And the earthquake has changed her profoundly.

She was in the garden on the day the earth roared. Thrown from the chair, she couldn't understand what was happening. The trees swayed madly above her. She scrambled on all fours to a clearing. Even the sky seemed to judder. When she looked out at the city, she saw dust rising from the fallen houses. She remembers screaming.

The house had minor damages: a few cracks, nothing structural. But the servants' quarters were reduced to a heap of broken bricks. Harihar escaped just in time to avoid injury. Mrs Thapa's house, next door, lost a front room. Ava offered Mrs Thapa her spare rooms, but her family chose to remain in their house with the gaping front room. Luna's family lost their rented apartment in the quake. In the first few days, she and her family—a husband and three children—lived with Harihar in a tent that they fashioned out of two pieces of tarpaulin in Ava's earthquake kit. Ava eventually moved Luna's family into the downstairs guest room. Harihar remained, out of a sense of duty—or perhaps under Mrs Thapa's orders—in the tent. He'll move into the servants' quarters when it's rebuilt in the autumn.

Tomás's apartment was also deemed unsafe after the quake: half the building, a late addition to the main structure, cracked apart. He moved in with Ava. They're living together, now, in an easy, platonic arrangement. Tomás's vow of celibacy remains unbroken. The earthquake made him pass on the job offer in Myanmar. He's working in earthquake-affected districts. One of the areas he works in is Langtang, where he and Ava were trekking two weeks before the quake.

At her family cottage, Ava thinks of Langtang. She wonders how the survivors are coping. News of the area reached her late, days after the earthquake. The entire village of Langtang was flattened by snow, ice sheets, loose rocks and boulders that came crashing off the surrounding mountains. More than three hundred people—residents, lodge owners, porters, trekkers—died there. The bodies were recovered slowly, over months, as the snow and ice melted. Some have never been found. The village hasn't been rebuilt yet. There are plans to do so, plans that Tomás follows. He tells Ava about them. He's planning to return there soon. He's asked her to come too.

Ava isn't sure. For her, Langtang holds the same kind of private confusion that the orphanage does. More than a year has passed, yet the trek is still vivid, like an image etched in her mind permanently:

the truth is, the jagged world claims her.

~

At the end of the block, Gyanu reaches the entrance to the subway station and takes the escalator down. This is the route he takes to work every day. The station is crowded. It's a long weekend: for what occasion, he doesn't know. He packs in against the wall beside two elderly women talking in bright, excitable tones among themselves. Beside him a young white man leans wearily against the wall. A black man in a business suit, headphones clamped over his ears, nods his head in rhythm. Three young women are talking in tones that dip and rise in a familiar cadence. Listening to them, he thinks of Maleah.

The places we come from, meri maya, the places we go.

His journey to Canada began, in a way, on the day he invited Ava to the family home in the village. The bond they formed propelled both of them forward in their separate directions.

After taking Chandra to the Sunauli border, Gyanu went on to Ava's house in Kathmandu. She opened her whole life to him. She installed him in a spare bedroom upstairs, and fed him a dinner of dal-bhat, offered him wine. 'Stay as long as you'd like, Gyanu, I have so much space, it's great to have someone to share it with,' she said, oblivious to the divides—of class, of station—that she would have been sharply aware of had she been raised in Nepal.

She left for work early the following morning. He spent the day in the city chasing the permit paper, visa, air ticket. It would take weeks for everything to come through. On his way back to Ava's house, he bought white beans, bacon, lettuce and herbs: he'd noticed, the earlier night, that she didn't like dal-bhat. He would cook for her as a way of repaying her kindness.

The guard, Harihar, was reluctant to let him back into the house. 'How long are you staying, Bhai?' he asked at the gate.

'I don't know, Dai, a week or two, maybe more.'

'There's a servants' quarters, you'd be more comfortable if you moved there with me.'

The maidservant's displeasure showed when he went into the kitchen. 'This madam, she's difficult to please,' Luna said, hovering over the stove, as if staking out her territory. 'The last madam was nicer. This one doesn't like our food. I have to throw out her portion from the refrigerator every day, Bhai.'

'Foreigners, they're not used to our tastes, Didi.'

'The thing is, even if she's hired you as her cook, Bhai, it's the landlady who pays my salary, and I'll still work here,' she said.

He had to reassure her: 'I'm only here for a few days, Didi.'

Ava seemed oblivious to the judgements around her in the house. Only the gardener, Jaleswar, kept to himself. Harihar was always prying. 'And how did you get to know this madam?' Luna loved to gossip. 'Is it just the two of you tonight, or is that white man also coming? What is it re, I forget his name.'

'Tomás.'

'He must be this madam's boyfriend, or is he her husband?'

'I don't know, Didi.'

'They have no decorum, hai, these foreigners? They do whatever they like, hai? What's her religion, Bhai? She must be Christian.'

'I haven't asked, Didi.'

'You must never cook beef in the house: the landlady forbids it.'

Gyanu still doesn't know whether or not Tomás is Ava's boyfriend. It doesn't matter to him. He knows that Ava has divorced her husband: she told him, one evening, that she was doing so. She treated Gyanu as a confidant, talking to him about whatever was on her mind. She's unguarded and open—by character, or perhaps by culture. She's liberated: she's the most liberated person Gyanu has ever known, freer than he's ever been or will ever be. He likes that about her so much.

~

As she watches the gate, people cross through: some go to India, others come over from there. At one point, there are so many vehicles coming and going, the gateway is jammed. The loneliness inside her to swell up like a bruise, tender and throbbing. Will it ever heal? How she misses Chandra.

From where she's standing, the lorry blocks the check post from view. The men are still loading it. The buffalo has ambled up to the front of the lorry. Sapana watches it carry on, through the gateway, to the other side.

She wants to feel what Chandra has felt. She looks around. No one's really paying attention to anyone else here. She crosses the road and sidles alongside the lorry. She reaches the gateway. Her heartbeat quickens. The heat rises with each step. From somewhere comes the sound of a dog barking. A minivan honks. There's a man shouting behind her: 'Stop!' She's almost in India. She walks on.

And when she crosses through the gateway and steps onto Indian soil, she can feel Chandra: she can feel her presence again.

'I told you to stop!' A man comes running behind her. He's a policeman. He's short. He's old. His face is contorted with the effort of catching up to her. 'Didn't you hear? I've been telling you to stop!'

Sapana looks at him coolly. 'Is there a problem, Police Dai?'

'You can't just go over, you have to show your papers at the post!' His voice is shrill.

'This is as far as I'm going,' she says.

'You can't even do that!'

It's strange how panicky he is, though he's the authority. Sapana feels like panicking him some more. 'I think I'll stay here awhile, Dai.'

He glares at her, exasperated. Then he whines: 'It's for your own protection, Bahini.'

Her protection? Sapana is amused. 'Do you know how many of us are already in India, Dai? Do you know how many of us go there, and never return? Don't worry about my protection,' she says. 'Go back to your check post. I'll stay here as long as I like.'

Now the policeman looks upset, as though having failed to reason with her, he's failed as a man. 'Don't go any further,' he says. 'I'll get in trouble. As will you—you'll get in trouble! It's the law!'

Sapana turns away, laughing.

The India side of the border isn't much different from the Nepal side. There are shops for food, clothes, pots and pans, electronics. It feels busier, though: more charged and energetic, somehow. Chandra lives amid this charge, this energy. She can feel that. Chandra is part of this energy now.

Something about the energy reminds her of Kathmandu. There was a vibrancy to the capital city, a vibrancy that Gyanu Dai had been part of early on, after leaving the village. Sapana missed him a lot when she was in Kathmandu. For the duration of her visit to the capital, she was part of his life's vibrancy.

And now, standing on Indian soil, she feels herself part of the big world, part of its charge and energy, part of the light that swirls around and the force that brings together constellations—of people, objects, circumstances—and draws them apart, making everything change, always change. Entire days pass, nowadays, without her thinking about Ba and Ma. Everything changes. She's changing too. Just as the world is Gyanu

Dai's and Chandra's, it's hers too. Her life isn't small; she swirls with the whole big world.

'Come back now,' the policeman whines. 'It's been a hard day. You're only making it harder.'

She turns to him, and sees a tired man with a tired job on a tired day in a tired old world.

'I haven't got all day,' he pleads.

It's childish to stand around daydreaming like this. She has her own life to tend to. She'll focus on that from now on: she'll think about herself, and about her own life, because you can't progress if you're always thinking about others. You must harden your heart and be selfish, Sapana thinks. Chandra's done so, Gyanu Dai's done so. She'll harden her heart and be selfish too.

She follows the policeman back across the border.

~

We're all survivors, truly. Indira makes a silent toast. To Nepali women. She takes a sip of wine.

And to women all over the world, she thinks. They're all survivors too. To Kadri Pütsep, her dear sister Kadri, and to the entire sisterhood of global change-makers. To Abena Kwasima, to Rudo Gamble, to W. Werry, to Mei Wang, to Juana Hernández...and also to Catherine Christy and Ava Berriden.

And to herself, too, for she, too, is a survivor. She survived the darkest shadow to ever pass over her life: the shadow cast by that excrement-filth, Vishwa Bista. He failed to sully her, and Chandi Shrestha failed too. She's moved up, and they're exactly where they were: Vishwa Bista at IDAF, Chandi Shrestha at WDS-Nepal, the co-director, her underling.

She toasts herself: to Indira Sharma.

It's important, she muses, not to be discouraged, no matter how challenging things become, and to move on, because what might have been is gone, but what there is now is still there, and who knows what might yet be? The entire plaza shimmers into soft focus. A lightness of spirit comes over her: her heart is full of wine. The sun is high up in the sky. It'll stay there forever on this long, glowing summer day of the northern hemisphere.

To women, she thinks. She sips the wine.

To women all over the world. To Nepali women. To me.

~

In the afternoon, she returns to the far side of the island. There's a blueberry patch beside the whalerock. She and Luke can pick them this evening: they can make pancakes for breakfast tomorrow.

From the granite rock she dives into the water, then comes up and floats on her back. There are a few plump cumulous clouds in the sky. They form and break apart and form again at a leisurely pace. A kite, or perhaps an osprey, circles overhead. A water plane glides by. The sun dips behind a cloud and when it reappears, it dazzles.

She feels as—high, or free, or light in the body—as she did on the Langtang trek. She started that trek overburdened with work and numb about the divorce. She and Tomás and two of his friends, a British expat Len and his Nepali boyfriend Bibek, were being led by a young guide named Kiran Magar.

On the first day, they took a battered old Jeep out of Kathmandu, to a road that led through high, rocky hills. The road was rough. At one point they had to wait for a digger to clear away a rockfall. There was a dizzying precipice on one side, with a view of high hills, terraced fields and isolated, scrabbly villages. Towards the end of the drive, they also saw snow peaks, but they vanished behind the hills as they descended into a narrow valley, to the trailhead.

They began to walk the next morning. Almost immediately, Ava's burdens began to fall away. There was something clarifying about the high-altitude air. Or perhaps it was something about walking. A serenity came over her. There was time and space enough, while walking through a narrow river gorge, to churn up emotions and to let them settle back down again. The land was vast, and everything else took its rightful place in that vastness.

By the third day, they were up at the base of the snow peaks they'd seen on the drive. They'd meandered through beautiful villages perched high on the hills. There were pine forests along the trail, and rhododendron trees. A cool wind whispered through the trees. The land looked intimate but was unending. It kept unfolding into new canyons and gorges and hills, new peaks kept appearing out of nowhere. Snow glittered on the Himalayas, and every small sensation—the cawing of crows, the heat of the sun—was electric.

Even Tomás was relaxed in the mountains. Late in the afternoon, the group would stop at a lodge for lunch, and in the evenings they'd chat over dal-bhat and beer, exchanging thoughts, quips, observations from the day. In the morning they had breakfast together, but outside of meals, they were on their own for most of the day.

By the time they reached Langtang village, they were fit and tired and exuberant. They avoided the larger lodges there, and stayed in a cozy stone house with a big, blazing fireplace. The sisters who ran the lodge told them about a prayer going on in a Buddhist monastery. After dal-bhat, Kiran took them to see it. They spent the night listening to monks chanting, beating drums, blowing trumpets, the sounds so thunderous they vibrated through the body.

That day the walk had been gruelling, and Ava fell asleep as soon as they returned to the lodge. The next morning she awoke to a blinding white light at the window. She stumbled over and opened the curtains to see the Himalayas looming directly above her.

They were right there, within reach: all that stone, snow, light. She'd never been spiritual—Mom and Dad had gone through a Buddhist phase, but she and Luke had always been secular—but the sight filled her with a wonder that bordered on reverence.

What a country, Nepal.

That morning they walked on to the final village, Kyanjin Gompa, and stayed there two nights. On the second morning, after breakfast, they climbed a ridge that offered a panorama of the entire range of the Langtang Himalayas.

On the way down from the ridge, Ava came across four children bundled up in sweaters and jackets, their faces ruddy with sun. They shouted 'Namaste,' and Ava said namaste back, and they scampered alongside her on the narrow trail.

The eldest, a girl, asked, 'Where from?'

'Canada,' Ava said. 'Where are you from?'

'Nepal!' The girl giggled.

'What are your names?' Ava asked.

All of them cried out at the same time: 'Pema!' 'Shambhu!' 'Chhakke!' 'Dorje!'

Then the girl pointed at Ava and asked, 'Name?'

'Ava.'

'Abha!' The others echoed her: 'Abha!' 'Abha!' 'Abha!' Then they turned off, yelling, 'Bye-bye-bye-bye-bye!' and ran down a steep side trail.

Floating on her back in the water, Ava wonders whether the children survived the earthquake. After they scampered away, Ava has often measured the value of their lives, and the value of her life, and realized: she could have been one of them, but isn't. She can understand, empathize, feel for or even feel like them, but she isn't one of those children at all.

She's about to swim back to the whalerock when she hears the drone of an engine. Her parents' powerboat is coursing up to the STOP THE DROP! sign. Mom's wearing an enormous pink hat, waving madly with both hands: 'Darling! Ava dear! honey!' Dad's at the steering wheel. Beside him, Mary is bundled up in a sweater, jacket and and toque. Luke has little BJ strapped into a carrier strapped on his chest. 'Auntie Ava!' he lifts the baby's hand and makes him wave. 'Say hello to Baby Jesus!'

'BJ, oh, my God, oh my God!' Ava begins to swim over to her family. 'Wait for me, I'll be right there, wait for me!'

~

The train screeches into the station. The doors slide open. The crowd presses in. He keeps in step with everyone else.

Inside, all the seats are taken, so he holds onto a strap.

The announcement of the stations is a familiar mantra: Keele. High Park. Runnymede. Under his breath, Gyanu murmurs: 'Come to me.'

He thinks: Ava must be in Canada now. She'll be north of Toronto, with her parents. She's told him where they live, and where they have a vacation home, but the names mean nothing to him. She's going to visit him at Kabob House next week.

He wonders if she's still as fragile as she was when she was in Kathmandu. Every day after work she talked to him about her project, which was changing rapidly, almost daily, as it came together. 'I'll be going back to Butwal a lot. I'm feeling really good about this, Gyanu.'

On his final day there, she came to his room looking particularly buoyant. She was going on a trek soon, with Tomás. She was excited about it. She sat on his bed and told him about their plans. 'We'll drive to a place called Syabrubesi—do you know it?'

'I have not gone that side.'

'We'll start our trek there—we'll go through a portion of the Tamang Heritage Trail. Have you heard of it?'

He hadn't.

They went to the kitchen. She opened a bottle of wine and poured them both a glass. He put a chicken to roast for their last dinner.

'No Tomás today?' he asked; for Tomás often dropped by.

'He might come later. You know what he's like.'

As he put together a salad, she asked him about Dubai: what he was going to do there, what he'd done before. He told her about Zafran, and about his old job at Five Spices. He talked about Jairus: what a friend he'd been. He'd told her before about Maleah. He talked about her again: 'We will marry soon.'

'Here's to a happy future for you two.' She poured them more wine.

Her face grew flushed, her eyes grew bright. She was in a mood to confide. She told him about her parents in Canada, and her brother and his girlfriend in America. They were expecting a baby. She wanted to know about his family too: she asked about his mother and stepfather. 'What about your real father?' she asked. 'Are you still in touch with him?'

'No, I—I do not know his name.'

'So does that mean you don't know your caste? How old did you say you were when your mom remarried, four or five, right? Do you remember much?'

'One-two things.' He said, 'I do not know my background.'

'Does that bother you?' she asked.

'It is not my choice, Ava.'

'But if you had a choice, would you try to find out more?'

She was probably seeking answers to her own life in his. He said, 'I think yes. And you?'

'I guess so too.' She said, 'For me too, if there were a choice, I guess I'd want to know more—though actually, I'm not sure.' She thought about it awhile. 'I mean, it obviously matters to me a lot to have a connection to Nepal, but I feel like I'm developing it through work, and through—well. I don't have to connect with my own personal past, do I?' She looked at him. 'Can you tell, Gyanu, from looking at me, what caste I was born as?'

With her sharp features, dark skin, and large, almond-shaped eyes, she could be of Newari or Dalit or Madhesi background, or, for that matter, from any number of other communities. He said, 'It is not possible to know.'

'There wasn't much in my records,' she said. 'My name is the only thing I've got from my past.' She pronounced it the Nepali way: 'Abha.'

'It means: when sun comes up in the morning.'

'Dawn.' She said, 'Will you say it again, Gyanu? I really like the way you pronounce it.'

They were standing side-by-side at the kitchen counter. When he said her name, she reached out and put her arms around him. Unused to Western-style contact, he braced instinctively. But her gesture was innocent. She laid her head on his shoulder. He put his arms around her uncertainly. She was small, all bones. He felt the softness of her short-cropped hair on his face and smelled her fragrance: a flowery perfume.

She stepped away. 'I'm sorry,' she said. 'I'm not—I really needed that.'

'It is all right,' he said.

'You've been so good to me, Gyanu.'

'It is all right.'

She nodded. 'It is all right, isn't it?' She smiled a little. 'I feel like I've found a brother in you.'

The train rushes on. The stations pass by. Jane. Old Mill. Royal York. Gyanu whispers, 'Come to me.'

The plane will land soon. In his mind he can see Maleah walking out, as he did, to the waiting officials. He went through the same routine a month ago. He showed the officials his papers. They sent him through long, empty corridors, to the immigration desk. From there, he was sent on to a separate room to process migrants.

That room was sterile and antiseptic, and crowded. The line went all the way to the back. He stood in line for nearly an hour. Some in line were here on express entry, like him. Others had come with their permanent residency status already secured. There were whole families in that room, waiting to begin their new lives.

The train pulls into Kipling station.

He gets off and takes the escalator up to board his usual bus. It's not crowded at this hour. He chooses a seat towards the middle of the bus. As he sits, a woman at the front of the bus catches his eye. She's standing, though the seats around her are empty. She's dark-skinned. Her hands are on her hips. She's fine-boned, her hair is dark, and pinned back in a braid. She turns, revealing the face of a stranger.

Regret catches him unawares nowadays. He thinks constantly of Sapana. The low buildings of his neighbourhood roll by as they pass his stop. This neighbourhood holds most of what he's seen so far of Toronto: a wide avenue, two highrise buildings, a traffic island, a No Frills, a convenience store. Sapana will do all right.

Maleah may get through immigration more quickly than he did. Her case is simpler: she's coming on a temporary visitor visa. The lawyer will help her obtain permanent residency as a spouse, and for Crisanto as their son. Crisanto is almost eight years old. They'll bring him from the fishing village as soon as possible. It might take a year, it might take two years, but they are determined to live here as a family.

The bus turns onto the broad highway to the airport. They pass the signs for the terminals.

'Come to me,' Gyanu murmurs. He sees Maleah in church, praying. *Our father who art in heaven.* As the airport sweeps into view, Gyanu prays for salvation. 'Come to me, meri maya, come to me.'

ACKNOWLEDGEMENTS

Thank you to David Davidar, Aienla Ozukum and everyone at Aleph Book Company for being kind and supportive through all stages of the writing, editing and publishing of this novel. This novel owes its inception to Ravi Singh, who commissioned it on spec for Aleph. I was fortunate to have received critiques by Johanna Stoberock, Lesley Grant, Barbara Weyermann and Wayne, Judith and Rachel Amtzis on crucial drafts. My deep thanks, too, to Carolyn Forde and the entire crew at Westwood Creative Artists, for being calm and steady when I've been neither.

This is my first novel after moving from Kathmandu to Toronto. I couldn't have written it, or indeed continued to write at all, without the support of some key Canadian institutions. Thank you to the Canada Council for the Arts for a grant and for the Joseph S. Stauffer Prize. Thank you also to the Toronto Arts Council for a grant to see me through lean times. I completed the first draft of this novel as a Writers' Trust Writer-in-Residence at Berton House. My time in Dawson City deepened my feel for Canada. For this I am indebted to the Writers' Trust, and also to Dawsonites Karen Dubois, Eldo Enns, Greg and Shelley Hakonson, Dan and Laurie Sokolowski, Lulu Keating, Glenda Bolt, Dan Davidson, Kathy Webster and Chere Wilson. I learned much from the Dänojà Zho Cultural Centre in Dawson City. In Toronto, Linda Robinson was terrifically generous in sharing the world of corporate law with me. I am also thankful to Diane Goodman, Allan Leibel, Natalie Munroe and Mary Abbott for giving me a glimpse into Bay Street. The bulk of my research on the aid industry took place while I worked in it, sporadically and mostly peripherally, in Nepal. My sense of microfinancing was gleaned as a researcher for *Unequal Citizens: Gender, Caste and Ethnic Exclusion in Nepal* for the far-sighted Lynn Bennett. I am grateful to Jasmine Rajbhandary for offering me insight into the aid industry's more powerful and opaque echelons. In this novel I've mentioned some of the books that have influenced my thinking on this industry, though this novel isn't, of course, a polemic on the subject. The term PEON, or 'Permanent Establishment of Nepal,' was coined by one of Nepal's clearest thinkers, CK Lal. One need only read national newspapers to learn of the risks that Nepal's migrant workers face in the Gulf. *Registan Diary* by Devendra Bhattarai has been particularly educative for me, as have Kesang Tseten's films *The Desert Eats Us, Saving Dolma,* and *In Search of the Riyal.* I've found Barbara Weyermann's views on the connections and divergences between migration and the trafficking of women clarifying. On the earthquake of April 2015: I owe the Nepali community in Toronto, and especially Asha Toronto, a debt, for supporting long-distance activism and critical engagement after the earthquake. Everyone involved in Rasuwa Relief and the Langtang Management and Reconstruction Committee have set an example of post-disaster relief and reconstruction. I've learned much from their work, and from the work done by other informal and non-government organizations in Nepal. Thank you to Farid Alvie and Elizabet Rhoden for allowing me to gain a first-hand sense of the UAE at the Sharjah Book Fair. The art installation I've described in the novel is *Bhumi: Where Do I Stand?* by Ashmina Ranjit. On the subject of adoption, I found *The Language of Blood* by Jane Jeong Trenka and *Lucky Girl* by Mei-Ling Hopgood helpful. The rape at the orphanage is based on real events: a report can be found in *Nepali Times,* Issue # 714, 4-10 July, 2014.

Finally, thank you to Daniel Lak for giving me Toronto and Georgian Bay; to my parents Bhekh Bahadur and Rita Thapa for giving me the world; to my siblings Bhaskar Thapa and Tejshree Thapa for blazing the trails that I, slacker youngest, follow; to Gord and Doreen Lak, Frank Thorneycroft, Sumira Thapa, Katie Parker-Lak, Brent Langille, Robert Parker-Lak, Barune Thapa, Maya Thapa-ÓFaoláin, Sidhant Thapa, Alexandra Langille and my faraway godson William Eric Hudson Schonveld and his sister Maya; and to friends far and near and also virtual. Ben Schonveld will recognize the stupor of sitting through Nepali-language meetings as an English speaker. Parag Shrestha will recognize the words 'artificial intelligence', uttered in a conversation about Nepal in Parkdale. Many others will, I hope, see our times reflected in these pages. This novel came together through our interconnections, for which I am extremely grateful.